When to Love Again

novel by

LAVETTE JOHNSON

Book design by The Troy Book Makers
Troy, New York • thetroybookmakers.com

Printed in the United States of America

ISBN: 979-8-218-21358-9

To my loving husband,

who listened and supported my dream

to become a published author.

Chapter 1

AS SHE STARED INTO THE CAMERA on her laptop, Ava was careful to mute her microphone when she wasn't talking. She was on another marathon video conference call. Her dad and everyone else on the call had an advantage: they were just starting their workday. Ava had already finished a grueling shift overseeing the new parts and equipment tracking system installation at the plastic manufacturing plant outside Beijing.

After working a full day, she should have been tired, but the reason for the call had amped Ava up to the point that she wanted things settled immediately. She rested her elbow on the table and rubbed her temple, weary from the endless legal talk of the attorneys.

Ava abruptly unmuted her microphone and broke into the conversation. "We know what is happening. Someone needs to get to Germany and put a stop to it right now. A good portion of our family business is at stake."

Their company, Brooks Manufacturing Global, had expanded too quickly, leaving her and everyone else distracted.

When the deal to buy the factory in Germany was in the final stages, Ava had just left for China to establish an Asia footprint by acquiring Gao Modern Plastics. Her brother, Danny, was in Brazil, and their dad, Clayton, was sidelined after suffering a mild heart attack. They all wrongly—and now regrettably—trusted their long-time advisor, Mr. Barton, to protect their interests. He had never disclosed his close friendship with the factory's previous owner, Hammet Vogel.

Fighting to remain calm, Ava glared into the camera. *Where the heck is Danny?* She wondered, biting her lower lip. She could use her big brother's help facing the stoned-faced attorneys crowded around their dad at the conference room table.

"It's been long enough. How many more hoops do we need to jump through to save our business?" Ava pressed as her temples throbbed. "We've talked long enough."

"I agree with Ava."

Ava's heart jumped upon hearing her brother's voice. Her backup had arrived. Danny joined the call while parking his car. He talked loudly to be heard over all the background noise in the parking garage as he made his way to the elevator to join their dad in the conference room.

"We need a solution *now*," Danny continued. "If Barton is cooperating, what are we waiting for? The longer we wait, the worse things are going to get."

Several months back, Ava had noticed some irregularities in the financial records of the factory in Germany. Upon closer inspection, the financials and other company records revealed a litany of small, illegal actions that made up an enormous web of embezzlement. One scheme sent scrap materials generated in the production process to a recycling business owned by the factory accountant's brother.

Vogal listed the scrap as "a sustainability donation." In reality, he had sold it for a profit and deposited his ill-gotten gains into three different bank accounts.

Another scheme—a classic mob protection tactic—involved a despicable employee "tax." An under-the-table cash payment for job protection targeted the low-skilled immigrant workers, who were too afraid of losing their jobs to not pay. The thieves also created "ghost" employees and fictitious customer accounts to pad the balance sheets. And of course, the outright theft of company equipment. The stolen items ranged from expensive mechanic tools to laptops to two-way radios, and so on.

Clayton slapped his hand hard on the table before he interjected.

"There is a great deal at stake here; we all know that! Our business, our reputation, and the livelihood of hundreds of people. I refuse to let this get any worse. We have built this business from one small metal fabrication shop in Texas to multiple manufacturing plants and factories worldwide. It may not mean anything to some people, but it means everything to my family. Legally, what do we need to do?"

The entire family, infuriated with their situation, was determined to make things right, no matter what. To have someone on the inside actively working against them and stealing from the company was unbelievable.

Still, there was never a doubt they would always have each other's backs. By the time the attorneys had laid out the legal requirements, Danny had joined their dad. Although out of breath due to running from the elevator, he managed to give an excited wave to his little sister. Ava returned a huge smile when she saw her big brother on camera.

One of the five attorneys in the room gave an update. "Yes, we're lucky Mr. Barton is fully cooperating, but we still need to be careful. We have to make sure no one at the factory gets tipped off."

Clayton fumed. "Is Mr. Vogal still living comfortably in the Swiss Alps on the money that belongs to the hardworking employees at the factory? For twenty years, Barton worked side by side with me. I trusted that man, and he goes and does this?"

Ava's dad rarely raised his voice, and he never cursed. His *tone*, however, candid and serious, cut a person down to size. She watched as her dad leaned back in his chair with his arms crossed over his chest. She could almost feel his blood pressure rising as he thought through the options laid out by the attorneys. If her dad had another heart attack over this disastrous mess, she would personally hunt Vogel down and make it her life's mission to destroy him.

She knew it hurt her dad terribly to have his best friend of more than thirty years and business partner of twenty betray him when he was at his most vulnerable. Eddy Barton was not only the family's most trusted merger and acquisitions advisor. He was like an uncle to Ava and Danny.

For him to conspire with Hammet Vogel and convince the family to buy Vogel's factory, knowing full well, Vogel laundered money through the factory, was beyond despicable.

Ava hated hearing their names. She hadn't let go of any of her anger and hatred toward the two most deceitful men she had ever encountered.

Everyone knew the plan and the challenge ahead. It was solid, but Ava saw one thing that was missing.

"We cannot do this remotely or just with the attorneys." She gave a sly glance toward the five suits staring back at her from the screen. "No offense, guys. Someone from the family needs to be on-site to see this through, or we will never build a relationship with our employees."

Clayton took a deep breath. He nodded his head back and forth and tapped his pen on the table, thinking.

"Danny's headed back to Brazil to cover things with the new plant, and I'm tied down here." He took another deep breath and rubbed his forehead. "Ava, I want you to go to Brazil, and Danny can go to Germany. I'm sure your brother would agree that there is nothing in Brazil you can't handle.

Plus, we're not sure what the situation is really like in Germany. It could get dangerous."

Ava was not fast enough to unmute her microphone again and respond. Danny was already rebutting their dad's solution.

"Ava is the one who alerted all of us to the problem. She's the most acquainted with the situation and qualified to represent the family. Plus, it's not like she's going in blind or without help. We have connected with all the necessary authorities here and over there. If things get dicey, she'll have plenty of help." Danny shot a raised eyebrow look Ava's way. "You're prepared, right, sis?"

"Yes, I'm prepared," said Ava with a wink, confidence rushing through her veins. "I can be in Germany by the end of the month after completing the transition here in China."

"No! It's too dangerous." Their dad refused to budge. "I don't want my baby girl in harm's way. Or you, Danny, so I'll go."

Ava clicked the unmute button with a vengeance. "Dad, you can't be serious." She opened her arms wide. "I'm here in China. Alone. Remember?"

Her dad shot back. "That's different, Ava, and you know it."

"Daddy, you know I can handle this."

"Yes. I know you can handle it, but it's simply too dangerous."

Danny tried to help bolster Ava's case. "Ava's been traipsing around the world just like me since she was twenty-four. Dad, you're not being fair or reasonable."

Their dad crossed his arms. He was done. "We'll discuss this later as a family."

The call ended without a clear decision on which Brooks was going to Germany. The formidable Mr. Clayton Brooks would not be rushed into making a decision. On Ava's first solo international business trip, his stomach was twisted into knots. He called, texted, and emailed every day until she was back stateside. It's gotten easier to see her leave over the years, but Germany would be different. Sending his only daughter, his little princess, to confront a bunch of criminals scared him to death.

For the rest of January, Ava, Danny, and their mother attempted to ease his fears and convince him that Ava should be the one to go. Ava took the rational approach. She drafted up an extensive project plan. She detailed how she would continue to gather evidence, safeguard assets, and connect with employees and customers.

Danny played the supporting role. He put together a list of every contact the family and their legal team worked with since discovering the schemes. FBI agents from the Dallas and Berlin offices, IRS investigators, German Federal Police (Bundespolizei), and the General Federal Criminal Police Office (Bundeskriminalamt) made Danny's list. After adding the fifteenth contact, Danny called it quits.

Rita, their mom, settled on the emotional play using a bit of reverse psychology. "It's best a man sees to the situation in Germany. Ava's a smart girl, but she just isn't ready. Our girl is one tough cookie. She's dealt with union bosses, sexist factory managers, and corrupt politicians. But you're right, Clayton. Germany would be too much for her."

The tag team tactic wasn't just about chipping away at Clayton's excuses for not sending Ava. It was more about giving him the confidence and peace of mind to say yes. Still anxious, he finally gave the thumbs up.

Traveling the world was Ava's life. The opportunity to meet new people and learn new things was a thrill that took her to many parts of the globe. Ever since she was twenty-four, she had hopped from one European or Asian country to the next on behalf of the family business.

Ava expected the worst for what lay ahead of her in Germany. The scheme was pretty sophisticated and had apparently been operating for years. At best, one or two employees would go to jail. At worst, production would come to a screeching halt. Never one to shy away from a challenge, especially when it came to protecting her family, Ava set out to do her job.

Thankfully, her flight from China to Germany was uneventful. Inside the gate area, Ava stopped for a second to get her bearings and give her blood a chance to circulate through her legs. Eager to get out of the airport and to her new apartment, she dreamed of a long, hot bath to wash away the hours of exhausting travel. She hustled to baggage claim. After waiting an eternity for her luggage, she went to the designated pickup spot for her ride.

Behind a roped-off area, a few feet past the terminal sliding doors, a surprisingly large number of men in black suits held up signs with people's names. Ava's eyes scanned the signs, hoping to see her name. There was a *Herr Richardson,* a *Herr und Frau Adelberg,* and a *Frau Rodriguez,* but not a *Frau Brooks.*

Then, an older man in the customary black suit with a chauffeur's hat tucked under his arm made his way to the front of the line. He held up an iPad with *Frau Ava Brooks* on the screen.

Ava's squinted eyes met the driver's kind gaze. She waved and walked forward to greet him.

"Hello, I'm Ava Brooks—" She paused, catching herself, and greeted the chauffeur in German. "*Hallo, ich bin* Ava Brooks."

Her driver, crowned with white hair, wore black-rimmed round glasses. A neatly trimmed mustache rested above his warm smile. He tipped his hat and responded in English— the upbeat, friendly tone of his voice comforting her.

"Hello, Ms. Brooks. Welcome to Germany. My name is Jack. I will be your driver during your stay."

The frigid German wind blanketed Ava's face like a sheet of ice as soon as she stepped out of the airport. *Ugh, Danny's in Brazil, and I'm here freezing my butt off in Germany. He owes me big-time.*

Ava braced herself, put her head down, and fought through the frosty gusts to make it to the car. Jack started the black BMW and turned up the heat before loading her bags into the trunk. Rubbing her hands together and shivering, Ava lamented, packing her winter coat and hat in her luggage. Her lightweight trench coat was insufficient protection.

Jack navigated the airport traffic to begin their two-hour drive to Ava's new apartment. Ava cradled herself in the heated seats as buildings whizzed past the tinted car window. She texted her family, letting them know she had arrived safely. Her eyelids drooped, reading through her mom's text again with the details about the apartment. She drifted off to sleep after reading the second line:

> The key will be in your mailbox.

"We're here, Ms. Brooks."

Ava shook herself awake when she heard Jack's voice from the back seat. She glanced out the window at the apartment building, relieved that her tiresome journey had come to an end.

Jack wheeled in the last of the bags and waited by the door. "Will you be going to the factory tomorrow, Ms. Brooks?"

"Oh! I didn't know you were waiting." Ava's droopy eyes popped open. "My apologies, Jack," she blushed through her brain fog. "What is today? Tuesday? Please pick me up on Thursday at 7 A.M. sharp." Ava had jam-packed her schedule with meetings and employee lunches, but she wanted at least one day to rest before jumping into the thick of things at the factory.

"Of course, Ms. Brooks."

"And Jack, please feel free to call me Ava."

After Jack left, Ava made her way to the kitchen. Someone had secured a note to the refrigerator door with a magnet of the German flag, the kind a tourist would buy.

Hello, Ms. Brooks,

I hope everything in the apartment is to your liking. A few of your packages have yet to arrive from China, but I have the tracking numbers. Your calendar is up to date with the meetings and lunches you requested. If there is anything you need, please do not hesitate to call or text.
Caroline Kraus
Administrative Assistant

Ava opened the refrigerator. Caroline had stocked it with fresh fruits, vegetables, and many of her favorite foods—with German labels, of course.

Ava then surveyed her new bedroom and the master bath and sent her mom another text.

The apartment is perfect.
Love you so much. 🖤🖤🖤

Ava only trusted her mom to arrange her housing if she wasn't doing it herself.

Hungry, but far too exhausted to eat, she turned the thermostat up, took a quick, hot shower, and crawled into bed. Eating, unpacking, and planning could wait until tomorrow.

Chapter 2

DeAngelo parked his gray Mercedes-AMG GT Roadster in the driveaway and strolled through the back door into the kitchen of his childhood home. A self-assured confidence radiated from him, yet when it came to his momma, a boyish uncertainty dampened his expression as he slipped into the house, quiet as a mouse.

"Ah, my boy!" was the enthusiastic shout from Momma Rosalynn. She wiped her flour-covered hands and attacked DeAngelo with a mama bear hug and kiss. "You didn't tell me you would be home today. What time did you get back?"

DeAngelo grinned and kissed his momma on the cheek. "I got back Friday."

Suddenly, Momma Rosalynn pinched his shoulder, an upset frown replacing the joy of the sight of him. He retaliated with another apologetic kiss on her cheek.

"¿Ves esto? Una semana entera y no una llamada y luego poof, aparece justo a tiempo para la cena."

"English, Rosalynn sweetheart, English," DeAngelo's

dad begged as he listened to his wife speak Spanish while he poured the wine at the table.

"Yes, yes, English." Undeterred, Momma Rosalynn proceeded with a second scolding of her son. "A week and not a single call, but on time for dinner!"

The whole gang was almost all assembled. Mrs. Gretta Kraus, aka Momma Gretta, and her husband, Albert, were making their way into the kitchen. Their daughter, Caroline, was dutifully setting the table. The only Krauses missing were Peter and his wife, Ingrid—Albert's son and daughter-in-law, respectively.

Since he was eight years old, DeAngelo could not remember a time when the Kraus family and his family, the Williams, did not have Sunday dinner together. Living across the street from one another, DeAngelo and Peter grew up to be like brothers.

Momma Gretta passed the platter of sauerbraten to Caroline before making her inquiry.

"Where is my ungrateful son Peter? I haven't seen him. Has he been hiding from me, too?" she said with a chuckle in her throat.

"I hope you left Peter in Italy," Caroline teased, responding to her momma's inquiry as Peter and Ingrid—his wife of two years—walked through the door.

Peter's ears turned bright red upon hearing the snarky comment from his little sister. He conceded with his hands raised in the air.

"Hey, I didn't do anything. I'm innocent." He tugged on Caroline's hair. "Glad to see you, too, little sister."

Momma Rosalynn untied her apron and hurried to take her seat at the table.

"Peter, tell us of your adventures in Italy," she pleaded.

With a wide, little-boyish grin on his face, Peter tipped his wineglass to DeAngelo.

"Our boy," he said with a knowing glance at his best mate, "as usual, owned the city. The production crew loved him, the Italian people loved him, and the ladies especially loved him."

"Yes sir, I had myself a grand time," DeAngelo gleefully admitted.

While in Italy, he and Peter filmed two television ads—one for an Italian sparkling water brand and the other for an athletic apparel company headquartered in Naples. A natural in front of the camera, DeAngelo had made an effortless transition from pro footballer to successful product pitchman. But, he was not interested in talking about his time in Italy. He turned his attention to Caroline.

"Who was that woman I saw you with?"

Caught off guard, Caroline swallowed hard. "What woman?"

DeAngelo's eyebrow raised. "The woman I saw you leaving the café with on my drive home from the airport. It was around one or so. A pretty but serious-looking one. Is she a Black American?"

Can't I keep some things to myself? Caroline gritted her teeth. "She's my new boss. Her family owns the factory where I work."

Unsatisfied with the lack of details, DeAngelo persisted. "So, is she a Black American? Tell me about your new boss."

Momma Gretta gave Caroline a little nudge on the elbow to coax her along. "Caroline, you have talked your dad and me to death about your new boss. Go ahead, tell the boys."

Caroline sighed and gave a reluctant smile. "Yes, Momma. Her name is Ava Brooks. She arrived three weeks ago."

Caroline had planned only to provide the basics, but her enthusiasm got the best of her. She giggled with excitement.

"Oh, and there is going to be a cocktail party in her honor this Friday. I can't wait. Ms. Brooks personally invited me to the party."

DeAngelo stared impatiently. He wanted confirmation of his assumption.

With an eye roll, Caroline confirmed. "Yes, Ms. Brooks is a Black American."

Not often was there an opportunity to meet a professional Black American woman in a large city in Germany, let alone in the small manufacturing town his parents lived in.

"A cocktail party sounds fun. I'll be your plus-one," DeAngelo proclaimed.

Caroline folded her arms, resisting the idea. "Who says I'm taking you to the party? I might have a date."

DeAngelo suppressed a laugh, but not the enormous grin on his face. "You don't have a date, Caroline. I will be your plus-one."

Caroline looked around the table for support or sympathy.

"Of course, Caroline does not have a date," Momma Gretta confirmed, smirking at such an absurd idea.

Embarrassment flushed Caroline's face pink, highlighting her freckles. "But Momma, she is not DeAngelo's type."

DeAngelo laughed out loud. "And what is that supposed to mean, not my type? I like all types of women."

Caroline rolled her eyes in frustration. It was out of the question. No way did she want to take DeAngelo as her plus-one. How silly and pathetic was she going to look, bringing DeAngelo? He was as much a brother to her as Peter. She dug in deeper.

"All women, yeah, right. Women who are fashion models, actresses, or swimsuit models. That's your type. Ms. Brooks is smart and professional."

Momma Rosalynn swooped in to defend her precious son. "Caroline, DeAngelo only dates nice women. Don't you, son? Besides, it's not often an American visits our little town. It would be a good gesture for you to introduce her to DeAngelo."

"Now that you're retired from football, you might want to think about settling down," Momma Gretta suggested as delicately as a sledgehammer.

Caroline's fight was over. Once again, DeAngelo got his way.

"So, what time do I pick you up, Caroline?"

Friday evening arrived, and as Caroline finished getting ready for the cocktail party, she tried to swat her momma's hands away from her hair.

"Please, Momma, stop. I'm not a little girl anymore. I'm a grown woman."

Momma Gretta continued to fiddle with Caroline's hair. Then she smoothed the back of her daughter's dress.

"Doesn't my little girl look pretty, DeAngelo?"

DeAngelo observed his dolled-up little sister with a scrutinizing but playful glance.

"Yes, our little Caroline is all grown up," he said in a squeaky babyish voice.

Annoyed, Caroline stormed out of the house to the car. *I have got to get my own apartment,* she thought to herself. DeAngelo followed at his own pace. By the time he moseyed up to the car, Caroline had already jumped in with her seatbelt fastened.

DeAngelo started to pull out of the driveway. "So, where's the party?"

"It's at Henry Müller's," Caroline mumbled under her breath.

DeAngelo slammed on the brakes. Caroline jerked forward, her seat belt locking tightly on her chest.

"Henry Müller's? You never told me the party was at that jackass's house! You know I hate that guy."

Caroline's hand was on the door handle. She would be more than happy to go to the party alone, as she had intended.

"You never asked. You were too busy having everyone gang up on me to make you my plus-one. Do you know how ridiculous I'm going to look? You're just as much a brother to me as Peter. I'll be a laughingstock bringing you to a work party."

Caroline turned to face the window. *It's all about DeAngelo all the time.*

Chapter 3

Ava disliked doing it, but she forced herself to participate in idle chitchat, a requirement at every boring office cocktail party she had ever attended. The mindless conversations would generally take one of three directions. First, she would often endure an abundance of questions about America and her home state of Texas. God forbid someone remembered the 80s TV drama, Dallas.

Second, and no less annoying, an office gossip would trap her, eager to tell her all the company business unsolicited. Ava suspected the gossip types because, in her experience, they were usually manipulative.

Third, and most tedious, the office "go-getters," the ones who found it necessary to tout every single one of their credentials and accomplishments in painstaking detail.

The evening left no hope of getting better. The food was bland, and the music dull. *Henry really knows how to throw a party,* Ava seethed while living out her worst nightmare. She found herself trapped in a conversation with the office gossip, who also just happened to be an American TV fanatic.

"Do people really live like that in Texas, you know, where everything is so big? I hear Henry overpaid for this house. Beyoncé is Black and from Texas. She's famous now, but did you know her when she wasn't?"

Ava was ready to unload professionally in response to the most insane, "You're Black, too?" question when her new German colleague was saved as everyone's attention turned to the loud cheers and laughter in the other room. Energy and excitement ignited throughout the house, providing a glimmer of hope that the otherwise lifeless party could be resuscitated.

A man swaggered into the party with an aura of magnetic confidence and a charming smile. Caroline trailed a few steps behind, dwarfed by the brightness of the man in front of her.

Still glued to Ava's side, the office gossip was on her tiptoes, trying to see who was making such a grand entrance.

"Oh my, I see Caroline has brought none other than DeAngelo Williams."

Ava stretched her neck forward. "Who is DeAng—"

Breathless, the office gossip leaned in, bursting with delight. "You see, Ms. Brooks, DeAngelo is a local and national celebrity. He just recently retired from football. I'm sure he has better places to be than here. Caroline must have begged him to come. She's very awkward, you know, for a girl in her early twenties."

As the crowd thinned, Ava met Caroline's wandering gaze. She smiled and waved Caroline over. Caroline grabbed DeAngelo by the arm and dragged him in Ava's direction. With a timid, girlish grin and brightened cheeks, she greeted her boss.

"Hello, Ms. Brooks."

"Caroline, I am glad you could make it," Ava warmly replied.

"Ms. Brooks, I would like to introduce my brother, DeAngelo Williams."

Ava, a master at controlling her emotions, believed no one could notice how surprised she was to be introduced to a tall, handsome, dark-skinned man with a charming smile.

The contrast between this brother-and-sister pair was striking. Caroline bore dark-brown hair, light, freckled olive skin, and a small nose and lips. DeAngelo, her brother, looked far from German. Maybe there was some part of African American in him, but maybe not.

There must be an interesting story around this unique looking family relationship, Ava wondered.

"It's a pleasure to meet you, Ms. Brooks," DeAngelo greeted Ava. His suggestive yet haughty expression captured Ava's attention. His voice was deep and silky smooth, and his accent stood out among the thousands she'd heard before.

Captivated by DeAngelo's brown eyes, Ava extended her hand.

"Likewise, Mr. Williams."

DeAngelo took Ava's hand. He almost enclosed it in a double handshake when she pulled free—wrong move. Ava despised a double handshake from a stranger. It either felt creepy, like a sleazy come-on, or an aggressive power play.

DeAngelo's forehead creased. He gave a respectful nod and turned to leave when none other than Henry Müller stopped him with a less-than-welcoming hand on his shoulder.

Ever the show-off, Henry had insisted Ava allow him to host a welcoming party for her. Henry's voice was suspiciously enthusiastic.

"DeAngelo Williams, what a surprise! This is quite the honor."

DeAngelo shifted his position so Henry's hand would fall off his shoulder. His suggestive tone transitioned to dismissive and rude.

"Good to see you, too, Henry. Caroline asked me to come."

Caroline excused herself with a shake of her head and a sigh of extreme annoyance at that lie. She left DeAngelo to face his nemesis alone.

Primed and ready to take things to the next level, Henry gestured wildly as he raved over DeAngelo's illustrious football career.

"DeAngelo is a national treasure. He led us to several football championships and to the World Cup." Henry said and turned to Ava. "You Americans call it *soccer*."

Henry looked back at DeAngelo. "I can't believe you're not in some more exciting place in the world with your supermodel girlfriend and movie star friends." Henry took a quick breath. He had more phony praise to pile on. Again, he turned to Ava with a wide-eyed, silly look on his thin face.

"You see, Ms. Brooks, DeAngelo travels in more high-class circles," he said and then faced DeAngelo. "I'm sure you miss the attention. You never shy away from the camera or your adoring fans. But I guess you have really settled down into an old man's retirement."

Ava was on the verge of howling with laughter, watching Henry make a fool of himself by repeatedly trying to embarrass DeAngelo. Henry insulted himself, her, and everyone he had invited to the party by insinuating they were mere peasants compared to DeAngelo's high-class circle of friends.

"Well, we all aren't lucky enough to have a low-level management factory job we can count on. The nine-to-five grind suits you, Henry. Lovely house," replied DeAngelo, who then gave another respectful nod to Ava. "It was a pleasure to meet you, Ms. Brooks."

It took every ounce of concentration for Ava to maintain a straight face. With all her other concerns—chiefly that of finding the scoundrels skimming money from her family's business—watching the ridiculous grudge match between two grown men was the momentary distraction she needed.

Ava watched for an hour as DeAngelo worked the room, pulling all the attention to himself. He was at ease with everything. There was nothing fake or forced about him. He genuinely enjoyed having people around him—an extrovert to the tenth degree. Every now and then, she would search the crowd to find Henry sulking amongst a small group he was able to peel away for himself.

Ava was too tired and disinterested to feel sorry for Henry. He brought it all on himself. She suppressed a yawn as she glanced at her cell phone. *Yes, two hours! My time is up,* Ava rejoiced. Her rule was that two hours was enough time to endure an agonizing work cocktail party. She was a firm believer that if you couldn't show proper appreciation to the host and meet and chat with all the guests within two hours, you were doing something wrong. She texted Jack and said her goodbyes to Henry.

Ava walked to the back of the house with Henry's wife, Abigail, to retrieve her coat. There was a small cry from the cutest little face poking out from one of the bedroom doors.

"Mommy, I can't sleep. You didn't tuck me in."

Abigail bent down to kiss her daughter's cheek. "I need to see to our guest. I will come to tuck you in soon," she promised before coaxing her back to bed.

"Please, Abigail, say a proper goodnight to your daughter. I can find my way," Ava reassured her and walked down the hall toward the foyer. She was about to round the corner when she heard a conversation in German. She peeked over and saw one of the factory supervisors had cornered DeAngelo and was pestering him with questions.

"You're a man of the world. Tell me, what do you think of the American businesswoman?"

DeAngelo shrugged his shoulders. "I don't think much of her."

"Can you offer any advice?" the factory supervisor pleaded. "I don't want to lose my job. I've never worked for a woman, let alone an American, before. I don't know what to make of her."

"I would say she's a typical American. She seems a little rude and strikes me as uptight." DeAngelo paused and thought for a minute. "I'd guess she's about twenty-eight years old. I suspect her father made her come for the international experience; let his daughter run the business for a while. You get what I mean? In a few months, she'll be back in the States."

Ava shook her head in disbelief. *The nerve of this man. We speak for two seconds, and he thinks he knows me.* For not thinking much of her, DeAngelo had an awful lot to say, and the only thing he got right was her age.

"Ava, wait! Let me walk you out," Abigail yelled after closing her daughter's bedroom door.

As they rounded the corner and walked past DeAngelo, Ava gave him a well-deserved dirty look. She conversed with Abigail in near-perfect German, conveying her gratitude for the party and the warm welcome.

DeAngelo stood alone. His companion miraculously vanished as Ava approached. Embarrassed, DeAngelo shrunk back into the party to find Caroline. He was ready to go.

Ava spent the weekend thinking about how strange the cocktail party had turned out to be. The one thought that kept rolling around in her mind was why DeAngelo had come to the party in the first place.

Clearly, he didn't like Henry at all. And what "brother" would escort his little sister to a work party? Strange. Unless perhaps, DeAngelo was somehow mixed up with the mess at the factory. Ava abandoned the idea; it was too far-fetched.

DeAngelo's perplexing presence at her party piqued Ava's curiosity. So she got down to the business of opposition research. DeAngelo's stunning good looks, sexy voice, and beguiling smile surely made all the ladies swoon but would not fool her. After all, he did bad-mouth her when he thought she wasn't around.

What a shame it was that the first Black man I met in Germany would turn out to be a bit of a jerk. But then again, all men have the capacity to be jerks. I've dealt with worse.

If Ava thought DeAngelo looked good at the party, she was not at all prepared for how good he looked in the seemingly thousands of shirtless pictures on the Internet.

My goodness, I need to start watching soccer. Oops, I mean football, she thought as she scrolled.

She read through DeAngelo's outstanding football records. His biography was extensive. He had retired last year, a few months before he turned thirty.

Unable to confine her thoughts in her head, Ava talked aloud. "He's American. African American—well, sort of."

To say DeAngelo was biracial was an understatement. His father was of African American and Jamaican descent, and his mother was Spanish and African.

The more Ava researched, the more the pieces began to fit together. She found a video clip of DeAngelo running arm and arm with his teammate, who bore a striking resemblance to Caroline. The caption on the video read *Best Mates DeAngelo Williams and Peter Kraus win their first World Cup.*

Ava followed that breadcrumb to Peter Kraus's online profile with a link to a podcast. *Now I get it.* It all clicked as she read the *About Us* section of DeAngelo and Peter's podcast. Ava scanned through a slew of photos of the two at football matches, hoisting trophies flanked by their families. The photographs chronicled their football career from pre-teen to university and to the pros. Clearly, Caroline's biological brother is Peter Kraus, and she considers DeAngelo her brother.

Of course, DeAngelo's popularity with the ladies crossed her mind, but the plethora of photos provided plenty of evidence.

It was crystal clear. DeAngelo and Peter were two handsome, athletic, and presumably, rich guys and very popular with all sorts of women.

Ava scrolled through a few more pictures.

"So, I have an international playboy on my hands."

Monday morning rolled around, and Ava needed to focus. She had been sent to Germany on a mission. However, she kept the whole thing secret from everyone outside of her family and close advisors.

Ava handed Caroline a sheet of paper with names, dates, and times she had scribbled down during the ride to work.

"Caroline, would you please schedule meetings with the management staff? Unless there is an urgent need, I expect everyone to attend. Make sure you also attend as well."

"Yes, of course, Ms. Brooks." Caroline hesitated before continuing. "But, I'm just an office assistant. I never attend management meetings. Besides, I don't think the men would like me being there."

Ava looked up from her laptop and leaned back in her chair. She saw fear and nervousness in Caroline's gaze.

"I'm not concerned with how the men will feel," she replied with a straight face. "You're my executive assistant, and I expect you to attend all management meetings unless I direct otherwise. And Caroline, you are welcome to call me Ava."

After squaring things away with her assistant, Ava was soon out of her office and onto the factory floor with none other than Henry Müller. She wanted to discuss several lean manufacturing changes, but poor Henry still had considerable heartburn over DeAngelo's surprise appearance at the party.

"I apologize for the disruption at the party. That DeAngelo Williams is too arrogant for his own good. I can't understand for the life of me why Caroline would bring him. He didn't belong."

Didn't belong. Henry said that with a healthy dose of venom. It sounded to Ava to be more than just jealousy.

Ava played nice. "The party was lovely, Henry. I had a wonderful time. And I got to meet your precious little daughter."

Henry complained more about DeAngelo but ceased whining when Charles Pfeiffer, the senior plant manager, approached.

Charles ignored Ava and questioned Henry. "What are you doing on the floor?"

"Good morning, Charles," said Ava. "I'm conducting a floor-walk and asked Henry to accompany me. Please join us, won't you?"

As expected, Ava found the employees to be rather standoffish. They seemed to get on well enough with Henry, but no one spoke without being spoken to first when Charles was around.

Ava requested the equipment repair log from one of the mechanics. The man glanced at Charles first before moving an inch. Charles tilted his head forward in a nod of approval, and then the mechanic retrieved the log, handing it to Ava.

This gave Ava more insight into how Charles ran things. On her second day at the factory, she experienced his rude and abrasive nature firsthand. Ava noticed his nasty habit of interrupting women and subordinates during their first finance meeting.

She had asked for an updated financial report when Charles cut her off mid-sentence. He heatedly claimed the information would not be ready for at least a week and that her request was unreasonable. She shut him down so fast everyone's head was left spinning.

After that, Charles sat silent until Ava called for a break. Once she did, he stomped off in the opposite direction of everyone else.

When he returned from break, he had a bandage on his left hand. Ava later found out from Caroline that Charles had punched the paper towel dispenser in the second-floor men's room.

On more than one occasion, Ava witnessed Charles hovering over employees, reprimanding them for little mistakes. He was a poison in the factory, and Ava would be glad to get rid of him.

With the floor walk over, Ava returned to her office to find a letter on her desk. Ignoring the letter, she quickly dialed into her weekly check-in call with her dad and Danny. The unopened envelope lay there as she finished the call, replied to several emails, and completed multiple employee reviews.

Her phone buzzed with a text. Jack was downstairs, waiting to drive her home. The stressful, back-to-back series of meetings had shortened the day but exhausted her as well. She tossed the letter along with her laptop in her bag and left for the day.

"Have a good evening, Caroline," Ava said as she walked past Caroline's desk.

"You too, Ms. Brooks."

Three hours later, at home, and after a nice, long, hot bath, Ava relaxed on the couch with dinner in hand. She pulled out her laptop; there was still work to do. As she did, her fingers caught the mysterious letter she had thrown in earlier. She sat her laptop aside to cut open the envelope.

Ms. Brooks,

It was a pleasure meeting you. I regret that our first meeting ended with a misstep on my part. I was out of line, and I apologize for my inappropriate comments. I hope that you will accept my sincerest apology.
DeAngelo Williams

His words sounded earnest, though a little formal. He had left his number, so Ava decided to text him to see how far DeAngelo's "sincere" apology would go.

> I appreciate your apology. No harm done. All is forgiven. Ava Brooks.

Ten minutes later, she received a reply.

> Would it be okay if I called?

Ava thought for a second, then replied with a thumbs-up emoji. Her phone rang a minute later.

"Hello, Ms. Brooks."

"No need to be so formal. Please, call me Ava."

"Well, Ava, I appreciate you being willing to talk and allow me to apologize. I hope I didn't come off as too big of a jerk." DeAngelo's voice was just as sexy over the phone as in person.

"It was a little bit of a jerk move, but I'll survive," Ava teased.

"Now I have to redeem myself. Would you allow me to take you out to dinner?"

Ava shook her head back and forth, signaling no, as if DeAngelo could see her.

"That really isn't necessary," she answered with more of a dismissive tone than intended.

"I'm not asking out of necessity. I would like to see you again. Are you sure you won't reconsider?"

An unexpected flutter tickled Ava's stomach. At that moment, she couldn't think of a reason *not* to reconsider DeAngelo's dinner invitation.

"Thank you for the offer. I accept."

Ava's answer sounded more like agreeing to the financial terms of a bank loan than accepting a date with a handsome man. It had been so long since a man had asked her out that she scarcely knew how to react.

After saying goodbye, she fell back on the couch. Looking up at the ceiling with her hands folded behind her neck, Ava wondered aloud, "I hope I didn't make a mistake."

Chapter 4

Ava couldn't remember how long it had been since she had prepared for a date. Two years working in China put a full stop to her social life. Not that it was that active even before China, but getting ready for a date had not been a part of her plan when she arrived in Germany.

This is crazy. She spent an hour debating over what to wear, shedding outfit after outfit until settling on a gray pencil skirt, a purple-and-gray V-neck, striped sweater with a fitted waistband, and heeled, leather, knee-high boots. She stared at herself with a critical eye.

"Yep, my butt looks good." Still, something was off. Ava faced the mirror, and it hit her.

"Geez, that's entirely too much cleavage for a first date."

She reworked her outfit, adding a white, wide lace-trimmed, V-neck camisole under her sweater. The touch of lace softened the look.

She let out a laugh as she looked in the mirror one last time.

"That's better, and my butt still looks good."

Someone knocked at the door. *He's here.* Ava took a deep breath, shaking her body to try and ward off the jitters.

When she invited DeAngelo in, he unexpectedly drew her into a hug. Was it his hands on her back, the richness of his baritone voice, or the woody-and-toasted spice scent of his cologne that made an otherwise friendly hug feel strangely intimate?

Caught off guard, she only expected a simple smile and "hello" at most. DeAngelo was presumptuous. This was too much, too fast.

She eased out of the embrace with a clumsy pat on DeAngelo's shoulder. A question loomed in Ava's mind. Was DeAngelo just a touchy-feely guy, or was he a playboy interested in getting as many women as possible?

Cocktail-party DeAngelo turned out to be sort of a jerk, but his handwritten apology note had saved him. Sadly, it seemed that handsy, first-date DeAngelo wasn't much better.

During the quiet drive to the restaurant, Ava tried to spark up a conversation when DeAngelo mentioned that the restaurant had a young chef with a modern take on traditional German food.

"I love to eat, and I especially love to cook. I'm looking forward to learning a few new German dishes."

DeAngelo kept driving and didn't respond at all. Ava fumed in the passenger seat. *I got dressed up for this?* She breathed a sigh of relief when they reached the restaurant.

If the food is terrible, this will officially be one of the worst dates of my life.

When the valet opened her door, Ava looked twice as she swung her legs out of the car. It wasn't the valet but DeAngelo standing there, offering his hand to help her out. A few snow flurries swirled in the air giving the evening a frosty bite.

Her cold hand rested in DeAngelo's warm one. She met his eyes and saw the same charming smile she had first noticed at the cocktail party.

Ava would have put her hand in her coat pocket, but DeAngelo kept a firm grip. He rubbed her icy fingers until they were warm and only let go to help remove her coat when they got to their table.

"Would a cup of hot tea help?" DeAngelo asked as Ava shivered. "I'm sure the weather is much colder here than in Texas."

Ava answered "yes" to both the weather and the tea. *How does he know I'm from Texas? What else does he know about me?*

"What do you recommend?" Ava asked after surveying the menu.

"You can't go wrong with any dish," DeAngelo said. "Every dish is traditional but with such elevated taste and preparation. I personally recommend the Holzfaellersteak and Tafelspitz."

When the server returned, Ava ordered the Tafelspitz—a round beef with creamy horseradish sauce. DeAngelo ordered the Holzfaellersteak, grilled pork loin with mushrooms and onions.

During dinner, DeAngelo leaned forward, making the distance between them smaller and more personal. She felt the lingering gaze of his brown eyes.

Is this a well-rehearsed game? Ava wondered. She wanted to move past the first-date chatter and get into a real conversation. She ate a few bites and waited for the right moment.

Maybe this will rub a bit of the smoothness off.

"Do you know Henry well?" Ava asked nonchalantly while sipping her sparkling water with lime.

DeAngelo looked up, his forehead wrinkling. His face was set in a hard expression, and the corners of his mouth turned down.

"I know him well. I never liked the guy."

Unashamed, she pressed a tad harder.

"Is there a particular reason you dislike him?"

Inch by inch, DeAngelo's mouth turned to a playful grin. He leaned in closer, like he was about to share a secret with her.

"Henry's been an ass since birth."

Ava's eyes lit up. She shook with full-body laughter that produced a wide smile on her face that hurt her cheeks. She had to hand it to DeAngelo; he was smooth, and he knew it.

Ava felt relaxed enough to start getting to the bottom of DeAngelo and Caroline's family dynamics. She had to know how they became close enough to consider themselves brother and sister.

"Were you born here in Germany?"

"No," replied DeAngelo. "We moved here from the States when I was seven. My dad was a contractor for the U.S. Army for a while. We were only supposed to be here for a year, but we stayed and never moved back. I think dad felt more respected here than in the States, but he never said."

DeAngelo paused to laugh. "After about six months, we moved out of temporary housing to where my parents live now. I thought my life was over. I hated everything about Germany. But the second week in our new house, there was a knock at our door. It was our neighbor, Mrs. Gretta Kraus, with a chocolate bundt cake in her hands and her son, Peter, grudgingly by her side. She prides herself on being the official welcoming committee of the neighborhood. Ever since that day, Peter and I have been like brothers, and our families are inseparable."

Ava gave a playful smile. "Is Caroline your only sister?"

DeAngelo took a few sips of wine. "Actually, no. My sister, Sophia, was three at the time. She lives in Spain with her husband. Caroline is the baby of the family, but not for long. Peter and his wife, Ingrid, are pregnant."

"First grandchild?" Ava asked with a laugh.

"Yes," DeAngelo answered with a noticeable sigh of relief.

"Peter's mom and mine have been itching for grandchildren since Peter got married two years ago. Sophia married early last year, so she has a little breathing room. All the focus is on Peter and Ingrid at the moment."

Ava couldn't resist teasing.

"So, you're going to be Uncle DeAngelo soon. That's a big responsibility. Nieces and nephews are good practice for the future."

"A future that is a long way off," DeAngelo replied. He changed the subject and started talking more about growing up in Germany and his football career. "The thing I missed most when playing football professionally was our families' Sunday dinners. No one cooks like my momma and Momma Gretta."

"I know very little about soccer. I'm sorry—football. May I ask why you retired?"

DeAngelo seemed surprised by the question. *Retired.* Just the word made him feel old, like a washed-up athlete well past his prime.

He hadn't talked to anyone but his family about his retirement. He tempered his urge to feel offended and answered as emotionlessly as possible.

"Well, I guess it was time. I love everything about the game, but I got tired of the grind. I don't miss it that much."

Ava sensed a slight change in DeAngelo's demeanor. He pulled back, putting some distance between them. His answer didn't sound right for a man so successful and competitive to be that comfortable with retirement.

"Maybe you haven't been away from the game long enough to miss it yet."

DeAngelo flashed his charming smile.

"Maybe not," he replied to Ava's wise observation.

The modern deconstructed Tafelspitz delighted Ava's tastebuds, and DeAngelo's flirtatiousness resurrected her dormant, womanly desires. Much to her surprise, she savored every moment of devoted attention DeAngelo paid her.

Afterward, while waiting for the car, DeAngelo's hands rounded her shoulders as he helped slide her coat over her. The heat of his stare sent a thrilling shiver down Ava's spine.

Despite DeAngelo's averseness to talk in the car, Ava chatted away to avoid a boring drive back to her place. The one-sided conversation hadn't prevented her thoughts from racing forward to how the night would end. Would he want to be invited up? Would he try to kiss her goodnight or would he want something more?

DeAngelo walked Ava into her apartment building and pressed the elevator button for the fourth floor. Ava had precious seconds to decide.

God, why is he standing so close? Why does he still smell so good? Ava thought as she fished her keys out of her purse. *No, I won't invite him in. It's too soon.* The elevator dinged on the fourth floor.

Ava hesitated. Goosebumps blanketed her arms, sensing the gentle touch of DeAngelo's hand on her back as they stepped off the elevator. Ava's apartment was a few steps away. She remained resolute as she unlocked the door.

"Thank you for a lovely evening."

Chapter 5

DeAngelo committed every moment of the date to memory as he drove home from Ava's place. He hadn't ended a date with just a hug since—well, he couldn't remember when—but tonight, that was all Ava had offered. Not even a simple kiss on the lips or cheek.

He hadn't expected to be invited in, but come on. Could he have misread things? Throughout the dinner, DeAngelo stayed fixated on the delicate lace trim that framed Ava's chest, hinting there was something extraordinary underneath he didn't have permission to see. That damn lace teased him all night.

Ava wore the hell out of her outfit. DeAngelo could still see the way her firm apple bottom swayed back and forth in that fitted skirt every time she took a step in her heeled boots. He wouldn't mind holding on to that nice, tight rear end.

Besides her sexiness, Ava's confidence intrigued him. He had to know more about her. The first thing DeAngelo wanted to know was what made her want to learn to speak German. Of course, their date was a result of him wrongly assuming she couldn't speak or understand the language.

So he asked, "How do you speak German so well?" He remembered her smile and the laughter in her voice as she relayed the story.

"You can blame that on my dad. He was adamant that Danny—my brother—and I learn at least two languages; an easy language and a hard one. Danny chose Spanish and Italian. He thought he could impress girls if he spoke Italian. It worked. I chose French and German."

"Why German?" DeAngelo asked.

Ava shrugged her shoulders and gave a flirtatious smile. "I have no idea. It was the first thing that popped into my head at the time."

"I didn't think many Americans cared to be bilingual. Your dad sounds like a serious man."

Ava thought for a second. "My dad is a serious man, but I would describe him more as focused. He has such an eye for the future and is a committed champion of education. It was hard to appreciate his vision when I was young."

DeAngelo noticed that when Ava talked about her family, her eyes twinkled.

"Danny and I never had a real break from school," Ava continued. "We had a full schedule of classes during the summer, all taught by Ph.D. candidates from the University of Texas, my dad's alma mater. And Mom had us in every extracurricular activity imaginable."

Ava gave an exasperated huff. "Equestrian, swimming,

debate, fencing—you name it, we did it." She gave another huff with her hand up as if singling someone to stop. "Fencing I only did for one long summer. I hated that silly mask."

Ava smiled and laughed more. "Of course, Danny played football," she said with a wink at DeAngelo.

"*Real American football*, that is. In Texas, it's God, family, country, and football. Not necessarily in that order," Ava pledged with a cute, Texan twang for effect.

DeAngelo had lived in Germany for the majority of his childhood and all his adult life. He had not been back to America for any length of time outside of a few football matches. His concept of the Black American experience was not at all what Ava had described. He thought the majority were working-class, the barely-making-ends-meet type. Maybe a few in the middle class. He never considered a Black family owning a global manufacturing company.

As Ava talked, DeAngelo swiped through a mental inventory of his friends. His circle was full of Germans and internationals, but sadly, very few Blacks or African Americans.

I don't have many Black friends. DeAngelo had no idea of the angry, eyebrow-raised expression he was making, but it was enough to stop Ava from talking.

"Is there something wrong?"

Damn it. Did I say that out loud? If he wanted to look like a total jackass, saying, "Oh, I don't have any Black friends," would do the trick.

"No. I was just thinking that spending the summer tutored by Ph.D. candidates seems intense."

From Ava's skeptical eye roll, DeAngelo could tell she didn't entirely believe him. Still, fortunately for him, she continued talking about her family, which she seemed fond of doing.

DeAngelo realized Ava liked to push buttons to see how much she could get away with. She enticed him, sitting across the table with a wicked grin on her face.

On the surface, Ava was different from the women DeAngelo had dated. Not that there was anything particularly wrong with the women he usually went out with. They were all the actress, model, and singer types. They dominated his social circle. If Ava was the type to enter his new social circle post-retirement, he would be happy.

The conversation. The gentle teasing. The subtle and not-so-subtle flirting. All the signs were there at dinner. DeAngelo was back to his original thought: *why did Ava end such a good night with just a hug?*

Two weeks had passed, and DeAngelo was still stuck, so he called Peter for advice.

"I need some ideas. Where should I take Ava on our next date?"

"What the hell, man? I don't know. Wait, are you talking

about Caroline's boss? Take her to dinner or something nice like that."

"Yes, Caroline's boss. And we already did that. Don't say anything to the family," DeAngelo warned. "I don't want to hear any of that when-are-you-going-to-settle-down talk. Besides, I think Caroline will be pissed."

Peter threw out the only other suggestions that came to mind. "Maybe you can take her sightseeing. You know, to all the touristy places. Or, maybe to the movies and then out to dinner."

Both ideas seemed rather lame to DeAngelo. Sightseeing was out of the question. He wasn't about to drive around playing the tour guide. Where would he even take her? To the zoo or some stuffy museum? There had to be more sophisticated places than tacky tourist traps.

DeAngelo ended the call with Peter, still clueless about where to take Ava on their second date. If Ava was any other woman, DeAngelo would whisk her off to a trendy nightclub—VIP treatment, of course—and then hang with his circle of the who's who of the international, elite crowd. He didn't peg Ava as the nightclub type. He learned from their first date she didn't even drink.

Frustrated, he couldn't think of a better date option. DeAngelo felt on edge driving to Ava's place. He kept thinking, *I'm taking a woman to the movies. This is just stupid.*

DeAngelo hadn't been to a regular movie theater since

he was a teenager, but he had been to plenty of red-carpet movie premieres with paparazzi swarming him like vultures.

The Saturday early afternoon overcast sky did little to lift DeAngelo's spirits as he pulled out of the parking lot of Ava's apartment.

"This should be fun. My first time seeing an authentic German movie in Germany!" Ava said once DeAngelo merged onto the main road.

While driving to the theater, Ava read the description of the two movies she was deciding between. "Which one sounds better to you?" she asked.

"Either one. You decide." DeAngelo hadn't paid much attention. He was too caught up in how stupid he felt. He selected a matinee to lessen his embarrassment, hoping to encounter as few people as possible.

Ava tried to make conversation again, but DeAngelo was less than receptive. Once at the theater, he squared his shoulders and walked more confidently, seeing far fewer people than he had expected.

Ava laughed when she saw a familiar smorgasbord of unhealthy snacks. She glanced up at DeAngelo.

"Germans like their sugary snacks at the movies as much as Americans."

"Yes, just like Americans," he whispered in her ear in German.

They stepped to the counter to order. Ava requested a

small popcorn and water as she gave a gentle rub on DeAngelo's muscular arm.

DeAngelo ordered, and as soon as he made eye contact with the concession clerk, he knew he had been recognized. The clerk stood there, shaking with a ridiculous grin on his face. A few seconds of silence passed between the gawky teenager and the world-famous footballer.

Then came the familiar, high-pitched, excited voice of a superfan speaking German. "Yes, yes! Anything for you, sir!"

DeAngelo held his breath and hoped the kid would let them go on their way. Fortunately for him, Ava was busy reading all the movie posters and making comparisons to U.S. theaters to notice his fan encounter.

The clerk stayed quiet, and with concessions in hand, DeAngelo ushered Ava in to find their seats. The theater was half-empty. DeAngelo's shoulders relaxed as he sunk into the leather seats. The lights dimmed, and the movie started.

The villain in the movie spoke in a weird, East German dialect. Ava leaned in to ask for a translation. DeAngelo whispered the answer and stretched his arm around Ava's shoulders, encouraging her to stay close.

This is nice. DeAngelo admitted to himself. No VIP treatment, just simple and quiet. Normal. He had forgotten what it felt like.

The movie ended with the bad guy in jail and the good

guy winning the girl. As the lights rose, the murmur from the audience indicated their approval.

"I don't think my Americanized German will do well in the East," Ava joked as the credits rolled and they exited the theater.

DeAngelo smiled. Before he could respond, a crowd of teenagers mobbed him.

Damn! That little concession-stand punk set me up.

Close to fifty kids came running up with footballs and posters, pressing up against DeAngelo and clamoring for autographs and selfies. That little punk got under his skin by getting the jump on him. Only a few months ago, he would have anticipated an ambush.

DeAngelo reached for Ava's hand, but the throng of teenagers separated them.

"Hey, hey! What's going on here?" yelled the manager, a red-faced young man with his hair tied up in a man bun, running out to the crowd. "Everyone without a movie ticket, get out!"

The kids didn't budge.

"Security! Come to the lobby *now!*" the manager shouted into his two-way radio.

The wide-eyed kids shouted a few choice words at the manager before dispersing in all directions, leaving DeAngelo catching his breath and straightening his shirt before giving the manager a "thank-you" slap on the back.

DeAngelo spotted Ava standing by the exit door. He headed towards her when the manager stopped him and asked for an autograph. He scrawled his name on a wrinkled piece of paper the manager was holding, then raced over to Ava.

"I'm really sorry about that. I didn't think something like that would happen," DeAngelo said as they walked to the car.

"Does that happen often?" Ava asked as DeAngelo opened the car door for her.

"No, not since I retired. I'm pretty sure the concession kid texted all his friends. Let me make it up to you. How about we get a bite to eat?" He convinced himself that Ava couldn't be that pissed. She agreed to an early dinner.

Over the next few weeks, Ava and DeAngelo continued to spend time together, squeezing in dates as their schedules allowed. This was their seventh or eighth date by now, but who's counting? Each date had ended more or less the same as the first. At least Ava had added a kiss on the cheek with the friendly hug. However, if DeAngelo had his way, there would be more soon. *Soon,* meaning, like, *now.*

DeAngelo swiftly led a freezing Ava into a small café. After over two months, he couldn't believe that Ava had still not adjusted to the weather. He smiled to himself. *It must be that hot Texas blood.*

DeAngelo ordered a black tea at the counter, and Ava ordered a lemon ginger tea and apple strudel. The strudel was ready, but the tea needed to be brewed and brought to the table.

The sparse crowd in the café left several tables open. DeAngelo, however, walked toward a cozy corner booth. The booth was situated in such a way he and Ava would need to sit side by side.

As they got seated, the server brought them their tea. DeAngelo sat close enough that his leg touched Ava's. He swung his arm around her shoulder. He glanced down at the shine of Ava's plump, slightly-wet lips and leaned in without hesitation. She gave into his kiss instantly.

He kissed Ava harder as her hand moved up his arm. Ava's hand reached upwards and massaged his neck. His entire body warmed. He wrapped his arm around her waist and pulled her even closer.

The roar of the espresso machine and the chime of the bell above the café door snapped them back to reality.

Without a doubt, DeAngelo knew that was a "yes, I want you" kiss. When Ava pulled back, he suppressed a laugh. Her face flushed and glowed with embarrassment.

He couldn't imagine why Ava would be embarrassed. It was a great kiss. Was it because they were in public? He attempted to decipher Ava. Is she hot, cold, or a constant lukewarm?

DeAngelo was at Peter's to record a few podcasts, but all he could think about was Ava.

He leaned against the wall of Peter's office and blurted out, "I think I'm going to stop seeing Ava. You know, Caroline's boss."

After several weeks of dating, he and Ava had only kissed. Things were moving far too slowly for his liking. Peter knew but had forgotten. He quickly thought up something to say.

"Maybe you should just let things cool off."

DeAngelo scoffed. "Cool off? The woman is practically an iceberg. The other night, I thought we were getting somewhere. I had her over to my place for dinner. Things were going in the right direction. A little something was happening, but her phone buzzed. It was her driver. At 9:00 P.M."

DeAngelo stopped talking to run a couple of microphone cords for the podcast recording. Disbelief covered his face.

"Get this. She says, 'Thank you for a lovely evening. My driver is here.' Can you believe that?" DeAngelo paced around Peter's cramped little office, shaking his head. "I knew it from the start, at the cocktail party. The woman is an uptight hard-ass."

Peter laughed so hard he was almost in tears. "She blew you off!"

None of this was funny to DeAngelo. He was not the type of guy to get blown off by a woman.

Chapter 6

Ava left work each day mentally and emotionally drained. The constant pressure of protecting the family business weighed on her. She lay awake for hours throughout the night, debilitated by blinding migraines.

As much as she despised Hammet Vogel, she knew he was the real mastermind behind all the nefarious activities. He had always been meticulously precise with his deception, but the nitwits he had left his criminal enterprise to were greedy and sloppy. They left a paper trail a mile long of forged timesheets, fake invoices, and falsified inventory records behind, documenting their underhanded reprehensible behavior.

She could no longer tolerate the small band of criminals that had a terrifying hold over the factory workers. Even with the factory only in her family's possession for a year, Ava still felt a great sense of failure. Good employees were quitting, and the factory continued to lose money and credibility with legitimate customers.

We should have caught this in our due diligence. The hours of phone conferences with her family and meeting after meeting with lawyers drove her blood pressure sky-high. Everyone was on edge, checking again and again that every "i" was dotted and every "t" was crossed.

After three months of work, the moment arrived. Ava, the authorities, and the lawyers all aligned. They now had all the physical and digital evidence to make the necessary arrests. Today was the day. The smug faces of the crooks, the fear in the employees' eyes, and the pervasive corruption would end. Ava felt relief, knowing that a major part of her mission for coming to Germany would be over soon. Afterward, more heavy lifting needed to be done, but Ava wouldn't be alone in that endeavor.

Ava had Jack pick her up at 5:00 A.M., a few hours earlier than normal.

"Good morning, Ms. Ava. You're headed to the office extra early today?" Jack greeted with a tip of his hat and opened the car's back door.

"Good morning, Jack. Yes, I need an early start today."

"Busy day, eh? Well, I suppose a woman with all your responsibilities, every day is a busy day."

Ava looked at Jack, knowing he had no earthly idea of what she would face in a few hours. "Yes, Jack. I have a very big day ahead of me."

"Well, ma'am, at least it's Friday."

Jack's optimism gave Ava some comfort. "You're right. I have the weekend to look forward to!"

With hardly any other cars on the road, they reached the factory in only fifteen minutes when it usually took upwards of forty-five minutes. Before she got out of the car, Ava instructed Jack to pick her up at the back entrance instead of out front after work. She spent the early morning hours in her office alone, sitting and thinking through as many different scenarios as possible. She started with the worst-case scenario: violent outbursts and fights, and ended with the best-case scenario: zero drama.

With her mind set and nerves stilled, Ava was ready. A steady stream of employees began flowing into the factory around 8:00 A.M. Ava could feel the rumble of machinery underneath her feet. The morning shift was up and starting their day.

Ava waited for the morning routine to settle before calling Caroline into her office.

"Caroline, schedule a management meeting in the boardroom for 2:00 P.M. Invite Henry Müller, Charles Pfeiffer, and Edward Wagner, the accountant. Hold the room for an hour."

Caroline jotted down a few notes in her notepad and turned to leave Ava's office. She stopped at the door, hearing Ava call her name.

"Oh, and Caroline," she added. "Be prepared to schedule an all-employee meeting for 4:00 P.M., but don't send out the communication for it until I give the go-ahead."

The rest of the morning and early afternoon ran their usual course. Half an hour before the management meeting, Caroline went to the boardroom to ensure everything was clean and in order. Her eyes widened at the sight of Ava already there with five other important-looking people.

"Caroline, this meeting may get contentious," Ava said, looking at her from the other side of the room. "I need you to stay sharp and learn how to handle yourself in stressful situations. Please, take a seat at the end of the table."

Caroline sat and watched Ava and the others talk. They spoke in half sentences of "yes," "understood," "it's taken care of," confirming previously-agreed-upon plans. She wondered what was going to happen next.

The clock struck 2:00 P.M., but none of the invitees had arrived. At ten after two, Charles, annoyed, pushed through the door with his puffy, rose-colored face and deep-set, beady eyes. Henry and Edward trailed behind him.

When everyone was seated, Ava began. She sat with her shoulders relaxed and her hands clasped and resting on the conference table. A smirk of satisfaction graced her countenance.

"Gentlemen, several months ago, my father and I, along with our finance team, noticed some irregularities with your accounting practices. After more in-depth forensics, we uncovered more than a few minor deviations."

Henry turned ghostly pale, and large beads of sweat formed on his forehead. Charles glared across the table at

Ava like a dog waiting to pounce. Edward's lazy eye began to twitch.

Ava slid a packet of stapled papers across the table to three pairs of stunned eyes glaring back at her. She then introduced the police inspector, someone from the prosecutor's office, and her legal counsel—the five who were sitting with her.

"I have worked with U.S. and German authorities. We have considerable evidence you and the previous owner, Mr. Vogel, have been embezzling large sums of money for years."

Charles snarled in response to Ava's accusation.

"How dare you accuse us of stealing! Vogel may have been a crook, but I'm not. You and this whole damn factory can go to hell!"

"You have used this factory as your personal playground. Your little criminal enterprise ends now," Ava replied, flipping through her packet of papers.

Charles exploded in a profanity-laced tirade, shouting and calling Ava the vilest of names. Ava's clasped hands tightened, and her eyes squinted. Charles jumped up, knocking his chair to the floor, and turned to leave the room.

"Sit down!" shouted the police inspector.

Ignoring the warning, Charles jerked around with his arms stretched forward, lunging across the table at Ava. Ava pushed back from the table and sprang from her seat, ready to defend herself. Caroline clenched her hands over her mouth to suppress a scream. Charles thrust his large body over the table, scrambling to get his hands around Ava's throat.

Ava cringed, hearing Charles gasp and seeing his beady eyes nearly pop out of their sockets as the inspector jerked him back and took him to the floor.

Henry, in true coward fashion, ran for the door. He came face to face with a uniformed officer on the other side, ready to arrest him. Edward remained in his chair until he was instructed to do otherwise.

Within twenty minutes, the tumultuous meeting ended. Tears ran down Caroline's face, and Ava took her by the hand.

"Come. Let's go to my office." Ava handed Caroline a tissue and waited until she could calm herself down. She pulled her chair around to Caroline, so they faced one another.

"How could you do that?" Caroline asked, talking through muffled tears. "Be so calm, especially when Mr. Pfeiffer came after you?"

Ava handed Caroline another tissue.

"It comes with years of experience and a career's worth of being in the trenches."

Caroline blew her nose.

"I could never be that brave."

"Listen to me, Caroline. You have been the most capable assistant I have ever had. From day one, you've followed my instructions to the letter. You've sat through countless meetings. And you never gossiped. I have counted on you for more than you know. Thank you."

Someone knocked at Ava's door before opening it slightly to enter. Ava brought Caroline to her feet and gestured for the attorney waiting outside to give her a minute. She instructed Caroline to send out the email invitations for the employee meeting and get a few other things prepared. Ava's words steadied Caroline's shaky hands.

By the time of the employee meeting, the news had spread throughout the factory. Many saw Charles, Henry, and Edward escorted away in handcuffs. News vans had also begun assembling in front of the factory. Ava and the attorneys were as transparent as possible, given the circumstances. Immediately after the all-employee meeting, an email was sent, reiterating the next steps and plans to move forward.

The day was almost over. *It's 5:30 P.M., thank goodness.* Ava flopped down in her desk chair, rubbing her temples. She could feel a migraine coming.

Soon, her phone buzzed with a text from Jack. From the window, Ava could see her driver standing at the exit door, looking around nervously.

Ava breathed in a moment of solace, gathered her things, locked her office, and walked downstairs. Jack opened the door when he saw her and shielded her until they reached the car.

"My God, Ms. Ava, are you okay? I heard some of what happened on the radio. There are still a few news crews out front.

I will take us out via the service road. There are cameras out front, I suspect, ready to broadcast live for the evening news."

"Thank you, Jack," she said, gratitude brightening in her eyes and lifting her spirits. "The quicker you can get me home, the better."

In the safety of her apartment, Ava called her parents. Her dad, of course, fumed. He had already talked with their attorneys and knew how Charles had gone after her. With her dad too angry to talk, Ava got off the phone. She sat on the couch, staring at the wall. For the first time since she had arrived in Germany, she didn't have any urgent business issues to solve.

For three months, she had poured all her energy into ensuring she got everything right concerning the family business, often feeling selfish for enjoying her dates with DeAngelo and splitting her time in half with him and the company. Now she didn't seem to have an ounce of strength to decide whether to fix herself dinner or not.

Layer upon layer of emotional strain had been building inside Ava. Since detecting the embezzlement, every meeting and conference call was one more layer on top of the last. Moving to Germany, another layer. Dealing with the arrogant attitudes, rudeness, and outright lies of those stealing from her family added a layer with every interaction.

Ava dragged herself to the bathroom. She hoped that

maybe a hot shower would help. The heavenly scent of eucalyptus and lavender bath salt, mixed with the shower's steam, enveloped Ava's body. The steaming hot water melted the blankets of stress. The jet spray kneaded the knots from her shoulders and back. Each layer of pressure, anger, and fear started to shift like massive tectonic plates.

Tears of relief burst forth as months of built-up tension dripped from her fingertips with each droplet of water. The shower relieved the stress, but now a crushing homesickness took over.

Too depressed to eat, Ava curled up in a blanket on the couch. She tried to watch television, but every channel failed to distract her. She skipped quickly past any news channel.

"I hate this stupid country!" Ava shouted, slamming the remote on the couch.

On one of the worst days of her life, her family was on the other side of the world. She desperately wanted a shoulder to lean on. Calling DeAngelo was out of the question. He stopped calling or texting weeks ago.

Of course, it disappointed Ava that DeAngelo couldn't hang on a bit longer, but she didn't blame him. She was more than a little fickle on their dates. Ava fought the urge to go as far as DeAngelo was willing on each outing. Their kiss in the café nearly shredded her resistance.

Ava's loneliness was one more sacrifice she had made for the family business.

Chapter 7

It was half-past six. DeAngelo was driving back to his apartment from a meeting with his agent. His phone vibrated back and forth in the passenger seat, blowing up with texts from his momma, Momma Gretta, and Peter. DeAngelo's eyes widened at the messages implying Caroline was in trouble.

DeAngelo didn't bother to text back. He immediately changed directions and headed to Momma Gretta's. As soon as he stepped through the door, his mom, Rosalynn, waved him into the living room with the rest of the family.

"Come, come, DeAngelo. It's on the news."

There were police cars and news vans crowded in front of the factory Caroline worked at. The words, "Breaking News," flashed in red along the bottom of the screen. A horde of reporters shoved each other and battled for position to get their microphone the closest. Each reporter shouted their questions, hoping for a sound bite.

The officers pushed three men through the crowd. Each one had their head lowered and arms cuffed behind their backs as the cops stuffed them into the patrol cars. The only one DeAngelo recognized was Henry Müller.

A more-experienced news anchor smoothed his hair back before thrusting the microphone into some well-dressed woman's face.

"I'm here with Brooks family attorney and spokesperson, Marcia Daniels. Tell me, Ms. Daniels, how well-organized is the alleged crime ring? Do the allegations extend to other factories owned by the Brooks family? Are you confident you have all the supposed members of the ring?"

The attorney, a Black woman with an American accent, remained poised under the aggressive questioning.

"The Brooks family is grateful for the support and professionalism of the German authorities. Their assistance was invaluable in this matter."

"Do you expect additional arrests?" the reporter continued.

"We trust the German authorities to continue their investigation. Thank you."

Highly satisfied, the news anchor looked as if he had scored the interview of the century. He held a gloating smile as he looked into the camera and then turned his attention to the communication director.

The only thing on DeAngelo's mind was he wished he could get his hands on Henry. He didn't believe he could hate Henry any more than he already did.

Ever since they were young, Henry had been an envious

little weasel, always trying to be more than he was and failing miserably. Never able to stand on his own, Henry glommed onto others, dying to feel important. DeAngelo never thought Henry was dumb enough to commit a crime.

"Henry Müller, that pathetic—" DeAngelo gritted his teeth and pounded his fist into his hand. He was at Momma Gretta's house, and she did not like foul language.

Caroline continued his thought. "Henry is a pathetic coward. He *actually* tried to make a run for it! What an idiot. The police were standing right outside the door."

DeAngelo scowled at the television screen, not blinking, expecting to see Ava interviewed. The only interviews given were by the corporate attorney and the communications director. He was furious. He wanted to do something, but *what*?

Through soft tears and a trembling voice, Caroline recounted the frightening events of the day. The entire family sat shocked. When Caroline described how Charles Pfeiffer had lunged across the table, everyone exploded with anger.

Rosalynn tried to calm and hush everyone so Caroline could finish, but to no avail.

"That bastard!" Peter yelled out. "He didn't hurt you, did he, Caroline?"

Infuriated, DeAngelo added to the uproar.

"Did any of them touch you, Caroline? Did they hurt Ava? I mean, Ms. Brooks?"

Momma Gretta had her arms around Caroline in a virtual death grip. Caroline could scarcely breathe, let alone speak. Rosalynn tried again to cool tempers with much better success.

Momma Gretta loosened her hold. Caroline took a deep breath and continued.

"Charles went after Ava, calling her the worst names I've ever heard. The inspector yanked Charles to the floor before he could reach her."

DeAngelo wanted to ask about Ava, but he thought it would seem strange if he showed too much interest in Caroline's boss. No one except Peter knew they had been dating.

Momma Gretta provided the perfect opportunity for him to hear about Ava, when she sympathetically interjected.

"I'm sure Ms. Brooks must have been scared to death."

"Oh, no, Momma," Caroline said. "I watched her. From start to finish, she was in control. It was like she was completely unfazed. If the inspector hadn't put Charles to the floor, I swear, I believe Ava would have. She was awesome!"

DeAngelo thought to drive over to Henry's house to see if he was out of jail. He wanted to bash that little asshole's face in.

Instead, he hung around the house for another hour or so until everyone had settled down, including himself. Before he left, DeAngelo gave Caroline a huge hug.

"I'm glad you're okay. Sounds like you handled yourself well."

DeAngelo drove off toward his apartment but turned around shortly into his journey. He headed over to Ava's. He knew he had to do something but wasn't quite sure what. For all he knew, Ava wanted nothing to do with him.

"Damn it! I shouldn't have ghosted her," DeAngelo argued with himself in the car.

He should have been more attentive, even if Ava didn't feel comfortable enough to confide in him about what she was dealing with at work. Still, DeAngelo figured he had to do something. He couldn't leave Ava alone with no one to talk to. That was too depressing.

DeAngelo made a few stops, then drove to Ava's apartment. He called her as he stepped off the elevator onto her floor. He was surprised but happy that Ava picked up. He spoke before Ava could even say hello.

"Hi, Ava. I heard you had a rough day."

There were a few seconds of silence before Ava replied.

"You could say that."

DeAngelo could hear the tiredness in her voice. The last thing he wanted to do was to make things worse. He took a chance that maybe an apology and "feel better" gift would cheer her up.

"I don't want to hold you up, but I have apple strudel and vanilla ice cream for you. I'll leave it at your door."

Ava opened the door to see DeAngelo standing there, holding a bakery box and a small brown bag. It was eight in the evening, but she was already in her black cotton pajamas.

Most of her curly hair was swept up and clipped, but several unruly strands hung loosely around her makeup-free face. To DeAngelo, she looked adorable.

She opened the door wide to let him inside.

"Please, come in and stay for a minute."

DeAngelo smiled, appreciative of the invitation. He thought "stay for a minute" sounded so American. Ava's face was too downcast for his smile to last for more than a brief second. She took the box and bag to the kitchen while DeAngelo made his way to the living room. Ava came back with a bowl of warm apple strudel and ice cream and plopped down on the couch next to DeAngelo, put her feet on the coffee table, and balanced the bowl on her knees.

DeAngelo fought the driving urge to kiss her.

"Caroline told us what happened, and we watched the report on the news. I'm sure it was awful."

Ava closed her eyes tight and drew in a deep, mournful breath. She then opened her eyes in sync with a long, slow exhale and punctuated it with a spoonful of strudel and ice cream.

DeAngelo struggled to keep himself focused. He knew he should allow her to talk, but what he wanted was to take Ava into his arms.

"You've been working on this for the entire three months?"

Ava sat back and leaned into DeAngelo. Her pink-painted toes peeked out from under her pajama pants.

"It's been much longer than three months. While in China, I started preparing to finally come and oversee the factory's integration into our business. I noticed some irregularities in the books. After some significant digging with our finance and legal teams, it was clear that the discrepancies were not simple oversights. We contacted the FBI and the proper local authorities here."

With another spoonful of strudel and ice cream, Ava settled her nerves. DeAngelo rested his arm on the back of the couch and softly twirled Ava's loose strands in his fingers. He listened as she continued.

"I came here to effectively close the case. I needed to help authorities build a case while protecting our clients, employees, and family interest."

DeAngelo put his arm around Ava's shoulders.

"You've been under enormous pressure. I'm sure I made things worse for you. I'm sorry for that," said DeAngelo.

"No, you were fine." The corner of Ava's mouth raised to a tiny smile. "Seriously, thanks for helping me focus on something other than the utter destruction of my family's business."

The whole situation bothered DeAngelo more than he expected. He didn't like the sadness in Ava's voice. He wanted to comfort her, make her happy, if possible.

Ava sat up a little.

"Goodness, I'm sorry. I've been eating ice cream and strudel, and I never thanked you or offered you any." Her beautiful, raven-black eyes showed a glimmer of brightness. She lowered her voice.

"Do you want a bite?"

"Just ice cream, please," replied DeAngelo.

Ava fed DeAngelo a spoonful of ice cream. When the utensil left his mouth, he had to have more, but not ice cream.

DeAngelo took the bowl and spoon from Ava's hand, pulled her close, and kissed her cold, apple-scented lips with determination.

He lingered on her neck and then kissed just below her collarbone, exposed by the open button of her pajama top. Ava's hands roamed over his chest, down his side, and along his thigh. A soft, dreamy look gleamed in her eyes, and her lips formed into a smile, drawing him in. DeAngelo brushed his hand against her cheek, and Ava kissed the inside of his palm.

"Make love to me," she whispered into his ear.

DeAngelo paused, thinking, *Was that a question, a suggestion, or a command?* Did it even matter? In his mind, he screamed, *Hell, yes!* A surge of energy raced through his body.

DeAngelo stepped out of his shoes by the bedroom door. Ava helped him take off his shirt. He watched her pajama pants fall to the floor. Ava's top was too long to see anything other than her beautifully dark, caramel legs. He hadn't imagined her to be this bold.

He watched her thin, feminine fingers free each button of her pajama top. The second button, third, fourth, and fifth—until her shirt cascaded to the floor.

DeAngelo ran his hands over Ava's smooth, shapely body.

"Damn, you look good."

He turned Ava onto the bed and thought this would be an amazing night.

Chapter 8

It was after midnight when DeAngelo woke with Ava draped across his chest. He knew he should leave, but holding her felt nice. He was determined to give himself fifteen more minutes, then wake Ava and go.

DeAngelo wasn't in the habit of staying at a woman's place through the night. He kept a very strict schedule during the football season when at home. Besides, the women he usually dated were as noncommittal as him. He started to count down the fifteen minutes in his head as he caressed Ava's back. His finger circled a rough patch of skin a few inches below her rib cage. He moved on, but his hand drifted back to Ava's imperfection.

DeAngelo was curious as his fingers traced along the rough edges of the scar. He conjured in his mind a hundred different situations that may have ended with such a result. After playing competitive sports all his life, he suffered more cuts, bruises, strains, and breaks than he cared to count, and each one had a story.

"It was a car accident. My scar. It's from a car accident," said Ava, her voice hoarse.

Embarrassed, DeAngelo dropped his hand to his side.

He hadn't realized Ava was awake or that he had paid so much attention to her imperfection she had noticed.

"I'm sorry. I didn't mean to—"

The accident happened so long ago it didn't bother Ava anymore to talk about it. She rolled onto her side, clinching the blanket close to her chest.

"We were all driving home from dinner. Mom and Dad were together in the car ahead of us, and I was driving back with Danny. The light turned green. Mom and Dad went through it first. Danny and I followed but were blindsided by a car that had run the red light."

Ava stopped. DeAngelo mirrored her movement so they were both sitting up and his arm around her.

"Our car flipped twice and landed upside down in the intersection," she continued. "I remember screaming out for Danny, him touching my hand and saying, I'm here, Sissy."

DeAngelo moved in closer. Ava leaned against his chest. "I can still remember hearing our parents' voices, but not what they were saying. I woke up two days later in the hospital with a dislocated shoulder, a few broken ribs, and multiple bruises and lacerations. Danny was in a similar condition, but he also had a broken leg."

Ava paused.

DeAngelo tightened his arms around her and kissed her forehead. He hadn't dreamed that the story would be so gut-wrenching.

"It must have been awful."

"It was, but we fared much better than the driver of the other car. She had her two small sons with her. Neither was wearing a seat belt. Her youngest, the two-year-old, didn't make it. She was drunk. Twice the legal limit."

"Is that why you don't drink?" DeAngelo asked without thinking.

Ava shook her head and thought, *Men have such few things to be concerned about.*

"No, there are more practical reasons I don't drink. I'm often working and living alone in different parts of the world. I want to always have my wits about me. A woman can never be too careful." She turned to DeAngelo, smiling. "You should know by now that I'm the conservative, disciplined type."

Ava's description of herself was a contradiction to her passionate kisses and her seductive moans when he touched in the right places last night.

Who is this woman? DeAngelo kissed Ava long and hard. She gently eased herself on top of him. His fifteen-minute countdown was soon forgotten.

DeAngelo's eyes watered, adjusting to the sunlight streaming into the room. He shook his head to clear the haze from his mind.

Damn it! He was still at Ava's and alone in her bed. *This must be her way of telling me it was time to leave.*

DeAngelo got out of bed and went to the bathroom. A new toothbrush, next to a clean towel and washcloth, lay neatly folded on the countertop.

What the—? DeAngelo arched an eyebrow, frowning. *What am I supposed to do? Shower, dress, and walk out like some one-night stand?*

When he saw his clothes likewise perfectly folded in a chair, he went from pissed to flat-out angry. He snatched up his pants and dressed, regretting not having left earlier like he had planned.

DeAngelo heard footsteps. He couldn't get his shirt on fast enough before Ava walked into the bedroom. The morning sunlight illuminated her face and her cream-colored silk robe that floated above her ankles.

Ava carried a breakfast tray.

"Good morning. Did you sleep well? I made a little breakfast." Cheerfulness coated her voice, and that sexy smile of hers brightened her face.

DeAngelo stood there with his shirt in his hands, watching Ava's every move. She turned with a glass in each hand.

"Orange or cranberry?"

He threw his shirt on and took the glass of orange juice. Ava handed him a small plate as they sat.

"I hope this is okay." Fruit, biscuits, sliced toast, and two small jars of jam filled the tray.

What the hell? Breakfast? DeAngelo's mouth hung open to speak, but he said nothing.

"I can cook a hot breakfast if you like."

DeAngelo forced himself to be polite.

"No, this is fine." He ate a few bites and watched Ava's face glow in the sun as she stared out the window.

"It looks like it's going to be a beautiful spring day," observed Ava.

Spring in Germany was a new experience for her, but it would be a day like any other for DeAngelo. He enjoyed seeing her excitement as her American eyes flashed with delight at the thought of a beautiful day in Germany. All she had known for three months was winter.

"I should go." DeAngelo surprised himself at how abrupt and harsh his words sounded. He knew he was running the risk of giving the wrong impression. He wasn't sure what kind of woman Ava would be now they had had sex. Still, he half-expected Ava to ask him to stay, but she didn't. She stood, wrapped her arms around his neck, and kissed him.

"Thanks for the strudel and ice cream."

His head was telling him to go before it was too late, but his hands were busy untying Ava's robe. They continued to kiss. The rapid beat of Ava's heart thumped hard against DeAngelo's chest.

Ava pulled back enough to speak.

"Don't you have to leave?"

DeAngelo felt a sting of disappointment that must have shown on his face.

Ava held onto him tighter.

"You could stay a while longer."

There was no more encouragement needed.

A few hours later, Ava hesitated before asking, "What time is it?"

DeAngelo groaned as he stretched to reach for his phone. Before he could read the time, a tirade of continuous pings of missed texts and voicemails broke the quiet of the morning.

"It's 11:00 A.M."

"Sounds like you're in trouble," Ava laughed as she snuggled beside him.

"Oh man," grumbled DeAngelo. "I was supposed to be at Peter's an hour ago to help him set up the baby crib. Peter is good at a lot of things, but he's not a man who builds stuff very well. I should be going."

DeAngelo rolled out of bed and went into the bathroom. Ava heard the shower turn on. She giggled at having a man in the house. If it all ended with their one night, it was worth it.

Chapter 9

The clock struck five past noon when DeAngelo left. Ava knew she should get dressed and start the day, but that was the last thing she wanted to do. She slipped back into bed to feel close to DeAngelo a little while longer. He wasn't gone ten minutes, and she already missed him.

Ava curled herself up nice and tight in the sheets and inhaled the lingering, woody, toasted spice scent of his cologne. She no longer had to dream about what it would feel like to be with him. All she had to do was close her eyes and remember.

She could still sense his touch, sometimes firm, sometimes soft, navigating the terrain of her body. At times, his touch was so wonderfully gentle; it was as if her body melted into his hands. DeAngelo left no secret place unexplored. The longer Ava lay in bed, the more she wanted him there with her.

A burning sensation pulsed through Ava's body as she stretched to get out of bed again. She blushed, thinking three passionate trysts through the night and early morning would definitely make a girl's muscles burn. She indulged in a hot, soaking bath before starting her day.

Ava kept her work laptop closed and instead grabbed her phone and happily searched, "Restaurants close to my location."

Several shops and restaurants were within walking distance of Ava's apartment. The cold, brutal German winter had kept her housebound, but not today. The warmth of spring had finally arrived. She was still a little sore but energized and ready to head out on an adventure.

Her first stop was at a small corner bistro. She sat by the window to people-watch, snacking on a charcuterie plate. Sliced capicola, rolled prosciutto, hard salami, kalamata olives, gruyere, and cheddar cheese filled the plate, along with an assortment of berries and crackers.

Amazed at the beauty of Germany, Ava realized how much she had kept her head down, plowing through work. She left the bistro and walked for hours, popping in and out of shops, buying things she wanted but didn't need. She found her way to the lingerie department of an upscale women's boutique.

She wandered around, brushing her fingers against the smooth silk and elegant lace. Would DeAngelo call her? How would he act now that they had been intimate? She wondered if he would turn out to be the type of man whose interest faded once he'd been to bed with a woman.

Ava could see it falling either way, so she set a deadline. If she hadn't heard from DeAngelo by the end of the weekend, he was sadly the "love 'em and leave 'em" type. As the cashier rang up 300 euros worth of purchases, Ava hoped DeAngelo would hang around for a few more dates. She laughed out loud at herself, thinking DeAngelo could be a little full of himself, but surely he would do the honorable thing and let her down easy.

By late afternoon, heavy bags weighed both arms down. Ava stopped herself from calling Jack to pick her up, even though her apartment was a kilometer away. The thought of another long, soaking bath reminded her she needed to pick up a few new bath bombs and essential oils.

After her last purchase, Ava conquered the walk back to her apartment with ease—much to her surprise. Her fingers tangled in her myriad of keys to unlock the apartment door when her phone buzzed. She gasped, fumbling with her bags, trying to answer in time. One glance at her phone screen, and she exhaled a pent-up breath. It was only a missed call from Danny.

Ava knew there were no missed calls or texts from DeAngelo, but she checked anyway. She tried to stop acting like an infatuated teenage girl, but she was foolishly enjoying the feeling.

She tossed her keys on the living room table, threw her bags in her bedroom, and dumped everything on the bed.

None of this is going on my expense report. She tried on every outfit again, pranced around in her new shoes, and daydreamed about when she would wear her new lingerie.

Ava spent the rest of the afternoon trying to avoid thinking about when DeAngelo was going to call. Under no circumstances was she going to make the next move. DeAngelo attracted her like no one else, but she wasn't going to chase after him or any other man.

Before taking her long-awaited bath, Ava caught up on her household chores. She switched out her bed linens, washed a couple of loads of clothes, and tidied up around the apartment. Ava took her bath and slipped into a comfortable pair of pajamas to relax for the evening.

It was no use. Ava sat on her couch, still needing a distraction. Her heart hurt with disappointment that DeAngelo hadn't called or texted. *No,* she thought, shaking her head, *I'm not going to call him.*

She picked up her phone. A bright 8:00 P.M. stared back at her. Too early for bed. Ava needed something to do. The idea of meal prepping popped into her mind. Hot baths and cooking relaxed her the most. Ava focused her attention on prepping meals for the coming week. She no longer cared if DeAngelo called or texted.

Chapter 10

An uncomfortably pregnant Ingrid, opened the door to let DeAngelo in.

"He's upstairs, and he's pissed."

DeAngelo gave Ingrid a hug and a kiss on the cheek.

"My goodness," she continued to lament. "He's been up there all morning, banging around. It can't be that difficult, can it?"

DeAngelo matched Ingrid's worried look, "Should I take him a beer? Maybe that will calm him down."

Defiant, Ingrid shook her head.

"Goodness, no. By my count, he's on his fourth already." She patted DeAngelo on the back as she pushed him up the stairs. "Good luck."

DeAngelo eased into the nursery to find Peter slumped over on the floor, surrounded by tools, a sea of parts to the baby crib, and a few empty beer bottles.

"Looks like you've been hard at it. You have enough tools to build a damn building," laughed DeAngelo.

Peter raked his hands through his hair, eyes bloodshot from stress.

"The baby is coming in a few weeks. As the future godfather, I expect a little more from you. What happened to you this morning?"

The beers had dampened Peter's anger some, and for that, DeAngelo was glad. He didn't want to put any more pressure on his best mate.

"When you called for the tenth time, I was headed back to my place from Ava's."

It took a few minutes, another symptom of too many beers, but Peter finally put it together.

"Wait, what? Didn't you dump her?"

DeAngelo didn't want to answer, but he didn't see a way around it. He waffled some.

"I wouldn't say dumped. I just kinda ghosted her for a couple of weeks."

Peter raked his hands through his hair again.

"What? Something's not right. You ghost the woman, and then you end up spending the night. What the hell?"

DeAngelo didn't answer and tried not to smile. Stunned, Peter continued his inquiry.

"No! I can't believe it. You stayed the night and half the next morning at a woman's place. What the hell, man?"

DeAngelo again ignored Peter's desire for the details. He buried his face in the assembly directions for the crib, but he wasn't going to get off the hook that easily.

"Aw, what the hell, man? The least you can do is give a

few details. This is big. You never spend the night."

"It's not that big of a deal," DeAngelo deflected. "Now, can we get to the reason why I came so my little goddaughter can have a bed when she arrives?"

At that moment, Peter needed the crib built more than he wanted details of DeAngelo's overnight stay at Ava's. He kept quiet and handed DeAngelo every tool he requested. In no time, they had built the crib, and as the finishing touch, DeAngelo was testing the safety locks.

Peter had held out long enough. Now, with the work of building the crib done, he wanted details.

"Was it that good?" he asked and waited, but no response. "The sex. Was it *that* good?"

"Would you shut up and toss me a beer?"

"Well, hot damn! The sex must have been out-of-this-world good," Peter pointed at DeAngelo. "Look at you. You're blushing. Holy crap, you really like this woman."

DeAngelo was convinced he wasn't blushing, but he wanted to change the subject anyway. "If you don't shut up, I will let you put the rest of the furniture together yourself."

Peter brushed off DeAngelo's idle threat.

"Yeah, you like her. Just go with it, man."

On his drive home, DeAngelo thought about what Peter had said. Was he becoming that type of guy? The "stay-overnight" guy? He took a quick look at his phone. Ava hadn't called or texted him. DeAngelo caught himself before running a red light.

Yes, Ava's beautiful, and last night was far beyond what I had imagined. The sex was fantastic, but she's just another woman. I'll wait a few days before calling. She'll probably call me first, anyway.

DeAngelo arrived back at his place. He fixed himself dinner and checked his phone. He sat down to watch television and checked his phone again, thinking that maybe he had missed a text. He lied to himself about the reason for his constant phone-checking vigilance. *It might be Peter texting that the baby is coming early. Maybe it's my agent. It's 10:00 P.M. I can't be the first to call. How would that look?*

The hell with it. DeAngelo made the first call. Hearing Ava's voice rushed him back to last night and that morning.

"Did you get the crib built?" Ava asked.

"The crib, the changing table, the rocking chair—everything is done. I never knew babies required so much new furniture."

"Little ones can be very demanding," laughed Ava.

"Are you free for brunch tomorrow? I can pick you up around 11:00 A.M.," DeAngelo asked on impulse.

To his pleasure, Ava agreed.

On his way over to Ava's, DeAngelo coached himself. He didn't want to look too eager. It would be embarrassing for Ava to think he was too into her this early on. DeAngelo made up his mind he would be his usual, cool self. He planned it all out. When Ava opened the door, he would step in, give her a hug, and maybe a kiss on the cheek. It all depended on the mood.

They would chat for a few minutes, then leave for brunch. After brunch, he would drive Ava back to her apartment and stay for no more than an hour. Done—a perfect, day-after-sex date.

DeAngelo arrived at Ava's apartment, full of confidence. All the initial nervousness was gone. He had his swagger back. He knocked on Ava's apartment door, at ease with his plan.

So much for his well-devised plan. DeAngelo did a double take when Ava opened the door. She wore a pair of dark-washed, skinny jeans cuffed at the ankles and a bright-white, fitted T-shirt.

He had only seen Ava's hair with curls, which he loved. Standing in the doorway, she stole his breath with her smooth, straight hair with a soft flip.

She greeted him with a big smile and a rub on his arm as she talked into a headset. "Yes, Daddy, I promise you I'm fine. Yes, I've already spoken to the lawyers this morning. The press conference is set for Monday. They will handle everything."

He heard a long pause in her conversation. Ava took DeAngelo by the hand and walked him into the living room.

"Of course, Daddy," she answered." If you want to fly over, you can. I'd love to see you, but there is nothing for you to do here. It's all taken care of, and I'm fine."

Another pause.

DeAngelo took a seat on the couch. Ava plopped down next to him with a little space in between. She made an attempt to finally get off the phone.

"Yes, Daddy, I love you, too. I should go. It's early in the States. Tell Mom and Danny I love them. Love you. Bye."

Ava ripped her headset off and threw it and her phone to the other end of the couch. She leaned back with a sigh.

"When Daddy is in the mood to talk, the man can go on forever."

"Is your dad flying over?" DeAngelo asked.

Ava shook her head. "I doubt it. He's been hyper-stressed with everything going on. He didn't want me, his little girl, to be in harm's way. It took everything for us to convince him I would be okay. He's double and triple-checking, like he normally does."

"Sounds like he loves his little girl," DeAngelo said with a bit of flirtatiousness in his voice. He was about to kiss Ava, but she made the first move.

She leaned in to give DeAngelo a proper welcome. A marvelously long, wet kiss. As they made out, DeAngelo pulled

Ava into his lap and ran his hand through her hair without thinking. He didn't plan on starting up, but he was willing to go with the flow. But Ava put a stop to his line of thinking.

She put her hands on DeAngelo's chest and pushed back. "We better stop before we get carried away."

DeAngelo pulled Ava in close again. "No, I think we should get carried away."

Ava blushed and laughed at DeAngelo's persistence. "Well, I haven't eaten all morning, and I'm hungry. Tell me. Where are you taking me for brunch?"

There was no wiggle room; unfortunately, DeAngelo was locked into their brunch plans. He gave Ava a quick rundown of their brunch destination. They were headed to a friendly, international, family-owned restaurant on the other side of town that had great food.

"If we time it right, we can beat the crowd."

He was slightly disappointed that Ava wanted brunch more than she wanted sex. But it pleased him that she didn't seem pissed about her hair. He knew some women would go insane if he touched their hair. Since Ava didn't, he hoped to try again later.

Ava hopped up off DeAngelo's lap. "Perfect, give me fifteen minutes to change."

DeAngelo insisted that what she had on was fine. Ava looked down at her clothes. She crinkled her nose, disapproving of her current outfit.

"No, I think I'll change."

True to her word, Ava came back in less than fifteen minutes. DeAngelo could feel the grin spreading across his face. Her long, caramel legs captivated him in a pair of crisp, navy blue shorts, accompanied by a floral silk blouse, a tan blazer, and a pair of heeled, tan sandals.

"Will this work?" asked Ava.

DeAngelo took Ava's hand and gave her another kiss. "You're the most beautiful American in Germany today."

DeAngelo started calculating how quickly he could get them through brunch and back here at the apartment to make love to Ava again without seeming too obvious.

Chapter 11

The smell of freshly baked bread, and the smoky char of a hot grill wafting from the kitchen increased Ava's confidence that DeAngelo had made a good choice.

As they waited for their table, DeAngelo stood behind Ava. He rubbed her arms or had his hand around her waist the entire time. Ava found it strange but satisfying. DeAngelo was far more comfortable being affectionate in public than she was.

Within ten minutes, the hostess indicated their table was ready. They heard someone call out before they could make it to their seats. A short, stocky man came walking fast toward them.

"DeAngelo, brother, I haven't seen you in ages. Your podcast is great. Your interview with Coach Dupuis was excellent. I may have a broadcast opportunity for you."

"Hector, man, it's good to see you. This is Ava Brooks," said DeAngelo with a grin. "Ava, this is Hector Garcia, one of my former conditioning coaches."

Hector wedged his way between DeAngelo and Ava, taking them both by the arm.

"Come on, you two. You have to join us. We're celebrating Millie's birthday. Everyone would love to see you, DeAngelo."

This was not what DeAngelo had planned. He looked at Ava.

"You good?" She nodded her head as her way of saying "yes." Hector opened the door to the party room at the back of the restaurant. For such a short man, his voice boomed across the room.

"Hey, everyone, look who I found."

All eyes turned in their direction and a loud round of shouts resounded.

"Hey, DeAngelo. Good to see you, man. Where you been?"

A woman with a pale face, aggressively-painted red lips, and thick black eyeliner came flying toward them, arms outstretched in an ornate kimono.

Her shrill voice of excitement cut through the air like a siren.

"Oh my God, as I live and breathe, DeAngelo Williams! You are the last person I expected to see on my birthday. You are a sight for sore eyes. We've missed you so."

DeAngelo wished Millie a happy birthday as she threw her arms around him like an animal attacking its prey. Ava had to step aside or get hit in the face with a flapping kimono sleeve.

"Millie, this is Ava Brooks," said DeAngelo.

Forced to be polite, Millie faced her with a snooty smile. "Ms. Brooks."

Ava caught a whiff of the strong odor of gin on Millie's breath and crinkled her nose.

"Come sit here. Let's get you some food," added Millie, grabbing a passing waiter by the arm. "Another gin and tonic for me and a plate for my friend."

"Order any drink. Hector has an open tab," said Millie, staring at DeAngelo.

DeAngelo took the liberty of ordering a beer for himself and sparkling water with lime for Ava. A confused look decorated Millie's face.

"Ava, darling, you don't drink?"

To Ava, it felt more like the exposure of a flaw in her character than a question.

"No," said Ava. "I never acquired the taste."

"Oh, my girl. What a pity. You don't know what you're missing. A little buzz makes the world that much more exciting," snickered Millie.

The waiter returned with the drinks and a small plate of food. Ava surveyed the meager assortment of appetizers which, at first glance, appeared to have made the journey from the freezer to the microwave and then to the plate.

Clearly, all Hector's money is going toward drinks and not feeding his guests.

"You two eat," Millie said with a wave of her hand. "And I will return promptly to show your friend, Ava, around."

DeAngelo watched as she left while guzzling her gin and

tonic. He leaned back with his arm on the back of Ava's chair.

"I'm sorry about that," said DeAngelo. "Millie can be a little much."

Ava continued to survey the room as she picked at her plate of sad appetizers. "I'm guessing she's an artist of some type. Maybe theater, painter, or perhaps, actress?"

DeAngelo laughed before taking a sip of beer. "Bingo, she's our group's resident stage actress and director."

Ava took a bite of some sort of beef tartlet. *Hmm this is delightful,* she thought, taking another bite.

"What's your history with the pretty brunette in the corner?" asked Ava with a raised brow. "She's been giving me dirty looks since we walked in."

DeAngelo looked. *Damn it!* This time, he swallowed a huge gulp of beer.

Ava noticed it took DeAngelo a few minutes to collect his thoughts, and she wondered why.

"That's Celine," said DeAngelo at last. "We were together for about a year. We split in January."

Ava munched on the other appetizers, finding them as bland and tasteless as they looked. "I don't need the details, but in general, what caused the split? It doesn't look like it was a mutual agreement."

The party was loud, so DeAngelo leaned in with his mouth, almost touching Ava's ear. Even talking about his ex-girlfriend, DeAngelo's velvety-smooth voice was seductive.

"The split was my idea. The relationship hadn't been good for months. She wanted more than I was willing to give. This is the first time I've seen her since then."

Ava had that ominous, creeping feeling that every woman gets when she knows a confrontation with a man's ex is imminent.

She didn't want to be more caught off guard than she already was, so she asked, "Is it over between you two?"

"Completely."

Ava's character refused to allow her to play the naive, new girlfriend role. She asked if he had a history with any other woman at the party. One ex was enough to deal with this early in her friendship and perhaps relationship with DeAngelo.

He promised that Celine was the only one. She still wondered how many more exs lurked around, ready to kill her with dagger eyes.

After about twenty minutes, Millie returned to the table a little drunker and a lot louder.

"Come, Ava. I have to tear you away from DeAngelo and introduce you to our circle of friends."

DeAngelo stood up to join, but Millie waved him away.

"No, no, no. You go talk to Hector. Ava needs to meet the girls."

Millie dragged Ava across the room to her little clique of girlfriends, each one sizing Ava up with every step.

"Ladies," said Millie. "This is Ava Brooks. I'm guessing she's DeAngelo's new friend."

Ava thought, for as drunk as Millie was, she managed to throw plenty of shade her way. One of the ladies greeted Ava. The others rolled their eyes or pretended not to notice her.

With great enthusiasm, Millie introduced the six ladies.

"I hear you have some big news, Lexi."

Lexi beamed, bouncing up and down in her chair. "I'm pregnant."

Right on cue, the gaggle of ladies screeched with delight. Millie, the loudest of all, yelled to her party guests.

"Everyone, Lexi is pregnant! Bruce, you sly devil. Drinks for everyone—except for you, love."

The waiter brought Ava and Lexi sparkling water to join in on the celebratory cheers. Millie quickly pulled the conversation back to herself and the new play she was directing.

"I insist all of you be there opening night. But not you, Lexi, if you're too far along. I simply must have the support of my friends. This play has been a bear to write, star in, and produce. I don't know why I get myself into these messes."

Again, right on cue, the gaggle of ladies doted on Millie with endless streams of praise and adoration. Millie's self-aggrandizing, overly dramatic, false modesty made Ava want to throw up.

She hoped it was the copious amounts of booze that skewed Millie's performance to the ridiculous and not an indication of her lack of talent.

Ava knew she was being set up when Millie insisted she "meet the girls." It didn't take long for Celine to approach with her head tilted high into the air, giving the impression she was above it all. The only question in Ava's mind was how nasty the confrontation would be.

Like magic, Millie slipped from glorious stage queen to bumbling flake. The closer Celine came toward the group, the more nervous Millie became. By the time the approaching woman was close enough to speak, Millie was in a full-on panic. Ava wanted to slap her and tell her to calm down and drink her gin.

"Millie, aren't you going to introduce me to your new friend?" Celine spoke in a proper, highbrow English accent.

"Oh, Celine, darling," said Millie with a nervous babble, arms flailing like a parrot, "Well, this is—that is, DeAngelo brought her. I mean, this is Ava. Ava, Celine."

Millie then strung her four beloved words together with clarity. "I need a drink!"

DeAngelo had made his way over to Hector, as Millie suggested. He recoiled as Hector's face turned an unpleasant shade of gray. Hector choked out his words.

"Oh my God, I forgot Celine was here. She's over with Ava. We better go intervene. I can see Millie is in a frenzy."

DeAngelo gestured to Hector not to move. "No, Ava can take care of herself."

Still jittery Hector didn't seem convinced, but stayed put anyway, wringing his hands.

Celine frowned at Ava and tossed her wavy, chestnut-colored hair. She spoke with a noxious, conceited tone to her English accent, which Ava now suspected was fake.

"DeAngelo was my man until I split from him."

Ava acknowledged the fact. "Yes. In January, I believe."

Celine's eyes narrowed, and her mouth tightened. She might put Millie and her small circle of friends in check, but Ava was another challenge altogether.

"I didn't think after I left him," said Celine, pausing to roll her eyes, toss her hair, and flash a malicious grin. "DeAngelo would lower his standards and hook up with darker, fatter women. Much less than what he is used to."

Ava heard a chorus of hushed gasps. However, for Ava, the insult rang hollow. She almost laughed.

Really? This is the direction she's taking? Dark (aka Black) and fat?

Ava was in no way insecure with her brown skin, which darkened into a rich chocolate in the sun, or her size-six figure. Ava guessed Celine had gotten by purely on looks. Her dyed, highlighted hair, fake boobs, and size-zero waist fed her ego.

Ava took a small step toward Celine, making the distance between them close but not too close.

"You don't know me," said Ava in a matter-of-fact tone. "And you're playing a very dangerous game, coming at me like you are. Before this turns bad for you, I suggest you walk away."

Celine's eyes popped. Her mouth opened in defense, poised to release another childish insult.

"Be careful, sweetheart," warned Ava.

Celine looked to her girls for support. Millie was trembling, and the other girls had their heads down or avoided eye contact.

Celine's green eyes twitched with anger. Livid, she clamped her mouth shut. She should have walked away, but no; she had to do another hair toss and shoot another dirty look at Ava.

Ava lost her charitable mood. She tilted her head to the side, smiled at the girls, and then aimed her pity-filled eyes at Celine.

"You poor thing. You really should stop pining for a man who clearly does not want you."

Once again, right on cue, as Ava could have predicted, the gaggle of girls giggled under their breath. Humiliated, Celine burst into tears and ran from the room. Millie immediately took her leave, raced across the room to Hector and DeAngelo, kimono sleeves flapping in the air, and grabbing another drink from a passing waiter.

Ava calmly excused herself from the group and walked over to join DeAngelo. She gave Millie time to render her account of the melodrama that had unfolded, arriving at the tail end of Millie's breathless retelling of events.

"Then Celine, as humiliated as she could possibly be, burst into tears and ran off. You saw her, right? Someone really should have gone after the poor girl to see if she was okay. I would have, but I can't leave my guests."

Ava had had it. She gave zero consideration as to whether DeAngelo wanted to stay at the party or not. She was more than ready to be as far away from his pompous, immature, drunk friends as soon as possible.

Inside, Ava was seething, but she managed a polite smile and warm handshake as she wished Millie a happy birthday and thanked Hector for the invitation to the party. She then turned to DeAngelo with the same gracious smile.

"We really should be going."

DeAngelo nodded, said goodbye and walked Ava to the car.

Chapter 12

DeAngelo started the car and eased out of the parking lot. "Do you want to try another restaurant?"

Ava shot him a deadly side-eye. "No. Just take me home."

Annoyed, hungry, and ready to leave, Ava refused to look at DeAngelo as she fumed and glared straight ahead. The lovely romantic brunch she had anticipated turned into a verbal smackdown with his snotty little ex-girlfriend.

Ava sat in the passenger seat, arms folded, her irritation building with each second that passed without DeAngelo saying a word. Why wasn't he asking what happened or if she was okay? Was he even going to apologize for his obnoxious friends?

DeAngelo glanced over at Ava from time to time. If he wanted to say something, Ava's clenched jaw and fiery eyes were intimidating deterrents. He couldn't have imagined a worse scenario: Millie drunk on gin and Celine out for revenge. What an utter failure! DeAngelo sighed, doubting he could get the day back on track.

As soon as DeAngelo parked the car at Ava's place, she had the door open. He took her hand before she jumped out.

"Can I at least walk you to the door?"

Ava rolled her eyes and got out of the car without answering. DeAngelo followed. They both remained silent in the elevator.

"May I come in so we can talk?" DeAngelo finally asked as Ava opened her apartment door.

She turned to face him with a smirk on her face that revealed a dimple in her left cheek.

"Talk? You want to talk? Now? Fine," said Ava with a shrug of her shoulders. A few feet into the apartment, she kicked off her shoes and tossed her jacket and purse onto a chair before heading toward the kitchen.

"Damn!" said DeAngelo. "She's pissed."

DeAngelo didn't hesitate to talk out loud. What did it matter? Ava wasn't there to hear him. He knew that if he wanted to try and make amends, he would have to do it on her terms. Everything was his fault, so he decided to man up and try to make things right.

DeAngelo walked into the kitchen. "Do you want to talk?"

Ava finished washing her hands, pulled out kitchen gadgets, and set everything in exact order.

She glanced up at DeAngelo and questioned, "So, is that your thing? Not talking in the car?"

DeAngelo leaned against the wall. Ava's questions caught him by surprise. Her stare felt like penknives, and only when she turned her attention back to cooking did he answer.

"Yeah, I kind of like to focus and think while driving. I know you're angry. I'm sorry. My friends can be a little much. I didn't mean for the day to be such a disaster."

Ava opened the refrigerator and took out an armful of vegetables and a container of marinating meat. Resting the food on the counter, she let out a deep groan. The kitchen had long been a safe haven where she could relax; anger could not dwell there.

"I'm not angry with you. I'm upset that all of it happened." She paused and gave a little smile. "Brunch was a disaster, but the rest of the day doesn't have to be."

After adding the rice to the cooker, Ava dropped the marinated meat on a hot, electric cast-iron grill. The meat sizzled, and the kitchen filled with the sweet-and-spicy smokey aroma of seasoned chicken.

"So, you *do* know how to cook." Impressed, DeAngelo stared as Ava arranged all the vegetables before pulling out a set of professional chef knives.

"Okay, now you're just showing off," DeAngelo teased.

Ava winked. "How about you make yourself useful and set the table?"

She sliced and diced the vegetables and drizzled the rainbow mix with a lemon vinaigrette, which she had just quickly whipped up. There was a glimmer of hope of getting back to a good place, but DeAngelo was too curious to let things drop. He wanted to know if Millie's version of Ava's confrontation with Celine was accurate.

"So, what really went down between you and Celine?" he asked.

Ava didn't want to talk about the brunch drama, but she would be straight with him since he asked. "Just a case of the queen bee trying to defend her hive."

Ava turned the chicken, kept an eye on the rice cooker, and continued. "It's clear to me that with her porcelain skin, snooty attitude, and tight circle of friends, she feels empowered to talk to people however she pleases."

With that, DeAngelo received a look that implicated him as a willing contributor to Celine's queen-bee complex. "Millie said Celine made some pretty nasty comments to you?"

The rice cooker popped and switched to warm. Ava put the cooked chicken on a platter and added the last batch of meat to the grill.

"A little immature for a grown woman. I don't think she has much experience in the world outside of swimsuit modeling."

Again, DeAngelo pressed the issue. "What made her run out crying?"

Ava had indulged his curiosity enough. She ignored the question. She had said all she cared to say about Celine.

The rice was finished with a rough chop of cilantro, some olive oil, a squeeze of lime, and a dash of salt and then added to the platter with the last batch of chicken.

"I hope you like jerk chicken, green apple slaw, and cilantro-lime rice," said Ava.

DeAngelo adored that Ava could cook. No woman had cooked for him outside of his mom and Momma Gretta. He dived right in.

"This is delicious," said DeAngelo between bites. "My dad is Jamaican. Well, Jamaican-American. Granddad moved the family to New York when dad was sixteen."

DeAngelo ate a few more bites. "Man, Dad would go nuts for this. According to him, there is no place in all of Germany he can get good jerk chicken. I think I just found a place for him. Where did you learn to cook it?"

Ava beamed at DeAngelo's raving reviews of her cooking. "Mom and Dad allowed me to stay on campus my freshman and sophomore year of college. My roommate, Sabrina, was Jamaican. I learned to cook jerk chicken from her eighty-year-old grandmother, Mrs. Zelda. I spent an entire summer bussing tables and washing dishes at Mrs. Zelda's restaurant in Kingston. A month into my second summer as a server, she let me prep dishes for the next day after the restaurant closed. That's when she started trusting me with her recipes."

"I thought women never gave away their family recipes," DeAngelo chuckled while continuing to eat.

"Mrs. Zelda was a generous lady. Besides, she knew no one could duplicate her dishes, even with the recipe. She had the experience and love that added that extra something to her cooking."

Ava's home cooking made it easy to forget about the

brunch debacle. After eating, DeAngelo and Ava relaxed on the couch and watched a movie. DeAngelo glanced at his phone to check the time, surprised at how quickly the day had whisked by.

"I should be going soon. Dinner is at Momma's in a couple of hours." He looked at Ava, but something seemed off. He tensed up and stuffed his phone in his pocket when Ava put her hand on his knee.

"I've really enjoyed spending time with you this weekend, but I need to discuss something with you."

She spoke with a sincere tone, and in return, DeAngelo's tone was harsh, almost mean.

"I need to leave." If he was her weekend fling, fine, but there was no way he would accept the "it's not you, it's me" talk.

Ava pressed down on DeAngelo's knee, a gesture asking him to wait for at least a second so she could complete her thought. She proceeded with caution.

Usually, the conversation Ava was about to have with DeAngelo would come a little further into their relationship. But in light of the day's events, Ava wanted to make things crystal clear. She was not a casual lover.

"I like us together, and I want to get to know you better. We can go forward as friends or as both friends and lovers. If we are going to continue to be lovers, then we need to be exclusive."

DeAngelo gawked blankly. He couldn't believe what was happening: an ultimatum. They had only been dating a few months. After one night together, she wanted to be exclusive. He didn't disguise his anger as he grabbed his keys from the table.

"Like I said, I need to go."

"Wait," Ava replied and walked off to the kitchen. She met DeAngelo at the door, handing a container to him. "Don't forget your dad's dinner. I hope he likes it."

DeAngelo walked into his parents' house, still shell-shocked by Ava's ultimatum. He moved through the kitchen by memory, only snapping to the present when his dad hollered out.

"Wah yuh have in dat box?"

DeAngelo looked down at his hands. He was holding the container Ava had given him.

"Just some jerk chicken for you," he replied, still looking at the container.

DeAngelo's dad gave a thunderous laugh. "Boy, yuh kno yuh can't find gud jerk chicken in Germany."

Skeptical, he took the container and lifted the lid. His chest rose with a deep inhale. His eyes closed and head swayed on the long exhale.

"Dis might be it."

He grabbed a fork from the table and tore into the chicken. No matter how long he lived in Germany, DeAngelo's dad still maintained his thick Jamaican accent.

"Lawd a massi! Dis is some real jerk chicken."

He had everyone's attention as he moved around the kitchen, practically dancing. "Dis take me back to my momma's kitchen in Jamaican Town."

DeAngelo's mom butted in. "Let me have a taste."

She had long since stopped trying to make jerk chicken. Her below-average attempts never got this kind of reaction. She wasn't about to admit it out loud, but Ava's chicken was delicious.

Between mouthfuls, DeAngelo's dad managed to ask, "Where yuh get dis? Whoever cooked dis know wah they do'n."

"A friend." DeAngelo could feel everyone's eyes and attention focused on him. He wanted to avoid the onslaught of inevitable questions like, *What friend? Who do you know that can cook jerk chicken?* The interrogation would be endless. So, he quickly redirected the conversation.

"Peter, you get the baby's room all setup?"

Peter happily came to the rescue. "We're all set, but now we need to decide on the right stroller and car seat. Have you seen these strollers? They are more high-tech than my car."

DeAngelo was off the hook. The future first grandbaby of the family got all the attention.

As distracted as he was, DeAngelo managed to make it through dinner without anyone noticing. He talked and joked around, but Ava was the only thing on his mind. He still couldn't believe it. She actually gave him an ultimatum: *"If we continue to be lovers, we need to be exclusive."*

He wasn't at the point of regretting he had slept with Ava but wouldn't have in a million years thought she would demand a relationship that fast. *What is with this woman?* He liked her, but being exclusive after a couple of months of dating and one night? An amazing night, granted, but it was way too soon.

Peter later found DeAngelo on the back porch. "So, you gonna tell me what's up?"

DeAngelo looked at Peter and thought for a second, he shouldn't say anything, but he needed to talk. He filled Peter in on the whole story: brunch, Millie, Celine, lunch at Ava's, and the ultimatum.

"She's basically asking for a commitment," DeAngelo added.

"That's usually how it works."

DeAngelo expected a different answer. "What makes you an expert?"

"You and Ava have been dating for a few months now, right?" Peter didn't wait for an answer. "You spent the entire night and half the next morning with her. Something you never do, right?" Peter glanced at DeAngelo.

"The very next day, you invite her to brunch," Peter continued. "You've already—"

DeAngelo squirmed in his seat. "Would you get to the point?"

"Okay, fine," Peter said before giving his opinion on the matter. "You take Ava to brunch, and your ex confronts her." Peter raised his eyebrow. "Your *very recent* ex." He paused. "I don't think she wants to be your rebound. She's smart. She's letting you know where she stands. You're not used to that."

DeAngelo had grown annoyed with everyone telling him what kind of woman he preferred and what he was used to. "What the hell, man? You're making me out to be some sort of player."

"Yes, you are, and you know it." Peter didn't tap dance around DeAngelo's feelings or ego. "You've never been one for long-term commitment, and I get it. I'm married now, but I was in the league, too. Things have changed. Maybe the way you look at relationships should change."

Scowling, DeAngelo wanted out of the conversation. His day had, yet again, taken a nosedive. Peter tried to smooth things over.

"Look, man, you know you have a reputation. Hell, you know Celine, and you and I both know she probably said some nasty things. Ava is not a foolish woman. It doesn't sound like she wants to play games. She might just be too real for you."

As annoying as Peter could be, he was the only one that DeAngelo could always count on to shoot straight with him. Peter never meddled or interfered in his life. Like a judge, he listened, weighed the facts, and then rendered an opinion.

DeAngelo stewed on Peter's last comment. It was time for him to be honest with himself. It was true; his life had changed dramatically. Being in the league was the perfect excuse for keeping things casual with the women he dated. Now retired, there were no more "real" excuses.

He had never dated the corporate, businesswoman type. And he sure as hell never dated a woman who had faced down a criminal enterprise to save her family's business. He smiled to himself with a sense of pride. Ava was kind of a badass and not nearly as much of the uptight, hard-ass American he had thought at first.

The problem wasn't necessarily the idea of being exclusive. DeAngelo's relationships may have been short-lived, but he never dated more than one woman at a time. It was that Ava had laid it all out. Just like that. No games. No pretending.

Chapter 13

It had been a long week of meetings and strategy planning. Ava had help, but it was still grueling to deal with the media circus, address employee concerns, and establish the new leadership team.

Caroline poked her head into Ava's office.

"Would you like to grab some lunch?"

Ava declined the invitation. She wasn't in the mood all that much. It was Thursday, and DeAngelo hadn't called or texted.

Well, I guess that is that. Ava was upset that she had fallen hard for DeAngelo. And she was angry he was ghosting her again. She was also hurt; he didn't want to be lovers, and she was disappointed he didn't even want to be friends.

She reminisced over the time they had spent together. It had only been three months, but she felt a closeness to DeAngelo she knew was real. The night they shared her bed changed everything, at least for Ava. She thought that maybe, for him, their night was more than just sex.

Her thoughts went to how the factory would be stable within the next few months and the new management team in place to take over more of the daily responsibilities. Then she would be free to leave Germany and move back home to Texas.

Now she was officially depressed. Ava didn't want to be alone anymore. She wanted someone in her life. No, she wanted DeAngelo in her life. Ava dropped her head on the back of her executive office chair and used her feet to spin it around.

Of all the men in Germany, why did I have to fall for Mr. "Love 'em and Leave 'em?"

Startled by a knock at the door, Ava looked up to see Frank, one of the young accounting interns, standing in the open doorway. In his hands was a gorgeous spring bouquet of pink peonies, white roses, and ruby-red hydrangea flowers.

"Hallo, Frau Brooks," said Frank in German. "Lieferung für Sie."

Ava stood up to greet Frank, a little dizzy from the spinning.

"Hallo, Frank," replied Ava in German, taking the flowers. "Vielen Dank."

Frank replied with a formal, "Auf Wiedersehen."

After taking the bouquet from Frank, Ava brought the flowers close to her nose and took a deep breath. The flowers smelled like happiness and pulled her from the depths of self-pity and internal whining. She searched for the card, surprised to find that it was sealed. She thought that was funny and assumed the flowers were from her dad. Ava's heart sank, depressed again at the thought of her dad being the only man in her life who would think to send her flowers.

Ava pried the card open. The handwritten note read:

Friends and Lovers,
DeAngelo

A grin blossomed across her face, her cheeks flushing as pink as the flower petals. Ava wasn't going to wait. She grabbed her phone and texted DeAngelo.

Thanks for the flowers. They're beautiful.

With the same apparent eagerness, DeAngelo didn't bother to text; he called instead.

"Are you free this weekend?" he asked.

"That depends. What did you have in mind?"

"A weekend getaway."

"I need more details than that," Ava teased.

"I'll tell you this much. It's about a three-hour drive, it's a luxury resort, and there will be at least one formal dinner."

"Oh, yes! I'm free. This sounds like something I'm going to enjoy."

They hung up, and Ava spun around and around again in her chair, talking to herself. "I need an evening gown, shoes, and the weather should be nice, so maybe a swim-suit, too."

The sun hung high in the bright blue sky as Ava waited with her packed bags for DeAngelo to pick her up and whisk her off to some wonderful destination. She didn't have to wait long. Five minutes after 1:00 P.M., there was a knock at her door.

DeAngelo stood in front of her with a light-grey suit and sharp-blue shirt. Ava had the same thought as when she had seen him for the first time: *Who is this outrageously handsome man?* He stepped in, kissed her, and then twirled her around.

"Don't you look beautiful!"

Ava wore a fitted dress with a white surplice top and a floral wrap skirt that fell just below the knee.

Eager to get the weekend started, DeAngelo and Ava kissed on the elevator ride down.

"What is this?" Ava asked, surprised to see Jack standing by a limousine with the door open.

DeAngelo leaned over and kissed her on the cheek.

"I hope you don't mind. I hired Jack to drive us. Three hours is a long time for you to be stuck in the car with me, not talking." Ava smiled and held on to DeAngelo's arm a little tighter.

With Jack in the driver's seat, Ava and DeAngelo could enjoy the time together. But before all the romance began, Ava wanted the practical discussion out of the way.

"Have you talked with Caroline about you and me dating?"

DeAngelo handed Ava a glass of sparkling water with lime. "No. Should I?"

Ava shoved DeAngelo's shoulder. *Men can be clueless at times.*

"Yes, you should. I would say something, but she's not my sister."

DeAngelo settled back in his seat and threw his arm around Ava. "I thought about it but wasn't sure where things were going with us."

"Oh no. You're not going to charm your way out of this. Promise me you'll talk to Caroline when we get back. I like and respect her very much, and I hate leaving things unsaid."

DeAngelo leaned forward and whispered, "I promise."

He then kissed Ava and gently eased her back into the seat and whispered again, "This weekend is all about you."

It seemed like they had just left her apartment when Jack buzzed on the car intercom.

"We are about thirty minutes out, Mr. Williams."

DeAngelo took out his phone and started texting. Ava guessed he was texting the resort to make them aware of their upcoming arrival.

The car stopped a short time later. Ava fluffed her hair and checked her face. DeAngelo leaned over and kissed her.

"Are you ready for this?" he asked before exiting the car.

A tall, lanky resort bellman opened the door for Ava. DeAngelo was there to take her hand. A distinguished, mature man greeted them.

"Herr Williams *und* Frau Brooks, *Willkommen bei* Wolff Mountain Resort. I am Louis Hoffman, Senior Manager. If you need anything during your stay, please let me know. Would you like a short tour of the property, or would you prefer to go directly to your suite?"

DeAngelo looked at Ava to let her make the decision.

"A short tour would be nice," she answered.

Mr. Hoffman waved his hands, and a young man holding a silver tray with two glasses of champagne appeared while two young men disappeared with their bags.

The resort was impeccably designed with modern, clean lines. The towering mountains in the background reminded Ava of a fairy tale.

As they toured the grounds, Ava became more aware of her new surroundings, and she better understood DeAngelo's question. She thought the question he should have asked was, *"Are you sure you're ready to be the only people of color in the entire resort?"*

They sipped champagne and meandered around the resort, by the pool and the garden, and then back to the lobby. They enjoyed a pleasant thirty-minute introduction to the fabulous Wolff Mountain Resort. Ava and DeAngelo followed Mr. Hoffman to an elevator. He waved his keycard in front of the elevator sensor and informed them it was for the presidential suite only.

When the elevator doors opened, Ava stood mesmerized. The sun hovered like an orange fireball over the majestic mountain peaks. Its brilliance flooded the room through the large, panoramic window that spanned the width of the space.

Mr. Hoffman introduced their private staff. "This is Rebekah, your maid, and Felix, your butler, sir."

Rebekah and Felix smiled politely. Ava was accustomed to shaking hands, so she offered hers to both.

"Nice to meet you, Rebekah, and you, too, Felix."

Both Rebekah and Felix answered in unison.

"Welcome to Wolff Mountain, ma'am. Please enjoy your stay." With that, Mr. Hoffman, Rebekah, and Felix left the suite.

Ava took DeAngelo's hand and dragged him over to the window to take in the heavenly view. She threw her arms around his neck and kissed him.

"This is the most beautiful place I have ever been to."

DeAngelo knew he had done well. Ava's smile proved it, but he had a lot more in store.

"What would you like to do until dinner?"

"Relax," she said, and that was fine with him.

They walked into the elegant bedroom. A fluted vase overflowing with at least three dozen red roses first caught her eye. She felt overwhelmed that DeAngelo would go to this much trouble and expense for her.

She didn't see their bags and was about to say something to DeAngelo, but she thought to open the closet first. Ava swung the doors open to a full-size, walk-in closet.

Even more surprising, all their clothes were freshly-pressed and hanging, and their shoes were perfectly organized. The maid had laid out Ava's jewelry in cushioned boxes on the island in the middle of the closet, along with a row of four pairs of DeAngelo's cuff links.

An unsettling thought crossed Ava's mind. She cringed, thinking that maybe Rebekah or, God forbid, Felix, had unpacked her underwear. She opened the drawer in the island to see her black silk garment bag still zipped tight.

Thank God. She was never more grateful than at that moment that she always packed her underwear and lingerie in a garment bag and not thrown them loose in the suitcase.

Chapter 14

An undercurrent of expectation filled their first night at Wolff Mountain Resort. DeAngelo waited for Ava in his formal dinner suit, checking his cuff links in the living room.

The taps of Ava's heels echoed on the marble floor before he heard her ask, "Do you like?"

He turned to see Ava in a dazzling silver, V-neck evening gown.

Damn, she knows how to meet the occasion, DeAngelo thought.

Ava twirled to reveal the gown's low back. DeAngelo thought of Peter's favorite phrase: *Hot damn.* DeAngelo loved to see a gorgeous woman in a sexy, low-back dress. He kept telling himself to just be cool and not get too excited.

He wrapped his arms around her waist.

"I like very much." He kissed Ava's neck. Then her shoulder. And then down her back.

Through much heavy breathing, all Ava could say was, "Oh, my goodness."

DeAngelo pulled her closer and rocked her in his arms. "After dinner."

The resort restaurant seemed fit for royalty. Enormous crystal chandeliers hung from the ornate, vaulted ceiling. Flawlessly pressed white linen dressed each table with delicate, bone-china place settings, genuine silver flatware, and Waterford glassware.

Both Ava and DeAngelo scanned the room. DeAngelo gave Ava a wink. She returned a coy smile. It did not escape their attention that they were the only couple of color dining tonight.

A stately maître d' greeted them at the open archway of the restaurant.

"Mr. Williams, Ms. Brooks, let me show you to your table."

In true DeAngelo style, he had reserved the best table in the house. Their spot was elevated off the main floor and situated privately in front of the bay window that overlooked the meticulous garden labyrinth illuminated with sparkling lights.

The maître d' introduced their headwaiter. "Paul will be your head server this evening. I leave you in good hands."

Paul promptly seated Ava and addressed DeAngelo. "Champagne, sir? Chef De la Rue has prepared an excellent menu for your dining pleasure. However, he is prepared to create a custom meal for you this evening if you wish."

Ava's eyes widened with delight. Traveling the world, one of her indulgences was to have the best meal she could find wherever she was and to learn as much about the local food scene as possible.

To have a renowned chef cook something special for her was a dream come true. Paul excused himself, giving them a moment to decide.

Ava beamed with excitement. "All of this is amazing. You didn't have to do this, but thank you!"

DeAngelo kissed her hand.

"Special meal from the chef?" Ava gave an enormous smile in agreement. DeAngelo loved seeing that smile. She giggled with a bit of embarrassment.

"I'll try not to eat too much, or I won't be able to get out of this dress tonight."

DeAngelo leaned back in his seat. His eyes focused with a serious, penetrating look.

"There won't be an issue getting you out of that dress tonight. Trust me."

His words rattled her. No poker face this time. Ava blushed uncontrollably. Her heart thumped in her chest, and her body temperature rose. She was tempted to fan herself but decided it would be undignified in such a grand place. She was so aroused that she didn't notice that Paul had returned to the table with a second server.

"May I, madam?" Paul asked as he took the dish from the

silver platter held by the server and placed it in front of Ava. "A amuse-bouche of blini with trout roe caviar and crème fraiche. Please enjoy."

"Thank you, Paul. This looks wonderful."

"Is that an American accent—"

"And for the gentleman," the second server interjected.

"For you, sir." Paul placed the amuse-bouche in front of DeAngelo, then turned back to Ava.

The man could at least have the decency to stop staring at her, DeAngelo thought before he refocused Paul.

"We accept Chef De la Rue's generous offer to create a meal as he sees fit."

Paul diverted his eyes from Ava. "I apologize, sir. Yes, of course, I will inform the chef."

Ava waited for Paul to leave before speaking. "I have one of Chef De la Rue's cookbooks. I've made his brown butter and sage roasted duck. It is delicious." Ava tried to contain her excitement, but she couldn't. She was bubbling over with anticipation. "I'm sorry, but I'm just so excited about this meal."

DeAngelo wanted to say something clever and romantic, but he was baffled by Ava's excitement. He hadn't expected her to be this thrilled and appreciative. He hated to admit it, but Celine would've treated his gesture of a romantic weekend as ordinary. If she wasn't put up in the presidential suite, doted on by staff, and offered a special meal by the chef, Celine would've made her dissatisfaction known.

DeAngelo's only disappointment was not selecting a booth instead of a table. He wanted to be closer to Ava so that he could touch her. Maybe stroke her arm. Perhaps even kiss her wonderful, soft lips. Their intimate table allowed for gentle hand-holding and whispered conversation.

Paul returned with their first course: a light, fluffy cheese soufflé. DeAngelo could see Ava was duly impressed as she savored the first bite with her eyes closed.

"This is divine," said Ava. "It's like a delicate cloud that melts in your mouth."

Course after course, the meal grew more extraordinary. At every interval, Paul presented each dish with exactness.

"Your second course: white crab meat and blood orange salad. Your third course: seared scallops with brown butter and lemon sauce. Your fourth course: wild mushroom ravioli."

Before he could try the fourth dish, DeAngelo felt a slight kick to his leg. He looked up to see Ava's questioning eyes staring back at him.

"Is something wrong?"

Ava held back a giggle. "This is all so delicious, but I don't know how much more I can eat. Would it be rude to ask how many more courses?"

DeAngelo winked. "I'll take care of it."

Paul later returned. "Your fifth course: grilled lamb chops with mint chimichurri. Chef De la Rue asks that you join him at his kitchen table for dessert."

As soon as Paul left, she whispered, "I never expected to meet Chef De la Rue. Did you arrange that, too?"

"I wish I could say I did, but no," replied DeAngelo. "I only asked if the chef would consider a custom dining experience. I wasn't sure if he would do it or not."

After finishing their fifth course, Paul appeared as promptly as before. "Are you ready for dessert, madam? Please, let me assist you." He pulled Ava's chair back and took her hand without asking or her offering. His thumb brushed over Ava's hand.

"No. I don't need your assistance." Ava pulled her hand free before Paul could enclose it with his.

What the hell? DeAngelo recognized that tone. Ava was pissed. Incensed, DeAngelo leaped to his feet. With one step, he was face-to-face with Paul.

"Look, you bast—" DeAngelo paused when he felt Ava's hand on his chest.

With his head lowered, Paul made his apology. "Sir. Madam. Forgive me. I meant no disrespect."

"The hell you didn't. You've been borderline disrespectful all evening."

Ava made a quiet plea. "DeAngelo, it's fine."

DeAngelo only noticed the maître d' standing next to him when he heard his question.

"Sir, may I be of service?" asked the maître d'.

DeAngelo glared back and forth between the two men.

He took Ava's arm and allowed the maître d' to escort them to the kitchen.

Besides thanking Chef De la Rue for the magnificent dinner, DeAngelo allowed Ava to do all the talking. He was still far too angry to engage in polite conversation. It was Ava's night, and he wanted to make sure it ended well. They posed for a few pictures and enjoyed an indulgent mille-feuille of peach and raspberry with a citrus cream dessert. Dinner had a delicious end.

DeAngelo sat alone in the opulent living room while Ava slept in the bedroom. From the green glow on the television console, he could see that it was 3:00 A.M. He needed to think. The events of the night were on constant replay in his mind.

When he first saw Ava in that dress with the low back, he felt pride in his step walking into the dining room with the most beautiful woman on his arm. Then, later on, he remembered how easily that dress fell off Ava's gorgeous body with one or two simple moves.

The more DeAngelo replayed the evening in his mind, the more his thoughts became exaggerated, and his frustration began to build. Paul, their head server, annoyed DeAngelo to no end with all his little, stolen glances at Ava. But he had crossed the line when he took Ava's hand. DeAngelo still wanted to smash the server's face in.

But it wasn't just Paul. DeAngelo saw how the men looked at Ava. He knew what was on their minds. They had the same thought as him: how Ava would look out of that dress. Of course, other men were going to look at Ava.

Hell, if she was with another man, I'd look at her. If I was alone, I would make a pass at her. If I wasn't alone, I would still be tempted to make a pass.

DeAngelo thrust his head back onto the cushioned chair. When he closed his eyes, he could still feel Ava's kisses. Her hands moving up and down his chest. The soft, dreamy look in her eyes when she was ready. The weight of her body on his. She had a sensual, soothing rhythm to her lovemaking.

Damn it! Everything about Ava felt good. It felt right.

DeAngelo wanted to convince himself he wasn't falling in love, but he struggled to make the case. He wondered if Ava was falling for him or if she had been this way with her previous lovers. He didn't know Ava's past, but that didn't stop his thoughts from running wild. He was falling hard for Ava, and now he was jealous.

Had the tables finally turned? Was DeAngelo becoming the needy one in the relationship? Being in love was a rare feeling for him. Being jealous was a new experience he didn't care for at all.

I can't be the jealous type. I'll just dial it back. I'm not going to be more into her than she is into me.

DeAngelo didn't hear Ava's soft footsteps, but he felt the tickle of her nails run along his shoulder.

"Is everything okay?"

He sat her on his lap. "What are you doing up?"

Ava kissed his cheek. "I was just about to ask you that same question."

"I couldn't sleep and didn't want to wake you." DeAngelo's forehead creased.

"Are you sure?"

Before he could stop himself, DeAngelo asked, "Do you always make love like that?"

Ava sat up with her back straight. "Like what?" she snapped.

"I don't know," answered DeAngelo. "Just like you do."

She hopped up off his lap. "I'm going back to bed," she yells as she stomped off.

Chapter 15

"Good morning, madam," Rebekah smiled. "Mr. Williams is on the balcony. Breakfast is ready."

Ava walked out to join DeAngelo. The smooth slate balcony floor cooled her bare feet, but the warmth of the sun melted her chills away.

"Good morning," murmured Ava, pouring herself a glass of freshly squeezed orange juice.

DeAngelo, on the other hand, was far too impulsive to keep his mouth shut. He squirmed in his seat, itching to speak.

"I'm sorry about last night. I was out of line."

Ava breathed in before drinking her juice. All she wanted was to enjoy a leisurely breakfast and pretend his criticism of her lovemaking had never happened.

"Can we talk about last night?" DeAngelo asked, ignoring Ava's blank expression of annoyance.

Ava already felt embarrassed and hurt. Now DeAngelo wanted to rub salt in her wounds and talk about how she didn't please him as a lover.

Ava took a deep breath and stared out into the land-scape. "If there was something I did you didn't like, you could have said so, and I would have stopped."

He recognized her tone and lowered his head. Because of his insecurities, he had humiliated her. How could he be so heartless?

He gathered her hands into his, hoping she would look at him. "No, Ava. Please don't think that."

She ripped her hands from his. Her voice raised in anger.

"What am I—" She caught herself and turned to see Rebekah still in the living room, cleaning.

Ava hushed her voice. "What am I supposed to think? If you don't like the way I make love to you, just tell me."

DeAngelo took her hand again, then caressed and tucked Ava's hair behind her ear. He loved how she never freaked out when he touched her hair. He stroked her face.

"Everything you do, I want and enjoy. I can't tell you how good you make me feel." His pulse raced. "I was overthinking it. I started not to like the thought of you having been with other men."

Ava's face tightened as she shook her head. Her mouth opened with a loud exhale of frustration.

"That's not fair. Neither one of us is a virgin," she said in a hushed voice. "You have a past which I was unmistakably confronted with at brunch." Ava rolled her eyes. "You may have forgotten, but I haven't. Remember—oh, about a week ago—my unprovoked run-in with your ex-lover?"

"I know. I'm sorry. I was an ass. I swear I'm not the jealous type. It's just that everyone kept staring at dinner. And Paul, that jackass. I wanted to smash his face in when he took your hand."

For the first time in his life, DeAngelo felt uncomfortable with other men staring at his date. In the past, with a well-known model or actress hanging off his arm, it was always a given that men would stare. He never had a problem with it then, but it was different now with Ava.

Ava was not flattered or impressed. "That's funny. I thought you would be used to people staring."

"I am, but it's different—.

"Please just drop it." Ava insisted. Frustrated at DeAngelo's childish jealousy, she didn't want to stay angry for the rest of the weekend.

After their awkward breakfast, they embarked on a spirited hike. The fresh air and exercise provided the perfect opportunity to work off a few calories from their exquisite dinner. After the hike and a poolside lunch, Ava indulged in a few hours of spa treatments while DeAngelo worked out at the gym.

The sun was beginning to set when DeAngelo led Ava to the lobby. "I hope you don't mind. Dinner is off-site tonight."

They walked out of the lobby to a car waiting at the resort entrance. The vehicle crested the hill to the top of a cliff, revealing a view of open land with the jagged peaks as a backdrop. A parted tent awaited them. Inside, the maids had decorated it with an abundance of embroidered pillows, a cozy loveseat, and a candlelit dinner. DeAngelo and Ava ate and watched the most brilliant sunset.

Ava kicked off her shoes and made herself more comfortable, cuddling up to DeAngelo. "Are you trying to make me fall in love with you?"

DeAngelo poured two glasses of wine, knowing Ava would only take a few sips. He looked at her with his signature smile.

"Is it working?"

"Maybe," Ava replied with a shrug of her shoulder and a mischievous grin. The staff had disappeared. The sun had set, and the sky sparkled with thousands of diamond-like stars. Ava shivered from the chill in the night air. DeAngelo spread a blanket over her shoulders and held her close.

Ava's voice was low and hesitant. "It's been three years." She tilted her head and looked at him. "It's been three years since I've been in an intimate relationship or a relationship of any kind. The way I make love to you is only for you."

DeAngelo's heart thumped as if he had scored the winning goal at the World Cup. Yes, he was being unforgivably male, but it was music to his ears. Ava was completely his and no one else's.

"Are we staying out all night?" she asked as she snuggled herself deeper into DeAngelo's arms.

DeAngelo laughed. "Not unless you want to. The staff left a car behind for us."

Ava kissed him. "Maybe not all night, but long enough for you to make love to me under the stars."

DeAngelo was happy to oblige. "You are an amazing woman, Ava Brooks."

Chapter 16

A few days after returning from his wonderful weekend with Ava, DeAngelo found himself on the brink of godfather-hood. The wait dragged into the fourth hour. DeAngelo had spent most of his time looking up at the television mounted from the ceiling in the far corner of the waiting room. He knew why the sound was mute; he thought it was pointless to have the volume off, though. The one source of entertainment, and you couldn't hear a thing. Annoyed, he vigorously worked to rub the crick out of his sore neck.

He glanced around the colorful room as he stood to stretch his back. He marveled at how his mom and Momma Gretta had made their peace with the waiting. Momma Gretta sat stone-faced with her back as straight as a steel rod, knitting with precision and speed. His mom flipped through cooking magazines, tagging pages, and making notes.

DeAngelo felt Caroline's pain as she twisted herself in knots, trying to get comfortable in the narrow, hardback chair. He glanced over at his dad, wondering how he was doing. The back of Rich's head rested on the wall with a nest of painted baby bluebirds as a halo. His legs were stretched out, and his arms were folded across his chest. Eyes closed, his chest rose and fell softly. Albert, Peter's dad, on the other hand, was glassy-eyed, watching the same soundless television.

A gush of cold air rushed into the waiting room as the automatic doors slid open. Peter stepped in. His eyes were bloodshot, and his face was long.

DeAngelo's forehead creased. *This can't be good,* he thought.

"Not yet," said Peter, shaking his head. "The doctor says the baby won't come tonight. You all should go home."

Knowing Peter, DeAngelo got up and began heading toward the door when he noticed everyone else was slow to move. He looked back, and his mom and Momma Gretta hadn't budged at all. The two were settled in for an all-nighter. DeAngelo gave Peter that same look he would give him on the field, as if to say, "I got this."

"Come on, time to go. Ingrid and Peter don't need us here, hovering."

DeAngelo shook his dad awake and helped Caroline dislodge herself from the torture chair. It took some prodding, but he was eventually able to unseat the steadfast, soon-to-be-grandmas as well.

Peter hugged the family as they got on the elevator. DeAngelo was glad to relieve some of Peter's stress. Two years of marriage and now their first child. DeAngelo knew Peter had to be a nervous wreck.

He texted Ava before pulling out of the hospital.

> False alarm, no baby tonight.

Then he texted again without thinking,

> Do you want to come to dinner Sunday?

As soon as he hit "Send," a feeling of utter dread hit him like a ton of bricks. He dropped his head on the steering wheel.

"What the hell did I just do?"

If ever he had wanted to retrieve a text, it was right then. Yes, everyone in both families knew he was dating Ava, but introducing her to them at Sunday dinner moved their relationship to the next level.

Within seconds, Ava texted back.

> I'd love to. ☺

DeAngelo woke up Sunday morning with the singular focus of getting through dinner as quickly as possible. That day in the hospital parking lot was supercharged with emotion; the long, tense hours waiting, the joy of the first grandbaby in the family, and seeing his brother becoming a father skewed his thinking. Why else would he be stupid enough to invite Ava to Sunday dinner?

He had not exchanged an "I love you" with Ava. They had not talked about the future. He didn't even know how long she planned to stay in Germany. He was just going with the flow of things. He assumed she would eventually want to move back home. Inviting her to Sunday dinner seemed like the most normal thing to do, and that reality startled him.

DeAngelo played the day out in his head. There were a few things working in his favor. One, like most babies, Emma Rose Kraus had arrived on her own schedule. She had come screaming into the world healthy and strong at 4:18 A.M. Friday morning.

The family would undoubtedly be too preoccupied with more baby talk to concentrate much on Ava. Second, Ava had no idea of the significance of the Sunday dinner. The unspoken rule was you only invited someone to Sunday dinner if you were serious about them. "Serious," meaning an engagement was imminent.

DeAngelo never felt this out of control with any woman. Ava had so quickly become a natural part of his life. He prayed his family wouldn't read too much into Ava coming to dinner.

DeAngelo planned to keep the mood light and bar his mom from smothering Ava with questions. He knew he could count on Caroline to run interference, if needed, but it was his mom and Momma Gretta who were the real hurdles.

"Are you okay?" Ava asked as DeAngelo parked the car in front of his parents' house. "You look a little weird."

He kissed her on the cheek. Looking weird was the least of his worries. He was a jumbled ball of nerves and guilt. He had done nothing to prepare her, but it was too late now. His hand paused on the doorknob. He breathed in, knowing that Ava was about to face the scrutiny of the entire family on the other side of the door.

"Are we going in anytime soon?" Ava's voice snapped him to attention. He nodded, turning the knob.

DeAngelo's steps were slow and deliberate as he walked Ava through the doorway into the kitchen. His mom leaned over the counter, juggling a couple of eggs in her hands.

He blurted out, "Momma, this is Ava."

His mom nearly jumped out of her skin. She cupped the eggs in her hand to avoid dropping them.

"DeAngelo, you nearly gave me a heart attack."

DeAngelo apologized with a hug and kiss. "Momma, this is Ava Brooks. Ava, this is my mom, Rosalynn Williams."

Ava extended her hand with a friendly smile and eager eyes. "Hello, Mrs. Williams. It is nice to meet you."

DeAngelo's mom sat the eggs down and pulled Ava into a rib-crushing hug. "It's nice to meet you, too," said Rosalynn with a grin. "Call me Rosalynn. I'm glad my son finally invited you over."

"Rich! Albert!" Rosalynn called out into the living room.

"DeAngelo and Ava are here."

The two men made their way into the kitchen. DeAngelo made the introduction.

"Dad, Albert, this is Ava."

Again, Ava extended her hand, but Mr. Williams was also a hugger. No doubt where DeAngelo got his affectionate nature from.

"I finally get to meet di lady my son tells me was behind dat wonderful jerk chicken. Call me Rich!"

Ava received a warm handshake from Mr. Kraus. "I'm Albert, Caroline and Peter's dad."

Ava congratulated Albert on his beautiful granddaughter and handed him a gift she had brought for baby Emma Rose. She then gave a bottle of wine to DeAngelo's mom.

"This is for you, Rosalynn."

Rosalynn took the bottle. "Thank you, sweetheart. With all the back and forth to the hospital, I'm behind on my cooking."

Rosalynn looked around at all the prep work that still needed to be done.

She wiped her forehead with a dish towel and asked, "Ava, do you mind helping out?"

Rosalynn ordered DeAngelo to get an apron from the pantry before Ava had a chance to agree and before he could object. DeAngelo put the apron around Ava's head and tied it around her waist.

"Sorry. I didn't bring you over here to cook." He placed his hands firmly on her shoulders. His voice was low as he stared into her eyes with a comforting gaze.

"Are you going to be okay?"

With her hands on her hips and a cross look on her face, Rosalynn yelled, "Get outta here, boy, we need to get this dinner ready."

"I'll be in the living room if you need me," DeAngelo said as he followed his dad and Albert out of the kitchen.

DeAngelo's mom blew all his plans to shreds. The one thing he wanted to avoid was leaving Ava alone with his mom. He sat in the living room, devising a way to get back into the kitchen without making his mom angry.

Rich sat back in his easy chair and glanced over at his son. "Son, ain't no use worrying yuhself bout it. I'm sure yuh momma and Ava will get on just fine."

DeAngelo relaxed a little and hoped his dad was right.

Chapter 17

Ava found it sweet that DeAngelo seemed worried about her being alone with his mom. It was like he had never brought a woman to dinner before. The first time meeting a man's family, there would be questions, but really, how bad could it be? Small talk about family and work, simple. It would be nothing she couldn't handle.

Ava took it as a good sign of being asked to help with dinner. Few women would invite another woman into their kitchen. Besides, if cooking was the test Ava had to endure, she knew she would pass with flying colors.

I've got this, she thought as she washed her hands and followed Rosalynn's instructions. When she finished the pasta dough, Rosalynn approved and handed Ava a pasta sauce recipe.

"Would you start this quick sauce, please, Ava?"

"Yes, of course," Ava agreed.

She diced the onions, chopped the celery, and minced the garlic. Everything went into a large skillet to cook until soft. The aroma rose and filled the entire kitchen with smells as tantalizing as any Italian restaurant. After a few minutes, she added the diced tomatoes and tomato paste. She let that cook, then added the dried herbs and seasoning.

Ava waited in anticipation for the motherly interrogation to begin as she cut fettuccine-sized noodles. Once Rosalynn finished seasoning the salmon and all the meatballs were in the oven, the vetting began.

"Did your mother teach you to cook?" asked Rosalynn.

"Yes, Mom taught me the basics. But my passion for cooking grew as I traveled for work. Learning to cook dishes in whichever country I found myself in helped me meet people and feel less homesick."

"So, tell me about your family," Rosalynn asked after handing Ava a glass of water.

"I have a brother, Danny. He takes care of our South American business."

"Older or younger? And is he married?"

Ava could feel the pressure building. "Older, and yes, Danny's married."

"Children?" Rosalynn questioned as she stirred the pasta sauce.

This lady's not messing around, Ava thought. "No ma'am, no kids yet."

Rosalynn then unleashed every conceivable question an overbearing mother would ever think to ask. She asked about how Ava was raised and her childhood, followed up by more questions about her family, religious beliefs, where she hoped to see herself in the next five years, and if she planned to return to the States soon. Ava was determined to draw the line if Rosalynn asked how wide her hips were and if she could bear healthy babies for her son.

The interrogation ended when Mrs. Kraus, aka Momma Gretta, and Caroline walked through the back door. Relieved, Ava hoped she had passed inspection.

"It's good to see you outside of work," Caroline said, rushing over to give Ava a hug. "Momma, this is Ava. Ava, this is my momma, Gretta."

Momma Gretta leaned in with a hug and kiss on the cheek. "I've heard a lot about you, Ava. Caroline talks about you nonstop. All very good things of course."

"Momma, please." Caroline blushed and pulled her mother to the table. "Let's get seated before you embarrass me to death."

"Dinner is ready!" Rosalynn yelled out into the living room.

"Ingrid and baby Emma Rose are home and doing well." Momma Gretta informed the family once everyone got seated.

"It's a shame how fast they send new mothers and babies home these days," Rosalynn opined before pouring herself a glass of wine.

The conversation took a sharp turn when, to Ava's surprise, Momma Gretta began her own interrogation. "How long do you plan on staying in Germany, Ava?"

"I'll be here for a few more months, maybe longer if my job requires it."

"I hear you speak German very well, you cook, and you're a good businesswoman," continued Momma Gretta. "You're quite young to be so accomplished. How old are you, again?"

Ava wished she had brought several copies of her resume to hand out. Being tag-teamed by Rosalynn and Momma Gretta was brutally excessive.

"I'm twenty-eight, ma'am."

Momma Gretta gave a commanding look to DeAngelo. "You're thirty. Peter got married at twenty-eight, and now we have our first grandbaby."

"The more grandbabies, the better. I want this house full of babies," said Rosalynn.

Ava's cheeks burned. All eyes were on her. She half-expected Momma Gretta and Rosalynn to march her and DeAngelo upstairs and demand they try for a baby that very moment. Ava felt DeAngelo's leg touch hers as he squirmed in his seat under the spotlight.

Thank goodness Albert came to the rescue. "I think that's enough baby talk for the moment."

Albert then asked Ava to tell him what the real Texas was like, because all he knew of Texas was from television. Rich then helped lighten the mood by asking Ava how she learned to cook jerk chicken.

The heat was off. The interrogation was over. Ava could enjoy dinner and the company of DeAngelo's family.

Fifteen minutes into the drive back to her place, DeAngelo asked, "Are you good?"

"I'm good." Ava paused to check her phone for messages. She looked at DeAngelo and rolled her eyes. "You could have at least told me I was walking in front of a firing squad. Your momma is one tough lady. She gets to the heart of the matter quickly."

She shot a glance at DeAngelo. "At one point, I swear I thought she was going to ask for my fingerprints for a criminal background check," Ava said, then burst out laughing. DeAngelo joined in. They both were laughing so hard that neither could talk.

When DeAngelo caught his breath, he asked, "Was it really that bad?"

Ava smiled widely, eyes twinkling with humor. She nodded her head.

"Yes. It was that bad."

They laughed as they parked and all the way up to her apartment, where they collapsed on the couch. She kissed DeAngelo and assured him that despite the intense scrutiny, she did enjoy dinner. The two families had such a loving dynamic. It reminded her of home.

DeAngelo brushed her hair back and slowly planted kisses all over her face. "How can I make it up to you?"

Ava had in mind various ways DeAngelo could make amends. All options ended with him staying the night.

"I'm going to get out of these clothes, take a shower, and go to bed. I would like it if you joined me."

With a naughty smile, she added, "But you have to promise there won't be any baby-making tonight."

Chapter 18

It was midweek. DeAngelo decided to text Peter. He hadn't bothered Peter for a few days. He figured his brother needed some time to settle into fatherhood.

> You up for working on the podcast today?

About twenty minutes later, Peter replied.

> Sure, come on over, but don't ring the doorbell.
> Ingrid and Emma Rose are sleeping.
> Just text when you get here.

DeAngelo pulled into Peter's driveway and texted before getting out of the car. As soon as he reached the front porch, Peter opened the door with enthusiasm, albeit hushed, and marched DeAngelo upstairs to the nursery. He opened the door wide enough for him and DeAngelo to peek in at his daughter sleeping in the crib.

"Look at my little princess. Isn't she beautiful?"

DeAngelo slapped Peter on the back. "Yes, she is the prettiest baby I've ever seen."

Peter slid the nursery door closed. "We have a few hours before she wakes up. We better get to work."

DeAngelo's first thought walking into Peter's office was: *You've got to be kidding me.* Peter had rearranged everything. The podcast recording equipment was on one side of the room, and a complete surveillance system was on the other. DeAngelo stared down at the monitor that showed four different camera angles of the nursery.

He looked back at Peter. "You're not overprotective in the slightest."

"No, no man, look." Peter rushed over and opened a binder, flipping through a mountain of spreadsheets. "I know it's early, but we have our schedule down. I'm charting Emma Rose's sleeping and eating patterns. By my calculations, Ingrid should get about six hours of sleep before Emma Rose's next feeding."

DeAngelo wasn't entirely convinced, but he had no experience with babies to question Peter's claim. His brother was always a numbers guy.

"Well, it looks like you've got everything under control."

A confident Peter leaned back in his chair. "Not to change the subject from my precious little princess, but I thought we were best mates."

Peter waited a minute to gauge DeAngelo's reaction. He didn't get a verbal response. The look on DeAngelo's face was enough.

"Don't give me that confused look," continued Peter. "Sunday. You brought Ava to Sunday dinner."

DeAngelo threw his hands in the air and paced around the office. "Man, I don't know. It was stupid. When we left you and Ingrid at the hospital that night, I texted Ava that Emma Rose hadn't arrived. Then, for some crazy reason, I invited her to Sunday dinner."

"Well, Mom brought food over on Monday, and that was all she talked about," said Peter, laughing. "Oh, and Caroline thinks Ava's too good for you. Why didn't you tell me you were that serious with her?"

DeAngelo admitted he avoided calls with his mom, opting to text to keep their conversations about Ava short. He then shook his head in frustration.

"That's the thing. We're not that serious. Ever since I met Ava, I feel like I'm off my game. I'm either acting like an ass or an idiot around her with just a few solid moments in between."

Peter again laughed not at DeAngelo but at himself. "I know that feeling. The only woman that can make me feel like an ass and a fool at the same time is Ingrid. That's when I knew she was the one."

DeAngelo shook his entire body, dispelling that notion. "Oh no. I'm nowhere close to talking about any woman being the one. It's this dammed retirement that has me off my game."

Peter smirked. "I hear you. Retirement is rough, but—"

DeAngelo quipped, "Rough? No, retirement sucks."

"True," said Peter. "But it seems like it's more than re-tirement. If Ava has you so out of sorts, why would you in-vite her to Sunday dinner when you know what that move means? She might just be the one."

"I came over here to work, not chitchat about—"

"Okay, okay." Peter flipped through his phone and then handed it to DeAngelo. "Just read. I don't need an answer now."

DeAngelo scrolled through the website open on Peter's phone. His head dropped. He huffed with exasperation.

"University! How long have you been thinking about this?"

Peter grabbed his phone back. "Since Emma Rose."

"So all of two weeks," said DeAngelo, having no aware-ness of how dismissive his words sounded.

Peter glanced over at the monitors showing Emma Rose still fast asleep.

"No, you ass, since Ingrid told me she was pregnant. Look, I need to start doing more with my life and this business. I have a little girl and a family to secure a future for. Doing podcasts won't cut it. We can grow this into a full media company, but we need to know a lot more about business to be successful."

DeAngelo was okay with growing the business, but he lacked Peter's drive for education. "But, hell man, go back to university? How's that going to look, two football world champions at university?"

Peter pointed to the website still open on his phone. "The undergrad and master's programs are one-hundred-percent virtual. Besides, who cares how it looks? We both left university to join the league. There is not much undergrad work we have left to do. I've checked."

With an eyebrow raised, DeAngelo still wore a skeptical look on his face. "I don't know. Sounds like a lot of work."

DeAngelo and Peter accomplished a great deal of work over the next few hours. They completed two podcasts, updated their website, and drafted three blog posts. Before Peter could get to an email from their agent, an ear-piercing shriek reverberated through the surveillance monitor speakers. Peter jumped up and noted the time in his binder.

"See? My little princess is just ten minutes ahead of schedule."

DeAngelo watched on the monitor as Peter lifted Emma Rose out of her crib and gently rocked her back and forth. For the first time that afternoon, DeAngelo saw Ingrid as she entered the nursery. She joined Peter, both doting on the tiny, wailing infant.

Soon, Emma Rose's roar calmed to a whimper. He peeked into the nursery to see his goddaughter and say his goodbyes. This was a first. DeAngelo finally saw Peter in a new light. A family man.

As he drove back to his place, DeAngelo couldn't help feeling how his life and everything around him had radically changed. Peter, his best mate, and brother, was now a dad. Long gone were the days they were two of the highest-paid, successful footballers living the bachelor life with the world at their fingertips. Peter was on diaper duty now and charting baby sleeping and feeding patterns, for goodness' sake.

DeAngelo moped around his apartment for the rest of the evening, reminiscing about the good old days. He flipped through a scrapbook his mom had put together of his World Cup winning season.

Damn! That seems like a lifetime ago, DeAngelo thought as he stared at the pictures. Officially depressed, there was one thing he refused to do. He promised himself that the moment he decided to retire, he would not turn into a washed-up athlete trying to stay relevant. The one speaking out on politics or stoking controversies hoping to get more Twitter followers.

He knew Peter was right. Their podcasting, random television interviews, and commercials were not a long-term business strategy. Yes, he wanted to grow their business, but he was still a hard "no" on Peter's university idea. To further complicate things, the other thought fighting for his attention was Ava.

Do I love her? I think I might love her.

DeAngelo oscillated back and forth on inviting Ava to

Sunday dinner again. On the one hand, it would undoubtedly confirm to his family that he was serious about her. The problem with that was DeAngelo wasn't sure how serious he was about Ava. He figured if he never invited Ava to Sunday dinner again, he could maintain that the first invitation didn't mean anything—but *did* he want it to mean something?

Chapter 19

"Isn't dinner at your parent's house?" Ava asked as DeAngelo's car passed by his folks' home and parked in the driveway of a house across the street and two doors down. DeAngelo hadn't mentioned otherwise, so she assumed Sunday dinner was at his parents', like the week before.

DeAngelo looked surprised at the question. "No. It's Momma Gretta's month of Sundays." He said it with a chuckle in his voice which annoyed Ava. He had neglected to share this important tidbit of information before.

Her brow raised with irritation. "You never told me that. Now, what am I going to do?"

"Do about what?"

"A gift, that's what. I'm coming to the Kraus' house for the first time, and I don't have a gift."

"No one is going to care about that."

DeAngelo's answer only irked her more. "I care about it. It's rude to show up empty-handed, especially at the first dinner invitation."

"You're right. I'm sorry for not letting you know. It's so

normal for me, I didn't think. I will let everyone know it's my fault."

"Don't you dare! God, no! That would be worse! Just let me handle it." Ava shook her nerves off. "Let's go in. I'm sure we look silly sitting here in the car."

Caroline met Ava and DeAngelo at the front door bursting with excitement. "Hey, come on in. Everyone's here." She grabbed Ava by the hand and rushed her across the room to a woman holding the tiniest and cutest baby. "Let me introduce you to my perfect little niece, Emma Rose."

"Hello, I'm Ingrid. Everyone gets introduced to Emma Rose, me, and then Peter."

"That's how it works," said Ava looking and waving at Emma Rose. "She is so beautiful. Look at those big, round, inquisitive eyes."

Ingrid kissed Emma Rose's forehead and moved closer to give Ava a side hug. "Thanks so much for the baby gifts. Albert gave it to Peter and me. You didn't have to go to the trouble. The picture frame is gorgeous, and the blanket is Emma Rose's favorite during nap time."

Ava turned, hearing DeAngelo's voice. "Ava, this is Peter, my best mate."

Peter was all smiles, as any new dad should be. Like Mr. Kraus, Peter was a hand shaker, not a hugger. "Nice to finally meet you, Ava. And yes, thank you for the gifts."

Caroline corralled everyone into the kitchen, where the

rest of the family had assembled. "DeAngelo and Ava are here."

Ava felt at ease with the warm welcome she had received. It was like coming home to a family anxiously awaiting your arrival. Rosalynn gave her a big hug.

"Glad you could join us, Ava," said Momma Gretta, enveloping Ava in a hearty embrace. "Did you meet my grandbaby?"

"Yes, ma'am. She is gorgeous."

"I can't wait to have more." Momma Gretta winked at Ava before yelling out that dinner was ready.

Everyone crowded around the table for a full, traditional German meal: juicy roast chicken, potatoes, and green beans. Peter dominated the table talk, eagerly detailing his elaborate feeding and sleeping scheme. The family's vocal skepticism and playful jesting rolled off him like water off a duck's back.

Emma Rose boasted Peter's credibility when she woke up with a whimper in Ingrid's arms.

"See, I told you!" declared Peter, looking at his phone, then at Emma Rose. "My little princess is just five minutes ahead of her scheduled feeding time."

Albert passed the roast chicken. "She must take after you, my boy. You always seem to know when dinner is ready."

Ecstatic they made Emma Rose the topic of conversation instead of her, Ava relaxed and soaked in the wonderfully cozy Kraus and Williams family vibe. She basked in the love swirling around the dinner table. She almost missed her family even more.

After dinner, Rich pulled Ava aside while everyone cleaned up. Her shoulders tightened with tension. She looked over at DeAngelo to get his attention, hoping he would come to her aid. Unfortunately, he was helping his mother with the dishes and didn't notice. Ava reluctantly followed Rich into the hallway.

"I used tuh host ah barbecue fram time tuh time. Been ah few years now. Wah bout—"

Excited to avoid answering relationship questions, Ava agreed to help Rich before hearing him out. She pulled her phone from her pocket and began to quiz Rich on the details. In five minutes of gleeful collaboration, Ava and Rich had planned the event of the summer.

The two returned to the kitchen. Rich knocked on the kitchen table to get everyone's attention.

"Everyone, I have an announcement. Da Fourth of July is inna few weeks. My fellow Merikan and proud Texan, Ava, has agreed tuh help me host a real, Merikan-style barbecue."

No one spoke. They sat with wide eyes and confused expressions. Concerned, Ava glanced over at DeAngelo to see his face drawn into a tight frown. She rushed to defuse the situation she saw brewing.

"This is going to be so much fun." She turned to Rich and then shot a big smile toward DeAngelo. "I am more than happy to bring a little bit of America and a whole lot of Texas to Germany."

Shortly after the big announcement, DeAngelo asked Ava if she was ready to leave.

DeAngelo didn't say anything until they got in the car. "You don't have to do this. My dad overstepped. He should never have asked you to plan a party with him."

"It's fine," said Ava. "I want to. It will be nice to do something other than work for a change. Besides, I'm a pro at throwing a party."

"The first time you meet them, Mom puts you to work in the kitchen cooking, and now, Dad is making you help him with the lame barbecues he used to have. They don't have to be all over you like this." He started the car, talking more to himself at this point. "They know you all of what three weeks, and now this?"

Ava sat back in the seat and let DeAngelo fume all the way to her place. He was clearly angry about something other than her helping plan a barbecue with his dad.

Once the big day arrived, everyone stirred with excitement; even DeAngelo stopped being a grump and warmed up to the idea. For weeks, Ava adjusted and re-adjusted her plans for the barbecue. The guest list went from family to family and a few friends to an open-door invitation. Rich had transformed the family barbecue into an all-out block party.

Ava employed Jack to drive her to DeAngelo's parents' place. She helped Jack load the car down with container after container the morning of the festivities.

"Sorry, Jack. I didn't think I had this much stuff." She threw the duffle bag with her clothes in the backseat and then jumped in herself.

Jack assumed his station behind the wheel. They were ready to go. Too anxious to be still, Ava wanted to talk.

"What are you doing today?" she asked.

Jack glanced in the rearview mirror to see Ava smiling, waiting for his answer. "Just hanging around the house until you call for a pickup. My son is home from university. He completed his coursework in computer science."

"Don't worry about picking me up. DeAngelo can bring me home. You and your son are welcome to come to the party. Caroline will have her friends there. They should be around your son's age."

Jack sounded a little apprehensive when he thanked Ava for the invitation. So, she applied a mild but effective dose of pressure.

"I'm not going to insist, but I would really like for you to join us. There'll be tons of food and fun."

Her sincere tone convinced Jack to accept the invitation.

Even with heavy traffic, their timing had worked out perfectly. The sun had risen on a gorgeous Saturday, July fourth, in Germany. Three hours before noon, the party event crew had pulled up and set up the lights, tables, jumbo projector, and sound system.

Men love their sports, so Ava made sure to have a second source of entertainment. She added a ten-foot outdoor projector screen system to the list of party essentials without Rich's approval—a personal touch to ensure the festivities' success. There was no way people would walk away and say the barbecue was boring. Besides, it was summer, and some sort of game was on nearly every channel to keep the men happy.

The crew was in and out within an hour. Ava enlisted DeAngelo and Rich to make a few subtle tweaks to the table layout to improve the flow.

The doors would open a little past noon. Guests could munch on snacks, mingle, and drink until the food was laid out an hour later.

A quarter til noon, Ava realized she still needed to clean up and get changed. DeAngelo took her upstairs, showed her the bathroom, and waited for her down the hall in his old room.

Ava gazed around the room as she changed clothes. Photos, ribbons, and trophies of DeAngelo as a young boy decorated the wall and bookshelves.

"Oh, this is so adorable. Look at all your little trophies. Oh, look how cute you were!"

She sat on the bed to rub on some sunscreen. DeAngelo had other ideas; he laid her back on the bed.

"Come on," urged DeAngelo. "I've never made out with a girl in my room before."

Ava smirked and rolled her eyes. "I don't believe you."

DeAngelo persisted as he worked on unbuttoning her blouse. He tried to look innocent.

"I swear. Momma would have beat me senseless if I had a girl up here."

Ava gave him one little kiss. "What would your momma do if she caught you up here with me now?"

DeAngelo thought for a second. "Probably beat me senseless or ask for a grandbaby."

They both laughed and headed downstairs.

The grill and the smoker were started. Ava's mom had shipped her four prime Texas briskets and several pounds of pulled pork. The meats were pre-cooked, but her mother had taught her to warm them up in the smoker, low and slow. A variety of German sausages and, of course, Rich's favorite, jerk chicken, sizzled on the grill.

Rosalynn, Momma Gretta, and Caroline made the lion's share of the side dishes and desserts. Ava contributed a few American favorites, like pasta salad and baked beans. She added peach cobbler to the dessert table. The last thing she wanted was to run out of food. Ava had been by her mom's side planning hundreds of business events. Her mom's number one rule was to never let a guest walk away hungry.

Rich kept hovering. Ava's brow crinkled with a strained

look on her sun-washed face. Her expression was more for effect than how she really felt.

"Rich, we have planned this out to the smallest detail. All the other meats are ready. This last batch of chicken will be ready in ten minutes. Everyone can start eating now." She turned him around and urged him toward his party guests.

DeAngelo saw his dad try to protest. "I don't want yuh cook'n all day."

With a final head shake and parting admonition, Ava convinced Rich to relax. "I have everything covered. Please go tell everyone they can start eating."

Rich wasted no time kicking the barbecue into high gear with a rousing. "Let's eat!"

The Williams house was the hub of activity with a steady stream of guests drawn by the irresistible aromas of grilled meat, sugary desserts, and the roaring sound of a good time.

Rounds of cheers and shouts erupted over whichever game boomed on the massive projection screen at the time. A backyard football match broke out with DeAngelo, the captain of one team, and Peter, captain of the other. Everyone was in too good of a mood for the game to get competitive.

The moon and stars shone above them when the party came to an end. DeAngelo showed the last guest out and then ran upstairs to get Ava's things. Ava stayed back, cleaning up the last of the stray dishes. Dancing to imaginary music, Rich swayed with Rosalynn on the patio to bring a close to their evening.

Before saying goodnight, Rich finished his dance and walked over to Ava.

"Dis have been one of di best nights I've had inna long time. Funny how yuh don't know ow much yuh miss a ting til someone brings it back tuh yuh."

Ava almost cried seeing how happy the party had made Rich. She grabbed her shoes while DeAngelo said goodnight to his parents.

"She's a gud woman, son," Rich whispered in DeAngelo's ear.

Ava and DeAngelo were the only two left. She smiled at him.

"This was fun."

DeAngelo put his arms around her. "It was amazing. You're amazing. You know I love you, right?"

Her heart burst at the sound of those three wonderful, little words leaving his mouth and wrapped in his smooth voice. Goosebumps covered Ava's arms. A chill ran through her body as DeAngelo's fiery brown eyes stared into her soul.

Her life had been so lonely for so long. Rich's words rang true in her soul. You *don't* know how much you miss a thing until someone brings it back to you. DeAngelo brought love and passion back into her life.

For once, she refused to deny her emotions. Her eyes swelled with tears.

DeAngelo rubbed her arms. "Baby, what's wrong?"

She was so in love with him it hurt. "I know I can love you forever."

Chapter 20

"Look at you, cooking breakfast."

DeAngelo turned his back to the stove to see Ava bare-footed, wearing one of his old jerseys and a pair of denim shorts. She looked way too sexy for ten o'clock in the morning, with her curly hair tied up in a loose ponytail and a big grin on her face that made him smile.

He flipped the skillet, and a fluffy blueberry pancake went spinning into the air.

"As a matter of fact, I *do* cook," he said, as the pancake dropped back down into the center of the skillet.

Ava clapped and giggled. "Bravo, bravo!"

He soon slid a plate with two blueberry pancakes in front of her, poured her a tall glass of orange juice, and gave her the most passionate good morning kiss of her life.

DeAngelo played with Ava's hair, kissed her face, and rubbed her arms, giving her just enough room to eat. After her last bite, they moved into the living room and relaxed. Moments after they had gotten settled, their phones buzzed with texts at the same time.

Caroline sent a string of photos of them together at the party the night before and a message:

> No Sunday dinner tonight. Everybody's still recovering from the best party ever!

Ava and DeAngelo laughed out loud.

"Oh my goodness, look at us. I never once saw Caroline take these pictures," said Ava, scrolling through the images.

DeAngelo declared his favorite was one of him holding Ava from behind and her head tilted to the side, laughing as he kissed her neck. Or maybe it was the one of Ava laughing with his mom and dad. No, it was definitely the one with Ava's arms around his neck looking up at him and his arms around her waist looking down at her. That was his favorite.

They stretched out on the couch. Ava laid back against DeAngelo's chest. She didn't have to see his face to know he was smiling.

"What's so funny?"

He smoothed her hair to stop it from tickling his nose. "Oh, nothing. Just thinking."

"You have to tell me what's so funny."

"Do you want to know when I fell in love with you?"

That had to be a rhetorical question. Of course, Ava wanted to know. She waited as he tightened his arms around her.

"It was when I saw you in that silver dress at the resort."

"When I asked you to make love to me for the first time,"

Ava replied. "That was when I knew I could love you. But our night under the stars, there was no doubt I was completely *in* love with you."

As the long summer days moved time forward, Ava began shedding more of her responsibilities at the factory. Caroline was Ava's right hand. She was always willing to learn and was enthusiastic about the business. Because of that, Ava was thrilled to promote Caroline to Junior Office Manager and establish her as part of the new management team.

DeAngelo's work picked up with several broadcasting gigs, but it wasn't full-time. In their free time, they spent every minute they could together, learning more and more about each other.

Ava learned that DeAngelo got grouchy if she woke him up too early for anything other than fooling around. Yes, he could cook, and yes, he would help when asked, but DeAngelo preferred to talk and watch while she bounced around the kitchen and cooked. Rosalynn raised him right. DeAngelo would always help clean up the kitchen without being asked.

She learned DeAngelo loved to touch and be touched. There was not a day that went by that he didn't hug or kiss her multiple times. When he walked by, he would rub her arm, run his hand over her shoulder, or give her a nice, soft kiss. Ava quickly adopted the same habit.

DeAngelo always liked to sit close, but with one exception: when he watched football. He would get so into the game, reacting to every play as if he were still on the field.

She was happy that, as much as DeAngelo loved to be around people, he valued his privacy. He wasn't one of those celebrities who posted every moment of their life on social media. Peter maintained their social media accounts and kept them strictly for business-related purposes.

DeAngelo appreciated Ava's willingness to cuddle but realized she liked enough room in the bed to have her own space and stretch out. He could see she wasn't as comfortable with public displays of affection, so he tried to tone it down.

He learned that when she had a particularly rough or stressful day, the thing that relaxed Ava most was a long, jasmine-scented bubble bath. Luckily for him, Ava's long, hot baths often put her in the mood for a bit of lovemaking.

He was still getting used to how honest she was when things bothered her. When upset, Ava avoided talking until she was calm, which was the opposite of DeAngelo. He was quick to talk and occasionally slow to listen. That was not always the right approach.

As time went on, the weather cooled, the days shortened, and the colors on the trees transformed to a yellow-and-red autumn radiance. On a Monday evening, Ava called and asked DeAngelo if she could come over to his place.

"I have great news," was the only thing she would tell him.

DeAngelo hoped the news was that she had either rented or leased a car. He was getting tired of driving her around everywhere. And he thought she was needlessly spending money having Jack drive her back and forth to work. He pushed the subject more when Ava told him she had a German international driver's license.

As soon as Ava walked through the door, she jumped into DeAngelo's arms. He spun her around, keen to celebrate her good news. Plus, he had a bit of good news to share himself. When her feet hit the floor, she gave him a big kiss and buried her head in his chest. Once she had steadied herself from being dizzy, she pulled DeAngelo to the couch.

Ecstatic, she kissed DeAngelo again before revealing the big news.

"It took a while, but we recovered most of what those—" She stopped, took a breath, and rephrased. "We recovered eighty percent of the embezzled money."

Ava's eyes widened, and her smile was ear to ear. "Now, we can give nice—very nice—salary increases and Christmas bonuses to all our employees at the factory!"

DeAngelo reached out to grab her for an embrace and kiss, but his actions were thwarted.

"Wait, there's more," Ava continued. She went on to detail how she was on a series of calls with Appliance International of France. They were one of the largest home appliance manufacturers in the country. They wanted to expand their manufacturing operations into Germany, and the Brooks family is who they wanted to partner with.

She shook with joy. "Do you know what this means? Only a very lucrative, five-year, multimillion-dollar deal and at least two hundred new jobs."

"Oh my God, Ava, that is fantastic news!" exclaimed DeAngelo. "I have some news to share myself. Peter and I secured a contract with our former football club to produce a commercial for its philanthropic campaign."

Ava gave DeAngelo a quick kiss and sprinted off to the kitchen to grab two glasses. Then, she retrieved a bottle of sparkling, nonalcoholic champagne from her bag left by the door. Big news deserves the popping of a cork in celebration.

DeAngelo popped the cork and filled their glasses.

"To our very successful careers," said Ava. "And to me finally getting a car this weekend."

August and September were a blur of activity. Everyone had their nose to the grindstone. Ava was completely consumed with building a partnership with Appliance International of France, and as a result, she and Caroline made many trips to France to meet with executives and learn more about their products and processes.

Ava knew that it would be the biggest break of her career if she could successfully broker the deal. Danny was making fantastic progress in South America. With both of their efforts, the family business could be a billion-dollar company by the end of the year.

DeAngelo and Peter's commercial project turned into something much bigger. They consulted on various projects, including a new marketing campaign, fitness and conditioning training, and a reboot of the club's youth football league.

October rolled around and life slowed down. Though they settled into a more reasonable schedule, Ava and DeAngelo struggled to get back into the carefree groove they had enjoyed over the summer.

Maybe it was the stress of the past few months, but Ava noticed a change in DeAngelo. He seemed distant, not as easygoing and laid-back. He was also less affectionate. Ava wondered if their "can't-keep-their-hands-off-each-other" phase had run its course. She hoped not. Every touch from DeAngelo made her feel alive and loved.

To regain the spark, Ava took matters into her own hands. She planned a romantic evening, hoping it would rekindle their spark. It had been two weeks since she and DeAngelo had made love, and she missed his touch and passion.

She donned her sexy little dress and lit the candles, but nothing worked. DeAngelo was quiet during dinner. He picked at his food and avoided making eye contact when Ava tried to start up a conversation.

She could deal with the silent treatment in the car but

not at the dinner table. She tried to stay patient, hoping for anything to bring them closer.

"Is everything okay?" Ava asked. "You don't seem like yourself."

"I'm fine," DeAngelo replied as he left the table and walked off toward the bedroom.

Ava followed and saw him looking around for something. "Can I help you find something?"

"I'm looking for my cuff links," DeAngelo barked back. "You know. The blue enamel, woven-knot ones. My favorites."

Ava calmly walked over to the dresser while DeAngelo opened and slammed another drawer. She had turned to hand him the box with his cuff links when she heard him mumble under his breath.

"I need to stop leaving my things here."

Ava tossed the box on the bed. "You can take your cuff links and all your things!" she shouted, storming out of the room.

DeAngelo came racing out of the bedroom like a raging bull, his eyes red and chest heaving in anger, ready to fight.

"What's the matter with you?" he yelled.

Ava's temper erupted at such a ridiculous question. She yelled back. "What's the matter with *me*? You're the one with the problem. I never asked you to leave your things here."

"Damn it, Ava. You know I didn't mean it like that."

He put the box in his pocket. Ava's voice was a little less loud, but she was still angry.

"Just how did you mean it?"

"I've got a lot going on right now," said DeAngelo. "The last thing I need is to not be able to find my damn cuff links."

Ava raised her voice again. "Really? We're fighting over a silly pair of cufflinks? What's your real problem? Is there something going on that—"

Shock rippled across DeAngelo's face. "What the hell is that supposed to mean? What are you saying?"

Ava narrowed her focus as she glared at DeAngelo. Her head was pounding. "I'm not *saying* anything. I'm *asking*. You're not as affectionate. We haven't made love in two weeks." She paused to build up her courage. "Is there anything you need to tell me?"

"No!" DeAngelo walked over to the table and snatched up his phone and keys. "I should go."

Chapter 21

Frustration and anger festered. Texting was as much as Ava or DeAngelo would commit to.

> Hi, how are you?

> Fine, and you?

was the extent of their communication. Both had retreated to their separate corners to cool off after their first fight. Their busy work schedule provided the perfect excuse for them to neglect seeing each other.

DeAngelo had attempted to make amends and end their two-week spat. He stopped by Ava's with flowers to apologize.

"I'm sorry for blowing up the way I did. Ava, the only thing I need you to know is that I love you," said DeAngelo, hugging her tight.

"I love you, too, and I'm sorry for letting things get out of hand," Ava replied with her arms around DeAngelo's neck, elevating herself on tiptoes to kiss him.

"Now, let's talk about something more exciting—the holidays. It's already November fifth, and we haven't made plans," she said as they relaxed on the couch.

DeAngelo's eyes stayed glued to the television, more interested in some movie than what Ava wanted to discuss.

"We're having Christmas at Peter's so Ingrid's family can join for Emma Rose's first Christmas," said DeAngelo. "But Momma insists on a small family dinner on Christmas Eve."

He turned to look at Ava with a blank stare. "You're staying here for Christmas, right?"

Working on the potential deal with Appliance International of France and falling in love kept her in Germany far longer than she had imagined. Ava was nervous. She hoped DeAngelo would say "yes" to the plan she was eager to propose. She rubbed his arm to soften him up.

"Well, I was thinking. How about I host an old-fashion Thanksgiving dinner here at my place? I can treat your family to a classic American Thanksgiving.

Ava had an innocent, pleading look on her face as she continued. "Things have been so crazy. We all haven't had time to slow down and have fun together. As far as Christmas goes, I was thinking of celebrating early with family and then flying back here to be with you."

Ava's eyes sparkled with anticipation. She couldn't tell if DeAngelo was open to the plan or not, so she added a bit more enticement.

"I also thought that maybe you could come to the States with Caroline and me in January to meet my family and have a little vacation. What do you think?"

DeAngelo adored the idea and realized he needed a change of scenery. He pulled Ava into his lap.

"I love the idea," he said. "And I love you."

The week before Thanksgiving, Ava worked tirelessly, planning every single detail. Her Fourth of July party was fantastic, but the Thanksgiving feast was going to be over-the-top spectacular. Hosting this dinner was her way of thanking the Williams and Kraus families for accepting her as one of their own. Without them and DeAngelo, her time in Germany would have been completely miserable.

Ava woke up at the crack of dawn to finish a few dishes and prep her twenty-five-pound, free-range turkey. The family was to arrive that afternoon, so her big, beautiful bird needed to be in the oven no later than 10:00 A.M.

After almost two hours of fussing, smoothing, and tinkering, Ava finished her gold-and-white tablespace, having accented it with mini pumpkins, candles, and beautiful, fresh fall flowers. Her design rivaled any *Better Home and Garden* magazine cover.

DeAngelo staggered into the kitchen at half-past ten o'clock, yawning and rubbing his eyes.

"Man, it smells good in here," he said, caressing Ava's back. "What time did you get up?"

She poured him some coffee. "Six this morning."

DeAngelo took a few sips of the brew, gave another nice, big yawn, and stretched. "Why didn't you wake me? I would have helped."

Ava bit her lip so as not to laugh. She knew that if she woke DeAngelo at 6:00 A.M. to cook and set the table, he would be the biggest grouch all morning long.

The closer it came to four o'clock, the more enthused Ava became. Nervous, she pressed her burgundy wrap dress smooth at her hips.

"How do I look?"

DeAngelo took her by the hand. "You look beautiful." He moved in for a kiss but felt Ava's palms firm against his chest. She wagged her finger at him.

"Just one tiny kiss. And don't you dare mess up my hair."

"Ok, but only because my family is coming," he pouted before kissing her again.

Hearing the oven timer buzz, Ava dashed off to the kitchen. She could see through the oven window that the star of the show was ready.

"Oh my goodness, he's beautiful."

The only thing left to do was pop the appetizers in the

oven and put the printed menus at each place setting. Ava put her hands together and said a quick prayer for everything to go well.

The entire family arrived together on time. Everyone shared plenty of hugs and kisses as DeAngelo took the coats to the back room while Ava helped Ingrid set up an area for baby Emma Rose in the bedroom.

The dinner party began with DeAngelo pouring drinks. There was beer, wine, and Jamaican rum-spiked hot apple cider. Ava made the spiked cider specifically for Rich. The cranberry Brie bites, roasted Brussels sprouts, and stuffed mushrooms appetizers were huge hits.

Everyone relaxed in the living room, noshed, and talked about what they were looking forward to during the holidays. There was a collective relief that work was behind them, at least until the New Year.

After about forty minutes, Ava invited everyone to the dinner table. With their guests seated, she and DeAngelo slipped into the kitchen. They returned with the first course.

Ava carried a large, metallic, gold pumpkin soup tureen filled with a creamy carrot ginger soup. DeAngelo brought the roasted beet and goat cheese salad in a matching salad bowl. After due praise was given to the hostess for her table design and food, the talk turned to baby Emma Rose.

To everyone's amazement, Ingrid managed to hold her sleeping daughter and eat simultaneously. Peter boasted about every little baby achievement, which wasn't many considering Emma Rose was only five months old. He swore he heard Emma Rose say "dada" the day before. Everyone laughed, but Peter stuck to his story.

Meanwhile, Ava was on the verge of exploding with pride to show off her golden turkey. "Is everyone ready for the main course?"

Again, she and DeAngelo slipped back into the kitchen. Ava let the latter carry the pièce de résistance—the bird—to the table. Not any old bird, but the most succulent, herb-crusted, golden-brown show-stopper that ever graced a table.

"Oohs" and "ahhs" welcomed his appearance. Then Ava brought garlic mashed potatoes and apple and sausage cornbread dressing to the table. She disappeared once more and returned with tarragon green beans with almonds and the cranberry orange relish.

After Albert blessed the meal, DeAngelo sliced the turkey. Ava beamed with pride seeing her moist, juicy bird carved. Each dish made its way around the table, and the feast began. The table talk dropped to a low rumble as everyone enjoyed the meal. About the time everyone was midway through their second plate of food, the table talk resumed.

"I have never had a turkey this moist before. Do you celebrate every Thanksgiving in America like this?" asked Momma Gretta between bites.

This was the third Thanksgiving Ava had been away from

home, celebrating in another country. As happy as she was, there remained a lingering feeling of homesickness in her heart.

"Yes. Thanksgiving is a big deal in my family. We all spend time volunteering at the local shelters or hospitals, serving meals in the morning. We eat in the late afternoon. And without fail, after dinner, we settle in to watch America's team: the Dallas Cowboys."

"I'm a Raiders fan myself," Rich piped up.

"A Jamaican and New Yorker not rooting for the Jets or the Giants. That's unheard of," said Ava.

The two had to laugh as DeAngelo and Peter boasted the superiority of European football over American football.

"You Americans and your NFL. With your helmets and your shoulder pads, it's too much," said Peter.

"We all know that real men play *real* football," said DeAngelo.

"Let's finish this conversation in the living room," Ava suggested.

The football debate raged on. However, when the conversation turned to basketball teams and which country had the best players, Ava was ready to defend her country to the death.

She could be a shameless, cocky American when she needed to be. "Clearly, no other country is better at basketball than America. Really, who can beat any of our NBA teams?"

Rich raised his glass of spiked cider and chanted, "USA, USA, USA."

Ava secured the victory. The conversation then moved from American sports to America in general. Surprisingly, for some strange reason, DeAngelo and Peter seemed to think they knew all about America. So, Ava proposed a "Battle of America" trivia game, women versus men. To make it a fair fight, Ava and Rich sat out.

"What about DeAngelo?" asked Momma Gretta. "He's American?"

Rosalynn laughed and patted Rich on the knee. "Our boy is a little bit of everything. American, Jamaican, Spanish, and African, but I think he's more German than anything at this point."

"I've been here in Germany since I was seven. I have no American advantage, but I still think Peter and I will crush the ladies," joked DeAngelo.

The guys' confidence bubble burst as the ladies got off to a fantastic start. Ingrid and Caroline answered ten questions in a row correctly. DeAngelo and Peter lagged behind with only three measly points.

Ava walked in with the dessert in time to hear the next question to DeAngelo and Peter.

"Are you ready?" Ingrid asked. "Here's your next question: Who was the first Black woman to become a NASA astronaut? Here's a clue: she went into orbit aboard the Space Shuttle Endeavour on September twelfth, 1992."

The score was now nineteen to eight, and the clock was

ticking with both DeAngelo and Peter asserting they knew but just couldn't think of her name.

Ava leaned over and whispered in DeAngelo's ear, "Mae Jemison."

"Mae Jemison!" blurted DeAngelo.

It was too little, too late, though. Time had expired. Ingrid answered her last question swiftly, leading to a landslide victory for the ladies. The guys demanded a rematch after dessert, with the trivia cards better shuffled next time. DeAngelo bemoaned the fact he and Peter got all the hard subjects like science, government, and obscure history.

"We could use a little help on the next game, Dad," Peter shouted at Albert, who was busy debating which dessert to choose.

Ava's dessert menu included chocolate bourbon walnut pie, southern sweet potato pie, and the classic of all southern classics: red velvet cake.

Albert had never had any of these desserts before, so he indulged in a small slice of all three. He turned to Peter with a full plate.

"I need a little sugar to help me think."

Everyone laughed. The boys fought their way to win the second game. They were in the middle of the tie-breaking death match when Ava went to brew a pot of coffee. As the coffee was going, she filled a thermos with the last few cups of cider for Rich to take home.

She turned around when she heard Rosalynn call her name. "Oh, Rosalynn, can I get something for you?"

"May I have a cup of Earl Grey if you have it?" asked Rosalynn.

"Yes, of course," Ava replied while Rosalynn took a seat at the kitchen table.

"Please, sit and join me," Rosalynn offered when Ava brought the tea over.

Ava sat down, her legs thanking her for the rest.

"This has been a marvelous dinner party," said Rosalynn, stirring her tea. "I am very impressed. Everything has been fabulous."

Ava breathed an internal sigh of relief, grateful for praise from DeAngelo's mother. "Thank you so much. I'm glad you enjoyed everything."

Tears watered Ava's eyes, and she looked away, attempting to hold it all in.

"I'm sorry. I don't know why I'm crying," continued Ava. "I just wanted to show you all how much I appreciate your kindness and treating me like family. It has been the next best thing to being at home."

Ava got up to fix herself a cup of tea. She returned to the table more composed. In the most loving, motherly tone, Rosalynn affirmed what she knew in her heart to be true.

"You love my son?" she asked.

Feeling loved and accepted, Ava did not hesitate to answer. "Yes, I love DeAngelo very much."

"Come." Rosalynn took Ava's hand and stood up. She held Ava's timid face in her hands. "I'm so happy he has you."

Chapter 22

DeAngelo came from the back room with the coats as Ava passed out the parting gifts. She had outdone herself with pecan bars and mini pumpkin bread loaves in gift bags for everyone to take home. Rich received the extra treat of the last of the rum-spiked apple cider.

Struck by all the silly looks on his family's faces, DeAngelo wondered what the heck was going on. Ingrid gave him a weird, wild-eyed glance as she put on her coat while Ava held Emma Rose.

Then there was Peter. He looked the silliest with a wide grin, winking eye, and bobbing his head up and down.

"I'm happy for you, man. She's awesome."

"I told you so," were Caroline's last words as she walked to the door.

DeAngelo thought it must be the drinks, the sugar, or all the calories that had made his entire family crazy.

Momma Gretta hugged and kissed him like she was never going to see him again.

"You're a lucky man," was all Albert said, and he gave

DeAngelo a congratulatory handshake.

DeAngelo held out hope his parents still had their senses about them. He lost that quickly, though. He could see the rum had his dad on cloud nine.

"I proud of yuh, boy. Yu have dun gud fi yuhself."

Surely his mom was still sane. As he helped Rosalynn with her coat, DeAngelo nearly hit the panic button.

"Do you love her?" asked Rosalynn.

What the hell? DeAngelo felt cornered. His mom liked to meddle in his life, but she had never outright asked him if he was in love with any woman.

"Ah. Yes, I love Ava." Hearing himself confess his love for her to someone else panicked him.

Rosalynn had made up her mind, and DeAngelo was going to hear it. "Ava's the woman for you. She needs to be your wife and my daughter."

DeAngelo knew he had to say something. He couldn't let his mom leave, thinking he was ready to get married. He chuckled to lighten the mood.

"It's way too soon to be talking marriage."

Rosalynn just smiled. She knew what was best for her son, and Ava was it.

Once the doors closed and the elevator began its descent, everyone gave their opinion. There was a unanimous agreement that a marriage proposal was on the horizon. It all added up. Ava was a regular at Sunday dinner and had hosted their first couple's dinner party.

Rosalynn proudly confirmed to the family. "I can tell you for a fact they love each other very much."

"Christmas!" a giddy Caroline yelled out. "I bet DeAngelo is going to propose to Ava on Christmas."

Momma Gretta joined Caroline's line of thinking. "Yes, he's going to the States with you two in January to meet her family. It makes perfect sense."

Rosalynn teared up and squeezed Rich's hand. "Our boy's getting married."

DeAngelo walked Ava back into the apartment. "Your first dinner party was an amazing success."

Ava held on tight to DeAngelo with her head buried in his chest. She was so exhausted she almost fell asleep in his arms.

"*Our* first dinner party was a success," she said, looking up at DeAngelo. "Now it's time for the cleanup."

"Absolutely not." DeAngelo picked a few roses from the table, took Ava by the arm, and walked her into the bedroom. He sat her on the bed, knelt down, removed her heels, and massaged her legs and feet.

"That feels good," said Ava, finally starting to unwind.

"You stay right here." DeAngelo went into the bathroom. He drew Ava a hot bubble bath and added rose petals for a touch of romance.

"You, baby, are going to relax," he insisted, leading Ava into the bathroom. "You enjoy your bath and let me clean up."

DeAngelo strolled into the kitchen and rolled up his sleeves. He had a big task ahead of him, cleaning up after a nine-person, multicourse dinner party. First, he cleared the dinner table and collected all the random glasses and plates in the living room. He put away the leftovers, but not before having another slice of sweet potato pie for himself.

Next, DeAngelo washed the pots, pans, and serving platters that were too big to fit in the dishwasher. He made one last trip through the dining and living room to wipe down the tables and put all the furniture in order. With one final sweep of the kitchen, he started the dishwasher and was done.

He couldn't help but smile when he saw Ava had slipped into bed after her bath and had fallen asleep. Of course, she had to be drained from the weeks of work she had put into planning such an elaborate meal, but he had hoped for some alone time. He leaned over and kissed Ava's lips to see what sort of response he would receive. Fingers crossed, she would return her soft, dreamy look of readiness.

Ava's eyes opened. She blinked and whispered, "I love you," before falling back to sleep.

DeAngelo brushed a few strands of hair from Ava's cheek. He sat back in the chair next to the bed and watched her sleep.

She really is amazing. He stared and wondered if she had thought about marriage. It seemed to be the only thing women getting close to thirty ever thought about. That was the problem with Celine. Well, that and a lot of other things.

DeAngelo couldn't look at Ava anymore. Marriage was something he wanted someday, but not now. He jumped from the chair and went into the living room to think. He paced. Guilt started to eat at him. He danced around the competing thoughts in his head about the slippery slope he was on, but not with Ava and marriage. He had been flirting with an actress on the commercial set.

Nothing has happened, DeAngelo thought to himself. *It's just been some innocent flirting. I flirt. That's what I do.*

One or two lunches don't mean anything, he continued, attempting to convince himself. *I'm still allowed to go to lunch with other people.*

DeAngelo fell back onto the couch with his hand on his head. *I should never have invited Ava to Sunday dinner. Regret twisted his stomach in knots. I knew that mistake would come back to bite me in the ass. Momma—and hell, the whole family—thinks I'm getting married.*

Like a slap to the head, it hit DeAngelo. He remembered Ava's correction. She said *our* dinner party.

Oh, hell. She wants to get married. Is that why she put on this big show and invited me to the States to meet her parents? Damn, she's hoping I'll propose.

DeAngelo felt trapped. He was speeding down the wrong road and thinking himself into a headache. At least with Celine, she had been the only one pressuring him to get married. Now it's his entire family. It was too soon for marriage talk.

I don't even know if she plans to move back to the States. He thought about everyone with those stupid grins on their faces. *"Ava's awesome" this, "proud of you" that. And Momma. How does she know Ava's the one for me? "Make her your wife."*

Like hell I will, at least not anytime soon.

The week after Thanksgiving, DeAngelo felt more relaxed now that Ava was off to Texas to visit her family. He slapped Peter on the shoulder.

"You missed another great dinner with the production crew."

Peter glanced up with a searching look in his eyes. He was going to say something, but bit his tongue. Instead, he turned his attention back to his daughter.

DeAngelo walked around the nursery with a grin on his face. "I've enjoyed hanging out with the team. Don't get me wrong; it's been a ton of work, but it's great being a part of everything again. I love the energy, the excitement." He turned to Peter. "Don't you miss it?"

"Miss what?" grumbled Peter without looking up.

"Hanging out with the team. Having fun. Being single."

Peter rocked back and forth with Emma Rose in his arms. His brow furrowed.

"What the hell, man? Are you crazy? I can't wait to get this project finished. Dealing with the egos, the drama, the temper tantrums. I hope to hell I wasn't that big of an ass when I was a rookie."

Emma Rose squirmed a little, so Peter lowered his voice. "I wouldn't go back to my single days for anything. I love my life."

DeAngelo brushed off everything Peter had said. "The project wrap-up party is this weekend. The entire crew and some of the players will be there. But I suppose that's too much excitement for a married man with a kid," joked DeAngelo. "Seriously, man, we're sitting here in a pink room with dancing animals in tutus painted on the walls."

"You shouldn't be going," snapped Peter.

DeAngelo knew what Peter was driving at. Ava had flown home to celebrate an early Christmas with her family. In two weeks, she would fly back to Germany to celebrate with him.

DeAngelo took a drink of his beer and smirked.

"Unlike you, I don't have to answer to a wife. Are you telling me you're completely happy?"

Peter put Emma Rose in her crib, furious at his friend. Brother or not, he wasn't going to allow anyone to disrespect him and his family.

"What the hell has gotten into you, asking me if I'm happy?" said Peter, his voice hushed and exasperated. "Hell, yes. I'm happily married to a wonderful woman and have this beautiful baby. You're acting ridiculous. Are you really going to risk messing up things with Ava for some actress?"

Peter had seen how the actress, Vivian, flirted with DeAngelo on set and how DeAngelo never once discouraged her, but rather soaked it up to feed his ego.

"You know it's not about hanging out with friends," Peter continued. "You're chasing after something you don't need."

DeAngelo's temper flared. He knew he should never have said anything. Peter was an old, boring family man now.

"What the hell do you know about what I need?"

Angry, both men squared off; neither intended to back down from the argument.

Peter glared at DeAngelo, shaking his head. "What the hell have you done? Please tell me you're not making it with that actress, Vivian."

DeAngelo finished his beer. He had a smug smile on his face.

"I'm not screwing her, if that's what you're asking. I've taken her out a few times for lunch over the past couple of months. So what?"

Frustrated, Peter ran his hands through his hair. "You really can't be this big of a jackass. You're cheating on Ava. Real classy, man. Real classy."

"I'm not cheating. I just told you, I'm not screwing the woman!" DeAngelo yelled from across the room.

Emma Rose squirmed in her crib. Peter shushed DeAngelo.

"Keep your voice down."

Peter walked closer to DeAngelo. "Are you out of your damn mind? You love Ava, right? Hell, the whole family loves her. You can't be this immature to still want to chase women."

DeAngelo had had enough. "Despite what you and the whole family might think, I'm not getting married anytime soon. Ava and I are just dating. That's it." He threw his hands in the air. "First, you all were quick to tell me she was too good for me. Now you all act like she's the only woman I could find. She's great, but—" DeAngelo stopped and set his empty beer bottle down, not wanting to continue. "I'm leaving."

There were times over the years when Peter disagreed with DeAngelo, but today he was disappointed in his brother and had never seen DeAngelo be so callous and mean. Like lit matchsticks, Peter's ears were ablaze with anger. He gripped DeAngelo's arm tight to stop him from going.

"I don't know what the hell your problem is, but I do know that if you mess things up with Ava, you'll regret it for the rest of your life."

DeAngelo's muscles flexed as he pushed Peter in the shoulder to free his arm. The two best friends locked eyes.

Each watched, poised to throw a punch at the slightest sign of aggression from the other.

"Go to hell, Peter, and mind your own damn business."

DeAngelo stomped out of the nursery. Peter started to head after him when Emma Rose stopped him with her cries.

Furious, DeAngelo ran down the stairs and stormed out, slamming the front door behind him. He jumped in his car and peeled out of the driveway.

"Damn him." DeAngelo's knuckles turned white as he gripped the steering wheel. "I'm sick of everyone prying into my damn business."

The drive back to his place did nothing to calm him.

Damn it. I just need some space. He didn't want to break up with Ava; just slow things down.

DeAngelo decided that in January, he would take some time for himself. Perhaps go to Greece or back to Italy for a few weeks to clear his head.

Chapter 23

After a few flight delays and twenty-five hours of traveling, Ava was home in the great state of Texas. Danny waited at the terminal exit to pick her up. Spotting him, Ava screamed and fell onto his shoulder. She had not seen her big brother in person for over a year. They hugged as her bags were loaded into the car.

"FaceTime calls are no match for the real thing," Ava cried.

As happy as she was to be home, Ava was glad her family made it an easy homecoming that night. With a deluge of hugs and kisses from her mom and dad, she ate dinner and then was ordered off to bed.

Ava texted DeAngelo to let him know she had arrived safely. She didn't expect a reply until morning, as it was late into the night in Germany.

Around noon the next day, Ava's mom, Rita peeked into the room. "You up, sweetheart?"

Ava's hair was in a towel and her body in a robe as she searched her suitcase for some clothes. "Yes, come in, Mom."

Rita entered and sat a tray overflowing with food on the bed. "I thought my baby girl might be hungry."

"You would be right," said Ava, squeezing her mom in a tight embrace. "I've missed you so much. It's good to be home."

Mother and daughter sat on the bed chatting, enjoying each other's company as Ava dug into her brunch.

"This is so good," said Ava munching on a slice of crispy bacon. "What's the plan for the day?"

"Never mind that," said Rita, waving her hand. "First, I want to hear all about this DeAngelo fellow."

Ava had talked to her mom many times about DeAngelo, but that was over the phone. Rita wanted to see how Ava felt about this new man in her life with her own eyes.

Ava lit up like a Christmas tree. She blushed and giggled when she talked about DeAngelo. She also nearly cried when she spoke about how hard it was to leave him to come home for a short visit.

"I can't wait till you all get to meet DeAngelo in January. I know you'll just love him."

"From all you've told me and seeing how happy he makes you, I love him already."

Ava's heartwarming visit with her family was short-lived, for a good reason, of course. On her second day in Texas, she received a wild, almost frantic call from Caroline. The CEO and Chief Operations Executive of Appliance International of France had planned to be in Germany that Friday and would love to see the factory and perhaps put the final touches on the deal.

Ava huddled the family together. "Dad, what do you think?"

Nodding his head in the affirmative, Clayton clearly liked the idea. "I think the CEO is trying to get the deal done to close the books for the year and end on a high note. It will be good for them and us to have this officially signed. We both can move into the new year with great momentum."

"We've turned this deal upside down and inside out to avoid another mistake like the one Ava had to clean up in Germany," said Danny. "We've all been on the calls. Our due diligence has been extreme. I say, let's do it." He raised his hand towards Ava for a high five. "Reel in that big fish, little sister."

Everyone agreed that the meeting was too important to pass up and would cement the biggest deal in their company's history.

Besides, once Ava had secured everything, Danny, their dad, and the lawyers would take over. Her return in January would truly be for relaxation with the deal closed.

Ava trusted Caroline enough to handle the details. Caroline was to conduct the tour of the factory Friday morning and arrange a dinner at a nice restaurant with an extensive wine menu for that evening. Mr. Blanchet, the Appliance International of France CEO, was a wine lover.

Within forty-eight hours of landing in Texas, Ava was on a flight headed back to Germany to land the largest deal of her career.

What a perfect way to end the year, she thought as she peered out at the clouds touching the plane's wing.

She was cutting it close, but fingers crossed, if there were no delays, she would get back in time to rest for a few hours before the dinner.

Ava arrived back in Germany with enough time to rush back to her apartment. After a quick shower, she dressed and texted Jack to pick her up. She needed to meet Caroline and the executives for dinner.

Once she arrived, the hostess escorted Ava through the sophisticated, Parisian-inspired restaurant to a private dining room.

"Aw, Ms. Brooks, I apologize for shortening your visit to the States. It is not in my nature to close business deals over the phone or via some impersonal, virtual meeting. I guess I'm old-fashioned. I still believe in the power of the handshake."

"Truth be told, Mr. Blanchet, so do I," Ava replied.

A tingling sensation ran through her body. The culmination of all her hard work was about to pay off.

"Well then, Ms. Brooks," Mr. Blanchet extended his hand, "Shall we shake on a successful partnership between

Appliance International of France and Brooks Manufacturing Global?"

"We shall," said Ava with a smile.

A waiter passed by with champagne. Ava, Mr. Blanchet, Caroline, and the other three executives raised their glasses.

"Thank you, Mr. Blanchet. We look forward to a long and prosperous partnership with Appliance International of France."

With the clink of the glass and joy bursting in her heart, Ava celebrated the proudest moment in her career. She wanted to shout from the rooftop, "I did it!"

The two-hour celebratory dinner ended with joyous Christmas wishes and plans to begin drafting the final contract in the second week of January.

As the group walked through the crowded main dining area to leave, a very pretty, tall, dark-skinned woman in a short-green sequence dress caught Ava's eye. Her hands rested all over a man as she laughed and tossed her hair. Ava thought the woman must be drunk. Why else would she make such a spectacle?

As she got closer, she recognized the confident stance of the man and the muscular arms resting around the woman's waist. The same lips which kissed her days ago were now locked in a lovers' kiss with a strange, drunk woman.

Ava froze and stared in disbelief at DeAngelo. *This can't be happening.* Her eyes remained transfixed on the scene like someone watching a horror film, and with each passing second, the harsh reality sunk in.

She wanted to run away from everyone, especially DeAngelo, but she couldn't. She had to play nice and get herself out of the restaurant before she lost every ounce of self-control. Ava intended to walk past without an acknowledgment, but Mr. Blanchet was not so inclined. A passionate football fan, he recognized DeAngelo immediately. Deflated, her body went numb, and her brain clicked into survivor mode.

"Look, look. DeAngelo Williams!" Mr. Blanchet shouted like a rabid fan.

Waving his cell phone, Mr. Blanchet approached DeAngelo with the gleefulness of a five-year-old.

"The great DeAngelo Williams! Please, sir, a photo."

Frustrated by the clamor of another annoying fan, DeAngelo turned from his lady friend to blow off whoever was yelling for a photo. Out of the corner of his eye, Caroline's enraged, contorted face startled him.

Damn it. That familiar, composed, and professional voice Ava used when she was beyond pissed rattled his chest.

"Mr. Williams, forgive us for the intrusion. This is Mr. Blanchet, CEO of Appliance International of France and an avid fan. Would you mind if we troubled you for a photo?"

Like a deer caught in headlights, DeAngelo stood there as Vivian, the actress from his commercial shoot, clung to him like a cheap suit. There was no way she was going to leave her prized possession unaccompanied in the presence of other women.

Vivian looked on with disgust. "My goodness. Take the picture and get it over with." She threw a contemptible look at Ava and Caroline and then gave a dramatic toss of her long, curly, black hair.

Of all the weapons in a woman's arsenal, Ava despised the snooty hair toss the most. Only simple-minded women used it as a means of insult.

Ava bit her tongue. She was not going to sink to the level of fighting another woman over a man. And above all, she wasn't going to jeopardize the biggest deal of her career and family business for DeAngelo.

Her mind flashed back to Celine. *Is this really the type of woman he prefers?* It was obvious DeAngelo had made his choice.

Vigorously shaking DeAngelo's hand, Mr. Blanchet noticed very little. He forced his phone into Caroline's hand.

"Picture. Please, take a picture."

To keep Ava's business meeting from derailing, DeAngelo smiled for the photos and made idle chitchat with Mr. Blanchet and the other guests. He managed to cast a guilty look in Ava's direction, but her face was devoid of emotion.

Caroline stepped in to end the torture for all of them. "Thank you, Mr. Williams. We appreciate your time."

Grateful, Ava hurried the group to their cars. Caroline lingered for a moment. She glared at DeAngelo and the woman clutching his arm. She wanted to slap the asinine, guilty look off his face.

"You should be ashamed of yourself. You royal *ass.*"

Caroline left him and rushed to catch up with Ava. "Oh my God, Ava, are you okay? He's an ass. A total ass."

A thundering pain ran wild in Ava's head. Her temples pounded like a bass drum. She rubbed her forehead and breathed out gently.

"I can't do this now, Caroline. I just can't. We have the deal in principle. Please see Mr. Blanchet and his team safely to the airport tomorrow."

Tears spilled down Caroline's cheeks. "But Ava, are you okay? I hate him. He is such—"

"I'll be fine," said Ava. "If anything happens workwise, call my family. I don't want to be disturbed all weekend."

Jack opened the car door. He had heard enough of the conversation to know something terrible had happened. Caroline was crying, and Ava looked pale and close to fainting.

"Home, Ms. Ava?"

"Yes, please."

"Are you okay, Ms. Ava?"

Ava hit "Send" on a text to her parents.

> Deal agreed in principle. Lawyers to work out the details. I'm going off-grid for the weekend. Text or call Caroline if you need anything. Love, Ava.

Ava turned off her phone, looked up, thought for a moment, and replied.

"No, Jack, I'm not okay."

Chapter 24

Not knowing what to do or think, DeAngelo retreated back into a sea of blurred faces and muddled voices. He was going through the motions. He had played this party scene over a thousand times before.

Suddenly, a rush of adrenaline raced through his body. The fog lifted. *I have to get out of here.* Despite her protests, he peeled Vivian off his arm.

"I need to leave." DeAngelo fled from the restaurant and sat in his car, desperate to wrap his mind around what had just happened.

What the hell is going on? Ava was back in Germany. She wasn't due back for another week. He took her to the airport and kissed her goodbye. He scrolled through Ava's texts. Had he missed something? Had she texted she was shortening her trip and coming back early? He checked. No, nothing.

There were three texts. The first was:

> I arrived safely. Love you.

The second was a selfie with a caption underneath:

> ♥ Wish you were here for this
> perfect Texas sunrise. Love you.

She looked beautiful and happy with the biggest, brightest smile in the full Texas sun. The third was a selfie with her family and the message:

> Everyone is looking forward to meeting you
> in January. See you in a week. Love you.

He had replied to all three.

> Glad you made it home safely.
> Love you, too. Texas looks as beautiful
> as you. Tell your family I said hi.

DeAngelo beat his fists against the steering wheel. He remembered that cold, emotionless look on Ava's face.

"What the hell have I done?"

He called Ava's phone. No answer. It went straight to voice mail. He texted several times with no reply.

"Damn it, Ava, pick up the phone. Please pick up the phone."

He tried Caroline. Thank goodness, she picked up.

"Caroline, is Ava with you?"

Dead air. Caroline didn't answer. He asked again.

"Why do you care where Ava is?" Caroline finally shouted back.

"Damn it, Caroline, don't start. Just tell me if Ava is with you. She's not picking up her phone."

Caroline had pulled into the driveway of her parents' house and parked.

"After what you did," she yelled, "I hope she never speaks to you again!"

"I didn't know Ava was coming back early. You knew. Why didn't you tell me?"

"You jackass!" shouted Caroline before she hung up the phone.

DeAngelo called Ava's phone again. Straight to voice mail once more. He threw his phone in the passenger seat and drove off.

He walked from room to room in his apartment, trying to force a clear thought. He was going crazy. He had to do something.

He grabbed his keys and ran back out to his car. He drove over to Ava's, sat in the parking lot, and waited. He didn't have the courage to get out of the car.

There was a sinking emptiness that stripped away all his charm and bravado. He couldn't believe what he had done. Driving back to his apartment, DeAngelo knew he had made the biggest mistake of his life.

Ava leaned against the back of the door. She stood there.

Not moving. Not thinking. Her chest burned as she struggled to breathe.

She took a step forward. Without warning, a crippling pain seized her stomach. She dropped her purse and doubled over in agony.

"Oh, God."

Her head continued to throb. Streams of sweat poured as her face flashed white-hot. Her vision blurred, and her mouth watered.

She ran as fast as she could to the bathroom. She fell to her knees, grabbed hold of the toilet, and heaved. Her throat was on fire, and her stomach muscles convulsed.

Still face down over the toilet, Ava gasped, fighting to catch her breath. She managed to peel off her coat and suit jacket. Her expensive silk blouse was soaked through with sweat. She flushed the toilet as she sat up. It was over. She breathed heavily and tried to stand.

"Oh, God."

The pain buckled her knees again. She hit the floor. Sweat mixed with tears. Again, everything came up. The long, torturous hours of travel. The stress of protecting the family business. The pressure of securing a multimillion-dollar deal. And the betrayal. The devastating betrayal from the man she loved with every fiber of her being. Oh, how she loved him.

Sensing no movement, the bathroom lights turned off as Ava lay motionless on the floor. The cool tile provided little relief to her fevered body. Several minutes passed before she found the strength to stand.

She cringed, and her stomach turned. She quickly flushed the multicolored mess down the toilet before another attack hit her.

She stripped off her clothes and rinsed her mouth. The sudden bright light in the bathroom made her eyes water and her mind swim.

Ava's head spun, and the ringing in her ears kept getting louder and louder. She hugged the wall and took in a few deep breaths to find her balance. She couldn't make it to the bed without help. She held tight to the dresser, then the chair, and finally, the edge of the bed.

Ava crawled into bed, exhausted, begging for relief from the pain rippling through her body. The bed was cold and lonely. All the nights she and DeAngelo made love, talked, and stayed wrapped in each other's arms meant nothing now.

How could he do this to me? To us? Ava curled herself up in a ball. Every moment they had spent together played in her mind like a movie.

She now knew why DeAngelo had stopped being as affectionate. Ava curled herself tighter.

"Why did he lie to me?"

Chapter 25

DeAngelo's body shifted back and forth. His head snapped back, and his eyes popped open. He rubbed his face and blinked several times to focus. He had been on the couch all night long. Texting. Calling. Waiting. Between intermittent dozing, he had gotten about two hours of sleep. Maybe. He stared down at his phone. It took him a few seconds to figure out if it was ten in the morning or ten at night. Hell, he wasn't sure what day it was.

"Damn, it's Saturday." DeAngelo's heart jumped. He couldn't believe it. He rubbed his eyes again to make sure what he was seeing was true. He had two voicemail messages. He took a deep breath.

"It has to be Ava." For a moment, he was angry with himself that he had missed the call, but at least she called. He rocked back and forth to compose himself. He had to calm down so he could really listen to the message.

"Damn it." The first message was from Vivian, and the other was from Peter.

Wait a minute. DeAngelo had renewed hope. *Maybe, Car-*

oline had Peter call instead of calling herself. That must be it. Peter is acting as a peacemaker. The thought made no sense, but DeAngelo needed something to give himself hope.

"Don't bother coming over today to work. I have better things to do." Peter's voice was cold and direct. He didn't mention a single thing about last night or Ava.

DeAngelo called and texted Caroline over and over, but she never responded. He needed to apologize, and just maybe, she would forgive him and help him get in touch with Ava.

All I need is one text, just to know that Ava is okay. Nothing. No one would talk to him. His thoughts ran out of control. Every worst possible scenario tormented his mind. Maybe Ava was hurt, and she couldn't come to the phone. Maybe she never made it home. DeAngelo ran through his contacts and called Jack.

"This is Jack Hartmann of—"

"Jack, this is DeAngelo. Did you drive Ava home last night?"

Jack immediately became alarmed. "Yes, sir. I drove her straight home. I could—"

"Are you sure?" yelled a distressed DeAngelo. "Straight home? Have you driven her anywhere this morning?"

Jack remained calm and spoke clearly. "No, sir. I have not heard from Ms. Ava. Is something wrong? I could tell things were not right last night."

"Damn it, man, what did she say? What did she say?"

"I asked if she was okay!" shouted Jack. "She said no. What did you do to her? What did you do?"

DeAngelo hung up the phone.

Ava woke up Saturday morning shivering. She rolled in the bed, wrapping herself up in the blanket, but it wasn't enough. It didn't help that she had stripped down to her underwear last night before crawling into bed.

She groaned when she remembered she had adjusted the thermostat before leaving to fly home.

"Trying to save on energy. Look where that got me." She didn't want to get up but also didn't want to freeze to death, either.

Still wrapped up tight, Ava inched herself to the edge of the bed.

You can do this. She sat up, put her feet firmly on the floor, and stood. A mind-numbing, razor-like pain shot to the top of Ava's head. The sting sent shock waves throughout her body, and she fell back.

Ava clenched her hands to her head.

"Oh my God!" she yelled in tears. A killer migraine was on its way if she didn't act fast.

She tried to stand again with much slower and more deliberate movements.

Victory, she was standing upright. Ava's head pounded, but no blinding pain, thank God. She shuffled slowly to the bathroom. Her eyes could tolerate the dim sunlight coming through the window, but the bright bathroom light would pierce her eyes like a knife. Ava didn't need the light. She knew exactly where her migraine pills were. She crept to the bathroom door, felt along the wall, then blocked the light sensor with her hand. She hit a little button to disable the sensor.

Ava didn't realize she was holding her breath the whole time until she exhaled a giant puff of air. The bathroom remained dark. Ava popped two pills in her mouth and swallowed them with a handful of water from the faucet.

She shuffled off to the living room, the blanket trailing behind her like a train, and stared at the thermostat.

"No wonder I'm freezing."

Angrily, Ava kept hitting the "up" button on the thermostat as she made the quick conversion from Fahrenheit to Celsius in her head. *Okay, 21 Celsius is roughly 70 degrees Fahrenheit.* "That should do it."

With the combination of migraine pills, frigid temperature, and complete exhaustion, Ava crawled back into bed. She fell asleep within a few minutes.

Three hours later, Ava woke up. "Let's try this again." Ava

threw her legs over the bed. She stood for a minute and waited. Nothing.

"Ah, that's better." No pain, only the steady throb of a typical headache. As an added bonus, the apartment was finally warm enough for her bones to stop aching.

Ava knew what she had to do, but first, she needed a long, hot shower. Her clothes scattered on the bathroom floor reminded her of the violent upheaval the night before. That nauseating feeling churned in her stomach again. She couldn't go through that another time. Ava stayed in the shower until the hot water started to run cold. It did little to relieve her mental and physical anguish.

Dressed, she walked into the kitchen. There wasn't much to eat. She had emptied the refrigerator before she left for Texas. Annoyed, she pulled out a can of chicken broth and a box of noodles.

"Chicken noodle soup it is."

In the quiet of her apartment, Ava sat at the kitchen table eating a bowl of bland, chicken-less chicken noodle soup. She took deep breaths every now and then to remind herself that, yes, she had made it through the night. Yet, there was an emptiness inside of her that kept her dazed.

Ava had dragged the morning out long enough. She couldn't avoid dealing with the seismic change that had shifted her life in a new and devastating direction. She checked her phone. It wouldn't turn on. The battery had run down to zero percent. She plugged the charger into the phone and began working on her action plan.

The only thought on Ava's mind was to leave Germany as soon as she could. She first made a list of everything she needed to do. Then, focused and almost robotic, she went room by room, cleaning and organizing things into three piles: "keep," "leave," and "return." Ava gathered up the "return" pile—a small assortment of DeAngelo's belongings—and placed them in the closet corner. She wanted nothing to do with anything that reminded her of him.

Ava returned to her to-do list, checked a few things off, and then continued on. She sent a few emails and checked more items off. *Almost done.*

A few hours later, Ava checked her phone at eighty percent to see twenty voicemails and over a hundred text messages. All but one voicemail was from DeAngelo. She listened to the one message from Jack.

She called Jack to let him know she was okay and needed him to pick her up as usual on Monday morning. She didn't have to ask or say a word. Jack understood.

"Your confidence is safe with me, Ms. Ava."

Ava refused to read any of DeAngelo's texts. She only sent one text to Caroline, asking her to come by the apartment on Monday before work. Ava grabbed her list, bundled up in her warmest coat, hat, and gloves, and braced herself for the ugly, cold day.

Chapter 26

On Sunday evening, the family had gathered for dinner. DeAngelo arrived early for the chance to force Caroline to talk and tell him if she had heard from Ava.

Caroline had stayed locked in her room all weekend. Fortunately, everyone was busy all day Saturday with Christmas plans, so no one bothered her, but today, Momma Gretta yelled upstairs for the third time, ordering her to come join the family.

One was expected at the dinner table if one was in the house. They would have to be on their deathbed or contagious to be excused from eating with the family, especially on Sunday.

Caroline stomped down the stairs. As luck would have it, she had to sit directly across from DeAngelo. Her eyes diverted to look at anyone or anything but him.

All the talk at the table was Christmas planning. No one asked about Ava. They all knew she had flown home earlier in the week to visit her family. Caroline kept quiet throughout dinner until DeAngelo dared to speak to her.

"Caroline, have you heard from Ava today?"

Caroline didn't answer. He asked again.

Momma Gretta, frustrated with Caroline's attitude, encouraged her to speak. "Answer your brother, girl."

Caroline looked at her. "I'm not speaking to him."

"What's gotten into you?" said Momma Gretta, raising a brow. "Why aren't you speaking to DeAngelo?"

The other voices around the table hushed. Caroline never talked back. This time, she stood her ground. Her voice was firm.

"I am not speaking to him, momma. If you want to know why, ask *him*."

Caroline turned a cold, hateful stare toward DeAngelo. "Tell everyone, DeAngelo, why I'm not speaking to you."

Caroline looked around the table, then back at DeAngelo. She was determined to speak her mind and, for once, and not care about DeAngelo's feelings.

"Since he won't say it, I'll tell you. I'm not talking to him because he's an ass."

Caroline brushed off every gasp and attempt to stop her. Again, she stood her ground.

"Ava had to fly back early to close the deal we've been working on for months. We saw DeAngelo at the restaurant Friday night, kissing and putting his hands all over some woman. It was disgraceful. He's been cheating on Ava."

"You don't understand," interjected DeAngelo, his voice

rising. "You don't know what the hell you're talking about, Caroline."

Caroline raised her voice, refusing to let DeAngelo or anyone talk her down. "I know what I saw. Are you really going to tell me you weren't with that woman?"

"Just shut up," said DeAngelo.

Momma Gretta grabbed Caroline by the arm, but she pulled herself free.

"Caroline, you must be mistaken," proclaimed Rosalynn, hands shaking.

"Oh my God," fumed Caroline. "I can't believe you all. Trying to calm me down—really?! He cheated on Ava. He's the one in the wrong, not me and not Ava. It's him."

"What do you care?" said DeAngelo, arrogance oozing from his words. "You're only afraid you'll lose your job or won't be able to go to the States to start that little leadership program Ava promised you. You're nothing more than an assistant, that's all."

Of course, DeAngelo had forgotten about her promotion to junior office manager. Why wouldn't he dismiss her opportunity to be in a leadership program and work for Ava in the States? The entire world *had* to revolve around him.

Caroline pushed back from the table and stood up to leave. She fixed her eyes on DeAngelo.

"You immature, arrogant ass. I'm not afraid of anything. I know Ava. Her word means something. She has been my truest friend, supporting me, encouraging me, and believing in me, which is something none of you do. You don't deserve her. She's too good for you. You're thirty years old. You need to grow up."

She looked around the table, sick of all her family treating DeAngelo like he was some precious little baby. "And you all need to let him grow up."

The table fell silent with shocked faces all around. Several minutes passed before anyone said anything.

Since Thanksgiving, everyone had been gearing up to celebrate a proposal on Christmas. Peter attempted to intervene, but Rosalynn silenced the group.

Her chair squeaked as she pushed back from the table. A look of disappointment mixed with disbelief darkened her face.

"We didn't raise you to be this kind of man."

DeAngelo drove to Ava's from Momma Gretta's. He refused to let the weekend go by without seeing her. He knocked on her door. No answer. He listened with his ear to the door and heard nothing. He knocked again and listened. Encouraged, he heard something, maybe footsteps.

He took out his phone and called. He could hear Ava's phone ringing. *Thank God she's safe.* The phone went straight to voicemail. He was about to dial again when the knob turned, and the door creaked open.

He waited about a minute before opening the door wide and stepping inside. Ava wasn't there to greet him. She was standing at the other end of the living room. He walked toward her but stopped abruptly. She put her hand up to keep him two arm-lengths away.

"I've been worried about you. You didn't return any of my calls or texts."

Ava's eyes were glassy. Her face was hard and fixed like stone. She stood glaring, saying nothing.

"Ava," said DeAngelo. "It's not what you think."

Ava closed her eyes. Her chest swelled with a deep inhale. Her eyes were laced red with anger, and her voice was monotone.

"How long has it been going on?"

"It's not what you think."

She asked again, enunciating every word. "Don't lie to me. How long?"

DeAngelo lowered his head. "Just a few dates over the last couple of months. Please, I can explain."

Ava's deep, slow inhale was the only sound in the apartment until she spoke again. "I don't need an explanation."

She choked out the next question and prayed for the answer she wanted to hear to ease some of her heartache. "Did you sleep with her?"

DeAngelo tried to give an explanation but struggled to get the words out. Ava's chest heaved. Her voice tore through the apartment.

"Did you sleep with her?" she screamed.

The vibration of Ava's voice thundered in DeAngelo's chest. There was a long pause.

"Yes," DeAngelo admitted, lowering his gaze. "But please, Ava, please let me explain."

"When did you sleep with her?" screamed Ava once more.

"I swear. It was just one time. Two days ago."

For a moment, DeAngelo may have thought Ava was laughing, but that was far from the truth. Ava clapped her hands together and rocked back and forth.

"I can't believe you," she said, her voice increasing in volume and intensity. "Two days ago. You mean two days ago when I was texting you from Texas at my parents' house, telling you that I loved you, you were in bed, screwing another woman?"

Ava's entire body shook with anger. She started to hyperventilate. A white-hot streak of pain hit the back of her head with the force of a lightning bolt. She reached for something to steady herself, but there was nothing. DeAngelo moved forward.

"Don't you come near me," Ava demanded.

She wobbled but regained her balance. She swallowed hard to suppress her tears and bit her lip to stop it from quivering. She balled her hands into fists to prevent them from shaking.

DeAngelo took the opportunity in the silence to plead for a chance. "Please, Ava. You don't understand. I swear I can explain. Baby, you have to believe me. It was a mistake. I don't love her. She means nothing to me. It will never happen again. I swear."

The more he talked, the more infuriated Ava became. She had to stop him, or she was going to lose all control. The more DeAngelo pleaded, the more his anger grew.

Why is she not talking, not listening, not fighting for us? He could only think of one more thing to say. Surely then, she would listen.

"Ava, I love you."

Ava's rage boiled over with such fury DeAngelo would forever regret every mistake he had made. She laid bare the truth of his betrayal.

"The hell you do! When, DeAngelo? Tell me, when did you remember you loved me?" Ava's voice was razor-sharp, slicing through DeAngelo's flimsy excuses. "So was it before, during, or after you screwed this other woman you happened to remember you loved me?"

Her voice rumbled throughout the apartment. "You lying, self-centered, arrogant bastard."

"No, Ava," DeAngelo pleaded. "No. It wasn't like that. I got caught up in the moment. What about us?"

Ava gave DeAngelo a frightening look of disdain. "Us? There is no more us. You have destroyed the possibility of an *us*. If it were a few dates, then maybe, but this I cannot forgive!"

DeAngelo scrambled for the right words. "I can fix this. I can make this right."

There was no fixing this, though. With her hands over her mouth, Ava took another deep breath. Her voice lowered with the sadness of a shattered heart.

"You love being DeAngelo, superstar ladies' man, more than you love being with me." She tried to wipe her tears away, but there were too many. "Why couldn't you see? I would have loved you forever."

It was a miracle DeAngelo made it home. He had driven like a madman, having no memory of the trip from Ava's apartment to his. He went straight to the kitchen to grab a beer. If ever he needed a drink, it was then.

He fell back on the couch, still in shock. The beer was at DeAngelo's lips when Ava's voice echoed in his mind and shook his soul. Frustrated, he flung the bottle. It shattered against the wall.

Everything hit DeAngelo all at once. The shame of his behavior. The staggering disappointment in himself. The disgust for having willingly thrown away the love of a lifetime. An emptiness closed in on him.

He paced the floor. His mind was bent in a thousand directions. He picked up his phone to call. He stopped himself. He snatched his keys to drive back to Ava's. He stopped himself again. He couldn't think.

"Damn it. What am I going to do? How can I win her back?"

The situation DeAngelo created had not yet matured him. He worked to convince himself that it was not too late. He reasoned that Ava just needed time. She was rightfully angry, but she wouldn't walk away. They loved each other too much. There was no way she could have meant everything she said.

"She has to still love me." He needed Ava to love him enough to give him a second chance. That's all he needed, one chance to make things right.

Hopelessness pulled at his heart. He wanted to break more beer bottles, smash windows, knock down walls, anything. There was too much desperate energy building up inside of him. But, there was no one he could talk to. Peter was still upset over their fight, and the rest of the family was furious with him, as well. So, DeAngelo grabbed his keys.

"This time, she will talk to me." His phone rang as he reached for the door. He saw it was his dad. DeAngelo didn't pick up. By the time he got to his car, there was a text.

Son, it will be all right.

That text saved DeAngelo from himself. Going back to Ava's would have been one more epic mistake piled on top of all his other devastating ones. He went back into his apartment and sat. He sat in all his loneliness, guilt, and shame.

He clung to the tiniest thread of hope that if he gave Ava a week to think and calm down, she would forgive him, and they could rebuild what they had lost.

Chapter 27

Ava reviewed her list and checked every room one last time. The only thing left was to say goodbye to Caroline. That was going to be hard. With the long hours of working side by side for months and sharing Sunday dinners like family, the two had grown close.

Caroline had promised herself to be professional when she reached Ava's apartment. She stuck to Ava's rule of never bringing up DeAngelo with her, and this was certainly not the time to bring him up. She still could not believe the man, who was like an older brother to her and who she idolized, would do such a horrible thing.

How could he be so deceitful? Caroline knew of DeAngelo's reputation with women; everyone knew. But Ava was different. She was so perfect for him. She was the first and only woman he ever brought to Sunday dinner, for goodness' sake. Ava was more than DeAngelo's new girlfriend; she had become a real part of the family.

Caroline's professional promise faded when she saw Ava's bags by the door, as well as the multiple moving boxes labeled and sealed. She threw her arms around Ava. Ava held on to Caroline a little tighter than she usually would.

They sat at the kitchen table, with Ava pouring Caroline and herself a cup of tea. "I'm going home to Texas, for good."

Caroline stared at her in disbelief. "You can't! What about the factory? We all need you."

It was nice for Caroline to say, but it wasn't true. "You, Ms. Junior Office Manager, and the rest of the leadership team have things running like a well-oiled machine."

"What about Appliance International of France?"

"Dad, Danny, and the lawyers are going to lead the implementation of the deal. Besides, it will probably work better with me being home with them if they need me."

Seeing Caroline's sad face chipped away at Ava's shattered heart. There was more in Germany than DeAngelo. She had work, friends, and a second family, but it would be impossible to extract DeAngelo from her life there. All the good and the bad were forever linked to him. Nothing could continue the same without him. She had lost what she valued most: love and family.

Huge tears ran down Caroline's freckled face. "I hate him for what he's done. I will never speak to him again."

Ava never asked herself whether things could get any worse, because she knew they could. Destroying a bond between brother and sister would be worse.

She cried with Caroline. "I know you feel a mix of emotions, but he's your brother. Don't ruin your relationship with him over this. Promise me you won't hold this against him."

After the tears subsided, there was business to settle. Ava slid a set of keys and some documents over to Caroline.

"I want you to have my apartment. It's a corporate expense, housing for corporate leadership. It's paid for until July of next year. I don't have a use for it now. Whatever isn't your style or you don't want, donate to charity. I'll coordinate with Jack and have him ship the rest of my things so they're out of your way."

Caroline refused to accept it, but Ava insisted. "Here is the paperwork for my car lease. I spoke with the dealership. It's up to you. You can trade your car in and buy the lease out. If that's not what you want, I have settled on a fee with the dealership for breaking the lease. Either way, it is up to you."

Caroline covered her face, weeping. Her voice was barely audible, but Ava heard every word.

"I can't accept any of this."

Ava gave Caroline another warm embrace. "From day one, I knew I could trust and count on you. You're no longer my assistant. You are the junior office manager of the factory. And that is your first promotion of many. After completing the leadership training, you will be a full member of our corporate leadership team."

Ava pushed the keys into Caroline's hands. "You deserve it. It is time for you to start enjoying the perks of your success."

After one final hug, Jack and Caroline helped Ava with her bags. Ava held Caroline by the shoulders.

"Don't cry," comforted Ava. "I'll see you in January. You're going to love Texas."

The closer Ava got to the airport, the more she could feel a treasured part of her life fade away. She had no hope she would ever love again. That real "jump-in-with-your-whole-heart" kind of love only happened once in a lifetime. Her chance had come and gone.

At the airport, Jack checked Ava's bags at the curbside while she took her last look at Germany.

"May I give you a hug? You have been the best client I've ever had the pleasure of driving."

Ava smiled and nodded. She embraced Jack and slid an envelope into his hand. There was a heartfelt "thank you, Merry Christmas, and Happy New Year," along with a very generous Christmas bonus.

Ava soon disappeared into the crowded airport. Everything moved in slow motion. All she could see were distorted faces and distant voices around her.

Ava had to concentrate to hear the jumbled gate announcements. She moved through the airport, feeling out of place and foreign. Not because she was American but because she no longer had a place in Germany.

Ava sat alone in the lounge to pass her three-hour wait until boarding. *Why couldn't he have just been honest?* It still would have hurt if DeAngelo wanted out of the relationship, but the betrayal cut deeper.

She had made so many plans for January. Ava had been excited for DeAngelo to meet her family. She knew they would love him. DeAngelo's high-octane personality would mesh well with her mom and Danny. Those two were always ready for a party or spontaneous adventure.

Her dad was more measured. It would take some time, but Ava expected he would've warmed up to DeAngelo in short order. It would have been a fantastic way to start the new year—to be in love with a wonderful man by her side.

She had been schoolgirlish and giddy, making plans to show DeAngelo all around Texas. Maybe, she thought, they would take a quick trip to Key West to soak up as much sun and warmth as possible before heading back to the bitter cold of Germany.

If he had only come to her after a few dates with the other woman, she would have listened. She would have heard him out, and they could have talked like adults.

I would have let him go. Ava thought DeAngelo to be a better man. She saw a future with him. She *desired* a future with him. She squared her shoulders and straightened her back, clearing her throat.

I will not cry in this stupid airport. Ava diverted her attention away from her expanding sense of loss. She ordered a few appetizers from one of the airport restaurants, pulled out her iPad, and read through drafted legal documents from the corporate attorneys. If she cried, it would be from absolute boredom and not from longing for DeAngelo.

Chapter 28

Caroline jumped at a knock at the door. *'Who can that be?'* No one knew she was there. She didn't feel the need to tell the family about the apartment. It would ruin Christmas if they knew she planned to move out when she returned from the States. Besides, the subject of DeAngelo and Ava was too painful. The entire family avoided it like the plague.

She went to the door and saw DeAngelo standing before her. The last time she saw him was at Sunday dinner when she told him exactly what she thought of him and what he had done to Ava. He looked surprised to see her open the door.

"I'm sorry, Caroline, I didn't know you were here. May I please speak to Ava?"

Caroline invited him in, not knowing how she would tell him. All her life, DeAngelo had always been *that guy*—the guy with all the good looks and fortune. His carefree energy was so infectious one couldn't help but be drawn into his enchanted universe.

The man avoiding eye contact with her was not the DeAngelo she knew. Caroline was stunned. Ava had only been gone for a week, which clearly had a devastating effect on him. His cheeks and chin revealed the beginnings of a scruffy beard. His normally bright, joyous eyes were dim.

"I'm sorry, but Ava's not here."

"When will she be back?" asked DeAngelo, disappointed.

Caroline's voice cracked.

"She's not coming back. She's gone. She moved back to Texas on Monday."

DeAngelo walked past Caroline and sat slumped over on the couch with his head in his hands, holding back his tears.

"I messed up," cried DeAngelo. "I can't believe she's gone."

Caroline sat by her brother and put her arm around his shoulder. "Do you want to talk about it?"

"You were right. Everyone was right. Ava was too good for me."

It was too heartbreaking for Caroline to watch. "Let me make you some tea."

Sitting in Ava's apartment, knowing she was gone, made the reality of losing her more agonizing. DeAngelo had pulled himself together when Caroline brought the hot drink.

"Our fight last Sunday was awful. I know I broke her heart. I thought she would give me a second chance. I should have known better."

Caroline listened. There was nothing she could do or say to make things any better.

"Did she say anything to you? Did she leave a note, anything?" asked DeAngelo.

Caroline went to the back room and returned with a large box. "She made me promise not to hold anything against you and not to ruin our relationship." Caroline paused, handing him the package. "She left this for you."

The taped box had DeAngelo's name written on the top. He ripped the tape, wishing there was something inside to indicate he still had a chance.

He lost all hope as he looked through a box of his belongings. He had left fewer things at Ava's than he thought. His three shirts and two pairs of pants were all neatly folded. Ava had folded his T-shirts, underwear, and socks and tucked away his cologne and cuff links in separate, smaller boxes.

DeAngelo rummaged through the box. "Is this it?"

Caroline jerked back. "What's wrong? Is something missing? I can look for it."

"No note. Nothing. Just my things folded in a box."

Caroline leaned back on the couch with her arms folded. "What did you expect? You cheated, remember?"

DeAngelo snapped. "I know that Caroline, but at least—" DeAngelo said snatching up the box and heading for the door. "If she can leave, so can I."

A bewildered Caroline ran after him. "Wait! Christmas is in two weeks. You can't miss the holidays with the family; you know this is Emma Rose's first Christmas."

Deep creases lined DeAngelo's forehead as he clenched his keys. "I need to get out of here. Don't worry. I'll be back in time for Christmas."

DeAngelo raced back to his place. He grabbed a carry-on bag from his bedroom closet and tossed it on the bed. He was almost frantic, carelessly throwing random items in the bag. He didn't know how long it would take for Caroline to alert the family he was leaving. All he knew was he wanted away from everyone and everything that reminded him of all the things he had done wrong.

After packing, he pulled out his phone and hastily booked a flight to Greece. Luck was on DeAngelo's side. He was able to book a flight that left in five hours. He immediately grabbed his carry-on, passport, and wallet and made his way to the airport. DeAngelo easily blended into the crowd of holiday travelers.

Irritated by the crowd at the departure gate, he waited at a bar across from the cramped seating area. He drank his beer and searched on his phone for the villa he had rented before outside of Athens. The views were spectacular, and it would be the perfect place to relax. It was a long shot, but DeAngelo hoped to book the villa up to Christmas Eve.

Damn. I can only book for a week. DeAngelo grew frustrated from waiting. His flight was supposed to start boarding forty minutes ago. He had been in the bar for an hour already. He looked at his phone and started searching for flights to anywhere that was leaving in the next fifteen-to-twenty minutes.

I need to get the hell out of here.

"We apologize for the delay. Our flight to Athens is now boarding."

DeAngelo ran out of the bar to the gate. He was the fifth first-class passenger to board. He got seated but was still on edge. He put his earbuds in to drown out the insanity of the boarding process.

Of course, there were the idiots who were too cheap to check their bags, slowing the boarding process and unable to find overhead space. Then you had the morons who couldn't figure out the aisle and seat numbers. And if things couldn't get any worse, there were at least two screaming babies on board.

"Sir, would you buckle your seat belt, please?"

DeAngelo opened his eyes to see a flight attendant smiling at him. He removed his earbuds.

"Excuse me?"

"We are about to take off. Please fasten your seat belt."

DeAngelo complied without saying a word. He leaned back and put his earbuds back in. The only other message he wanted to hear was, "Thank you for flying with us today. You are free to move about the cabin and exit safely."

The agonizing flight was worth it once DeAngelo pulled up to the villa. The building's superintendent was there to greet him.

"Mr. Williams, welcome back to Hyacinth Hills."

DeAngelo followed the superintendent in. The villa was as he remembered. He stood on the balcony as the man blathered. As soon as food was mentioned, DeAngelo gave him his full attention.

"I took the liberty of preparing a mezze platter for you, sir. If you would follow me to the kitchen."

"Thank you. I will also need dinner in a few hours."

"Yes, of course, sir. Simply ring the staff and order what you like."

The superintendent made his exit, and DeAngelo was finally alone. He opened a bottle of wine, poured a glass, and took it and the mezze platter to the balcony. The temperature was mild 15°C. Perfect.

Chapter 29

For hours, Ava replayed every moment she could remember spending with DeAngelo on her seemingly endless flight home. Her first memory was not her favorite. She could still see DeAngelo with all his swagger, captivating everyone at the cocktail party. He was every bit of a superstar—charming with a substantial ego. But his attempt at a double handshake was a no-no.

God, I should have known better. Ava's most cherished early memory was the sensual coffee-shop kiss. From that moment on, she had struggled to maintain control and not throw herself at him.

She had never cried on a flight before—except now, as she thought about the apple strudel and ice cream night. She was in a first-class cabin, so no one noticed except the flight attendant, who pretended he didn't.

Her next memory was of Wolff Mountain Resort. Then she thought about the first time DeAngelo said, "I love you." She took out her phone and scrolled through their pictures. There was no sound, just a river of silent tears.

God, why didn't I know better? Ava turned and stared out the window into the open sky. She was at the point where her pain was so agonizing her heart felt numb.

She thought of the last time DeAngelo said, "I love you," just after he had admitted to sleeping with another woman. No, "sleeping with another woman" sounded too tame. DeAngelo didn't innocently find himself in bed with someone else.

He chose to betray me. He had casual, pointless sex with another woman. That's what happened. I hate him.

Once the flight landed, Ava made her way through customs and then to baggage claim. She didn't take the time to text or call her parents. She hustled to the rideshare pickup and drop-off. Ava longed for the comforts of home; no more temporary housing in foreign countries. She wanted Texas. She wanted her family.

Ava knocked and waited with her suitcase on her parents' doorstep. She was using the last bit of strength she had to hold back her tears.

"Ava, honey! What are you doing back?" said Rita after she had answered the door.

Ava threw her arms around her mother. "There is nothing left in Germany for me."

Ava's dad came walking down the hall. "Rita, who's at the door?"

Rita turned to wave him back. She then wiped Ava's tears away.

"Go upstairs, sweetheart," said Rita, cupping her daughter's face. "I'll be up soon."

Once Ava was out of sight, Rita took her husband by the arm and walked him into the study. "It looks like things are over between Ava and DeAngelo," she whispered.

"What the devil did that man do to my daughter?" asked Clayton, heading for the stairs.

Rita pulled him back. "Clayton, calm down. Ava is hurting right now. Let me at least find out what happened."

Ava's dad backed down to let his wife handle the delicate situation first. Rita then went to the kitchen to put together a few snacks. She imagined her daughter was hungry after the long flight. Plate in hand, Rita knocked and then stepped inside the bedroom. Ava's luggage was open and picked through.

Ava walked from the bathroom in a pair of flannel pajamas with her hair pinned up. Rita stretched out her arms, wondering what horrible thing had happened for Ava to get on a plane and fly back home without a word. Ava held onto her mother and soaked in her love.

"Come eat something," urged Rita. "And tell me what's going on."

Ava didn't know where to begin. It was all so painful and embarrassing. She lowered her head, covered her face, and choked out the words through hot tears.

"DeAngelo cheated."

Rita held Ava in a tight embrace. *That lowlife hurt my baby girl.* All in an instant, she hated DeAngelo for what he had done to Ava.

"I'm so sorry, honey. I'm so sorry."

"I saw him with her the night of my business dinner," said Ava, her voice strained as her tears stained her mother's blouse. "He said he only slept with her once, but how can I believe him?"

Ava's voice started to weaken. Jet lag was creeping up. All the emotional upheaval was weighing on her.

"He was the one, Mom. I really thought DeAngelo was the one. And the worst part is, I still love him."

Ava sat out on the back patio by the pool, enjoying the warm, seventy-degree temperature. Of all the things she would miss, the brutal cold and snow of the previous winter were not one of them. She had experienced her first and last German winter.

Never again, she thought, as she enjoyed her frosty glass of sweet tea. *I'm home. Right, where I need to be.*

It was still hard to believe her life had fallen apart not quite two weeks ago. Ava wished her feelings hinged on a light switch. Then, she could simply flip it and *poof!* No more loving a man who broke her heart.

No one, not even Ava, as determined as she was, could

escape the stages of grief. She had a long, challenging journey of healing ahead, and she had made up her mind to face things head-on like she always did. She knew the truth. Once DeAngelo admitted it, denial was impossible. Maybe if she had stayed, she could have convinced herself for a little while.

"Ava honey, come on in. Dinner is ready, and everyone is here."

"I'll be right in, Mom."

Christmas arrived. Not the Christmas she had planned, but at least she was with her family. She wanted to think about anything else but DeAngelo, but he was the only thing on her mind. She wondered if he was still with her, Vivian. Ava knew it was a mistake to google her, but she couldn't help herself. Vivian Abara touted the sexiest Nigerian model and actress, according to her online brand. Her perfect face and perfect, tiny body were plastered all over social media.

I was never really his type, Ava thought, staring at Vivian's picture before turning off her phone.

Ava sat down to dinner with her family and wondered if DeAngelo had taken Vivian to dinner at his parents' house. She couldn't imagine why he wouldn't. Vivian was now his new plus-one. Of course, she would be by his side for Christmas, too. The more Ava thought about it, the angrier she became. She aimed every bit of that anger toward DeAngelo, who was one-hundred-percent responsible.

Ava knew it was late evening in Germany, but she still texted Merry Christmas to Caroline. She hoped that Caroline would drop some hint about whether DeAngelo was there and what might be going on. Caroline texted back almost instantly.

Merry Christmas. I can't wait to
see you in a few days.

Ava went through the motions of dinner and opening gifts, but her heart wasn't in it.

God, why did I trust him? Never again.

Chapter 30

DeAngelo had arrived back from Greece a week before Christmas, but he kept that fact to himself. His getaway did little to improve his mood. He still needed time to talk himself into going to the family's first Christmas Eve celebration with the new grandbaby.

The thought of trying to make it through Christmas Eve with the family stressed him out. DeAngelo wasn't happy, and he didn't want to pretend. He knew they all blamed him for the breakup. No one stopped to ask what really happened. They just assumed from Caroline he was wrong.

"Everybody's life has to change because of Emma Rose," DeAngelo grumbled to himself. The whole idea of getting together for Christmas Eve and again on Christmas Day seemed silly. The pressure to fake the holiday spirit for two days irked him. As much as DeAngelo wanted to, he couldn't ditch Emma Rose's first Christmas. After all, he *was* her godfather.

He arrived late at his parents' house, praying that at least dinner was half over. The less time he had to go through the motions, the better. Arriving late and leaving early was his plan.

As usual, DeAngelo entered the kitchen. He looked around, surprised to see the place empty. An abandoned, half-eaten chocolate cake sat on the table with a few plates.

What the hell? They actually ate without me. He followed the sound of voices coming from the living room. The laughter and fun of opening up Christmas gifts stopped when he entered the room. Everyone froze. They all looked nervous and a little ashamed.

Rosalynn got up and gave DeAngelo a big hug. "We didn't think you were coming."

DeAngelo frowned at the accusation that he wouldn't come to dinner. Yes, he was an hour late, but still—to assume he wouldn't come at all was mean.

"Why wouldn't I come? It's Christmas Eve."

DeAngelo heard Peter's voice from the other side of the room. "Maybe because you're over an hour late. Did you really expect everyone to wait on you?"

Rosalynn tried to turn DeAngelo back toward the kitchen. "Let me fix you a plate."

DeAngelo looked at Peter and then around at all the guilty faces. "What's going on? We don't open gifts on Christmas Eve. Is this our new tradition now?

"What the hell? Are you serious?" said Peter, shaking his head.

Caroline tried to break the tension, so she bravely spoke up. "It was my idea. We're only opening the gifts Ava left behind."

DeAngelo wanted to storm out. *Of course, she left gifts behind.* He knew Ava well enough to know that when she left Germany, she was gone for good. But now she was front and center on Christmas Eve, making him look like the bad guy all over again.

He tried. He begged. He promised it would never happen again if she would just forgive him, but all of DeAngelo's bargaining fell on deaf ears.

But no, Ava is too self-righteous to forgive. He hated Ava for being so damned unyielding to her principles. Yes, he made a mistake, but it was only once, and with a woman, he would never see again. Besides, things like this happen in relationships. People stray, but it shouldn't be the end. At least she could have tried if she really loved him.

"Here, she left this for you." Caroline handed DeAngelo a small box. "Are you going to open it?"

DeAngelo didn't answer. He jammed the box in his pocket and went back into the kitchen. Peter followed.

"Why don't you say it, Peter? You and the entire family think I'm the bad guy."

"Why don't you for once own your shit? You know this is all on you, nobody else. I get it. We both had egos back in the day, but you're thirty years old. It's time to grow up. If you don't, you're going to spend the rest of your life trying to recapture the past, and you'll be miserable."

DeAngelo stood at the counter, staring down at the sink.

"I'm already miserable," DeAngelo shouted. "Damn it. Don't you think I know I screwed up? What am I supposed to do?"

"For starters, stop acting as if it's everyone else's fault and not yours. This is all on you," replied Peter.

Peter's words punched him in the gut. DeAngelo couldn't continue lying to himself and playing the victim.

"Everybody's right. Ava was it. She changed everything, but I was too arrogant, vain, and immature to handle it. I'm going to regret this for the rest of my life." He took a deep breath, lifting his face to meet Peter's gaze. "I have to go."

Peter put a hand on his arm to stop him. "You need your family, man. We're here for you if you want us to be."

DeAngelo hugged Peter. "You're my best mate. I need tonight to settle a few things in my head. I promise I'll be okay. Tell everyone I'll see them tomorrow."

DeAngelo drove to his place. He had taken Ava and her love for granted. Now the only things he had left of her were memories and a little, perfectly wrapped gift with a red bow that was crushed after he had stuffed it in his pocket.

He opened the box. Inside, there was a note and a gorgeous pair of 14-karat, white-gold monogram cuff links.

I hope these cuff links will be your new favorites.

Love always, Ava.

If I ever get another chance, Ava, I swear I'll be a better man.

Chapter 31

"Dad, I can't do this anymore."

Clayton looked up from his laptop to see Ava standing in the doorway of his office.

She walked in, waving a handful of papers. "I can't read another business proposal or financial report. It's been over a year since I returned home and was sidelined from the business."

To be more precise, it had been one year, two months, and eleven days since Ava left Germany for good. She flopped down in the chair across from her dad's desk.

"If I have to proofread one more report, I think I'll scream."

Clayton closed his laptop and pushed his glasses up off the bridge of his nose. "You can do whatever you want, Ava. You know that."

"Really, Dad? Every time I mention going on the road again, you, Mom, and Danny about have a fit. You all keep telling me to take time for myself, and then you give me this nauseatingly busy work to do."

"We love having you home. For three years, you were overseas. First in China and then in Germany, doing a lot of heavy lifting for the business. We want you home with us and not so burdened with the family business."

"But I'm miserable, Dad. I'm sick of relaxing, eating, and catching up with friends. I want something to do." Ava waved the reports again. "Something more than this."

The truth was that there wasn't much to do. The business was running along smoothly. Danny settled the South American business, and Caroline and the leadership team in Germany successfully managed the Appliance International of France deal.

"I hate to tell you this, sweetheart, but there's not much going on right now. It's pretty much smooth sailing."

Ava crossed her arms and huffed. "There's got to be something more I can do. I'm going crazy!"

"Well, I might have something for you." Clayton opened his laptop and searched for an email.

"Here it is." He read for a second or two in silence, then asked Ava, "Do you want to take my spot on the hospital subcommittee?" He printed the email and handed it to his daughter.

Ava listened to her dad as she scanned the document.

"The committee has stalled raising funds for the new Texas State Pediatric Oncology Center and Family Housing Complex. It's the housing complex they need the extra push with."

"Yes, yes, yes. I would love to. Dad, this is perfect."

"Okay, then it's yours. Next month in mid-March, the committee will conduct final interviews for contractors for the family complex. You can sit in for me on that, as well."

Ava jumped from her chair, ran over to her dad, and hugged him tightly. "I love you, Dad."

Ava had sat in on four contractor interviews and was not impressed by any candidates. One particular candidate, McMillian and Company, Ava wanted to vote down immediately. Ten years ago, Ava's dad fired McMillian for running an unsafe construction site when building the Brooks family's new parts distribution center.

In the spirit of fairness, Ava listened to the presentation. She noticed they neglected to provide their safety records or protocols, solidifying her belief that McMillian and Company was still a shady outfit.

The last candidate was Keith Walker of Walker Construction, a native Texan who had worked in construction and ranching all his life. He stood over six-feet with broad shoulders and solid arms.

Mr. Walker engaged the committee in a collaborative and productive conversation. He highlighted his firm's experience, knowledge, and zero-injuries safety record for the past fifteen years.

At the end of his interview, Mr. Walker's words to the committee impressed Ava: "I give you my word. This project will come in on time and under budget."

Ava had negotiated with many contractors, and they all had promised to finish the job on time and under budget. Mr. Walker was the only one to ever provide proof. He offered a portfolio of various projects over the past five years with a summary of his bids, project schedules, and references who were well-known people in the community.

The committee took less than a week to deliberate. Walker Construction won the contract with a unanimous vote.

Ava turned her attention to the fundraising efforts for the next several months. She poured all her love and every ounce of energy into the three-million-dollar target. Her first course of action was to review years of donation records identifying the top donors. Ava never liked charitable organizations cold calling and asking her for money out of the blue, so she wasn't about to do that to other people.

Ava wanted to put a more personal touch on her fundraising efforts. She wouldn't dare ask for money from people she didn't take the time to know. So, she hosted several intimate dinner parties to meet with the top donors at her own expense.

Ava and her team planned events and campaigns for the entire year. They designed the first huge event: the Fourth of

July Family Festival. A month before the event, Ava needed to build anticipation, so she launched radio and television ads. As a result, ticket sales climbed. Now she could focus on the big donors.

"Hey, Mom. I'm off to hand-deliver these last few invitations!" yelled Ava, rushing out the door.

The cool morning air refreshed her skin and excited her for the possibilities the day would bring. She drove around town, stopping by business offices to hand-deliver "Fourth of July Family Festival" invitations. Later that afternoon, around two o'clock, she had one last stop.

"Yes! No meter," said Ava, ecstatic to find a free spot in the lot at the back of the building.

As she headed inside, she read the building directory: "Walker Construction, Suite 501." On the elevator ride to the fifth floor, she remembered a different Fourth of July party she had planned in Germany two years ago. She closed her eyes and was almost there again. The tantalizing smell of barbecue, the shouts of DeAngelo and Peter as they played a backyard football match, and the immortal image of Rosalynn and Rich dancing to the sound of their heartbeats.

She still could hear DeAngelo's soothing voice say, "I love you." Ava was happy it didn't hurt to remember anymore. A little sadness remained, but no pain or grief.

She shook herself to the present as the elevator jolted to

a stop, and the door opened. With a bright smile as big as Texas, she greeted the receptionist.

"Hello. How are you this afternoon?"

"I'm good, ma'am. How may I help you?" the receptionist replied with a cheery voice.

"I'm Ava Brooks from the hospital fundraising committee. I stopped by to hand-deliver Mr. Keith Walker's invitation to our Fourth of July Family Festival. Would he happen to be in?"

"Oh, yes, ma'am, Mr. Walker is in. I will ring him for you."

"Thank you so much. That would be wonderful."

Ava stepped back from the receptionist to avoid hovering. She occupied herself during the few minutes of waiting to look at the beautiful artwork on the walls. Soon, she heard a man's husky voice speak.

"Ms. Brooks, it's good to see you again."

Dressed in a white golf shirt that hugged his well-defined, strapping arms and a pair of black pants that hung just right, Keith Walker extended his hand. His perfect, white teeth and welcoming ebony eyes put Ava at ease.

"Likewise, Mr. Walker. I don't want to take up too much of your time. I wanted to drop by and personally invite you to the Fourth of July Family Festival benefiting the hospital." Ava handed Keith the invitation.

"Thank you," said Keith. "I look forward to attending."

"I look forward to seeing you. Thank you for your time."

She turned to leave, and Keith walked with her to the door and then to the elevator.

The elevator door dinged, and the door opened. To Ava's surprise, Keith stepped onto the elevator with her.

"Are you parked in the garage or the back parking lot?" he asked.

"The parking lot."

He pressed the button for the ground floor. "I was headed out for a late lunch. Would you join me?"

What? A lunch invitation never crossed Ava's mind. She thought Keith asked to be courteous.

"I apologize for interfering with your plans," said Ava.

"No interference at all. Please, Ms. Brooks. Join me for lunch."

Ava used the lunch opportunity to learn about the construction progress and talk up the fundraising efforts. They returned to the office building, and Keith walked Ava to her car.

"Would you have dinner with me tomorrow night?"

Ava focused on maintaining a calm face. Inside, she was shaking like a leaf. *Oh, my goodness. This man is asking me out on a date.*

Her hesitation was long enough for Keith to approach from a less direct angle.

"If you're not free tomorrow, is there another evening this week that works better?"

Without thinking, Ava accepted Keith's dinner invitation for the following evening.

Chapter 32

DeAngelo's phone buzzed with a text from Peter.

> We did it!

DeAngelo texted back.

> Hell yeah, we did it. I'll be
> at your place in an hour.

It had been a long and frustrating journey, but the day had finally arrived. After fourteen arduous months of online courses, DeAngelo and Peter had earned their degrees. DeAngelo earned a Master's in Sports Administration, and Peter earned one in Sports Marketing. It was time for a well-deserved day of celebration.

Dropping out of college early to go pro was an opportunity DeAngelo and Peter had refused to pass up. In their early twenties, the lure of fame and fortune as pro footballers was too tempting. They had left college behind without a second thought.

This go-around, their college experience was completely different. In their thirties, there was no campus life with parties or pro football scouts vying for their attention. Those days were long over. It was all work and no play, precisely what DeAngelo needed.

What remained the same was DeAngelo's determination to succeed. The moment he joined the league, he set his sights on being one of the best players of all time. It was football, family, and football again. Now, DeAngelo was singularly focused on building the media empire he and Peter had discussed. First things first, he needed his degree.

DeAngelo set a rigid schedule for himself. It was course work, family, business, and nothing else. He occupied every second of his day, not allowing his thoughts to stray far from the path he had laid out. Yes, a large part of DeAngelo's focus was on building his future, but there was that part that kept him from dwelling on the past. He knew his guilt would break him if he let up for a single second. He needed every possible distraction from his pain. He had not just broken Ava's heart but his own as well.

As much as DeAngelo had hated it in the beginning, his new routine proved profitable. In a short fourteen months, he and Peter had graduated. They both decided to skip the official ceremony and instead opted for a family celebration. In true Kraus-and-Williams style, all their celebrations involved food. The plan was to meet at Peter's and drive to the restaurant together for the celebratory dinner.

It was a quarter to one on a cloudy but warm, Saturday afternoon. DeAngelo needed to pick up the pace in order to be at Peter's in an hour. Luckily, all he needed to do was put on his cufflinks, grab his jacket, and head out.

He opened the top dresser drawer and stared at the little box in the corner that had sat closed and undisturbed for over a year. DeAngelo hesitated for a second before opening the box that kept the cuff links Ava had given him as a gift.

Should I wear them? DeAngelo wondered as he stood with the box in his hand. As he pondered, memories of him and Ava flooded his mind, washing over him like a tidal wave. He embraced the pain of a still-open wound in his heart. He missed her touch, laugh, and the joy that radiated throughout her body while she cooked. Most of all, he missed the way she loved him.

DeAngelo knew, without question, that if he and Ava were still together, she would be right there by his side, ready to celebrate his accomplishment. She would have encouraged him, forced him to study when he would rather go out, and done whatever she could to support him every step of the way. In retrospect, DeAngelo saw it was Ava's selfless nature that had drawn him to her. He had not found that in himself or the other women he had dated.

He bounced the cuff links back and forth in his hands and chuckled. He never thought his mother would share her kitchen with a woman he had brought home for dinner. But it happened the first time he took Ava to Sunday dinner with the family. Scared out of his mind, he left Ava to cook and endure his mom's interrogation.

DeAngelo sat the cuff links down and grabbed his phone. He scrolled through a mountain of photos to find his favorite: the Fourth of July barbecue photo—Ava's arms around his neck, looking up at him, and his arms around her waist, looking down at her. Alone under the night sky, he told Ava he loved her that night.

He released his sadness in a deep exhale, trying to expel the heaviness in his heart. It still hurt. He had come to terms with what he had done, but that hadn't erased the grief. There remained an emptiness in his heart. Fourteen months later, he still loved her.

He shoved his phone into his pocket. *Damn it! Why does it still hurt this much?*

DeAngelo picked out a simple pair of silver cuff links after putting the ones from Ava back in the drawer. As much as he wanted to wear them, he couldn't. He still carried too much guilt for what he had done.

When DeAngelo reached Peter's, he joined everyone in the living room. Emma Rose was entertaining everyone with her new skill: walking. Well, at least making two or three steps and then promptly falling on her butt.

Peter looked at his watch. "If we don't want to miss our reservation, we have to leave now. Where's Caroline?"

"She just texted. She's going to meet us at the restaurant," Momma Gretta replied as she scooped up Emma Rose.

Once at the restaurant, the hostess escorted the family to a private room decorated with balloons and an enormous congratulation banner. Caroline was already there with her eyes flashing and her arms in the air.

"Surprise!"

The stunned faces didn't damper her enthusiasm. Everyone was in awe, especially Peter.

"Wait a minute. I only made dinner reservations, not all this," Peter said, rubbing his forehead.

Caroline popped the cork on a bottle of champagne and poured everyone a glass. "My big brothers deserve a little more than ordinary dinner reservations. I'm so proud of you two!"

"We all are!" shouted Albert. "Cheers!"

DeAngelo watched, amazed, proud of his baby sister, now grown into an accomplished businesswoman. No thanks to him or anyone else in the family. Ava was the only one who treated Caroline like an adult. Now look at her. She was managing multimillion-dollar factories and business deals.

DeAngelo knew Caroline and Ava were as close as ever. He heard tidbits of her conversations with Ava every now and then. Hearing Caroline's excitement whenever she returned from a trip to the States comforted him. He would never forgive himself if he had destroyed her relationship with Ava.

Chapter 33

"Am I even ready to start dating again?"

Ava ransacked her closet, looking for something appropriate to wear.

"No. I'm not ready to date. It's too soon."

Ava questioned if she had fully gotten over DeAngelo. Love and affection for him still lingered in her heart. Keith had called to ask if she was okay with a casual, family-style restaurant. Ava readily agreed. She felt that would take the pressure of this being a real date off her shoulders.

But still, she couldn't decide what to wear. It was June in Texas and as hot as the devil. Finally, she chose a breezy, halter-top sundress.

The doorbell rang. "God, I'm not ready for this."

Keith stepped in with flowers in his hands. "These are for you."

Keith's chivalrous, romantic gesture caught Ava by surprise. These were no wilted, clinging-to-life flowers from a gas station; Keith handed her an exquisite bouquet with baby's breath, a silk ribbon, and tissue paper.

Ava couldn't help but smile. She loved flowers.

"Thank you, they're beautiful."

Ava returned with the flowers in a vase. She glanced up to see Keith staring at her.

"You look lovely, Ava." Keith's words seemed so sincere. Ava thought he actually meant it and wasn't just flirting.

The restaurant, Low Country Kitchen, looked like a converted house. Ava absorbed the rich, soulful aromas floating in the air and almost salivated.

Keith asked for a table on the back patio. Ava winced at that idea.

What is he doing? It's hot as fire. She soon realized Keith absolutely knew what he was doing. A massive oak tree with expansive leaves canopied the patio, blocking the direct heat of the blazing sun.

Ava couldn't see the small fans concealed in the branches but could definitely feel the gentle breeze they produced. She had to give Keith props.

"This place is wonderful," said Ava, her hands flattening her dress as she sat down. "I'm excited to taste the food."

"Is this your first time here?" Keith asked.

"Yes. I've been working out of the country for a few years. I feel like I'm discovering Texas for the first time."

Ava regretted mentioning her overseas work when she

saw Keith's eyes blink with curiosity. She tried to be as casual as possible, hoping he wouldn't pry for details.

"I lived in China for two years and Germany for one."

"What type of work? Is your family expanding your business?"

Ava had a short reprieve when the waitress came over for their drink and dinner selection. She ordered the herb-crusted, black sea bass over parmesan grits and raspberry sweet tea. Keith ordered the diver scallops atop goat cheese risotto.

"Would you like me to order wine?"

"No, thank you. I rarely drink."

Keith responded by ordering an unsweet tea with his meal, which raised Ava and the waitress's eyebrows. Unsweet tea in Texas was almost sacrilege.

We all have our faults Ava thought. Keith immediately circled back to Ava's international travels once the waitress had left.

"So, China and Germany. Spending years living and working in another country seems exciting and challenging. What was it like?"

Ava stuck with safe topics, like getting used to the work culture. She talked about the expansion of their family business and her love for cooking. She stayed far away from anything that might lead to a more personal line of questioning.

Surprisingly, Keith turned out to be more inquisitive than Ava had imagined. "What brought you back?"

There was no way she was going to say it was a devastating, soul-crushing breakup. "The business was stable, and I missed home." Ava felt nervous. She wasn't ready to date. She looked at Keith's calm face and understanding, watchful eyes. "And a painful breakup."

Mortified, Ava looked away. She couldn't believe she said that out loud. Thank goodness the waitress saved her again.

"Your drink, ma'am."

Ava prayed Keith would be polite enough not to say anything. She would be happy to eat in complete silence. She felt stupid and exposed. Then, she heard Keith's consoling voice.

"Parting from someone you care about is difficult."

They gave each other a polite smile and a knowing nod. Soon, the waitress was back with their meal.

"You may not remember me, but I attended your walk-through at the oncology center," said Keith.

Ava closed her eyes as the series of the five walk-throughs flashed through her mind. "Oh, wait. You were there when the older lady kept complaining about the heat, and I had to get a wheelchair for her. Why she decided to dress in her Sunday best to walk a construction site, I'll never know."

Ava shook her head and chuckled before continuing. "Mrs. Mabel is quite the character. But she is one of my more loyal and bossy volunteers."

Keith laughed as he remembered the drama of that day. "Yes, I was there. That was my second walk-through."

Ava's eyes widen with interest.

"When I saw you at my interview, I assumed you were a board member," confessed Keith. "After winning the contract, I met with the board again, and you weren't there. That's when I discovered you had sat in for your expertise." Keith stopped to eat a few more bites of his dinner.

Why is he telling me all this on a first date? Ava watched Keith closely, analyzing his words and tone to figure out what was going on. He was too sincere and straightforward. Flirting seemed to be the least of his concerns.

"I have been trying to figure out a way to meet you, and then you showed up in my office."

Ava had no witty comeback. She was about to stammer out something foolish, but Keith's gaze stopped her.

"I'm glad you walked into my office yesterday."

Ava needed to change the subject fast. She started to feel a certain kind of way, and she hoped it was food poisoning. That she could deal with. A few days of stomach cramps wouldn't be too bad. But no, it wasn't undercooked sea bass that fluttered her stomach and warmed her cheeks.

Ava found herself attracted to Keith's mellow spirit. His husky voice and kind, ebony eyes drew her into a safe and protected space. It scared her to feel so comfortable.

She pulled herself together. "What do you do when you're not working?"

There was no hesitation. No inflection in Keith's voice,

just a natural, transparent reply.

"I stay busy raising my son."

Ava kept her face in check, trying not to show the shock she was experiencing. The fact that Keith had a son was far more of a surprise to Ava than it should have been.

Keith was probably thirty-five. That was plenty old enough to have children. Ava realized that just because she never considered children didn't mean no one else did.

"How old is your son?"

"Malcolm turned twelve in May. Technically, he's my nephew and godson. He's my sister, Monica's, boy." Keith leaned forward. "Monica passed away when Malcolm was four. He's been with me ever since."

Ava detected a raw edge of sadness in his voice that made her grieve with him. "I'm sorry for your loss."

Keith changed the subject to Ava's Fourth of July fundraiser. Happy for the redirection; Ava extended an invitation.

"Please, bring Malcolm and anyone else you would like. It is going to be a family event. If you need additional tickets, let me know."

Ava kept their conversation on the event for the rest of dinner.

As Keith drove Ava home, they chatted about the new food scene and other random things. Ava debated if she should invite Keith in for coffee and made the split-second decision as she unlocked her door.

"Thank you for a nice evening," she said. "You have great taste in restaurants. I think we will get on nicely." Ava could have slapped herself for saying that. She didn't want to encourage another date. She wasn't ready.

Keith's low, raspy, thundering laugh made Ava think twice. "I can't cook, but I do have great taste in restaurants. Good food is a must for me."

Keith leaned in for a hug. "I would like to see you again, maybe next weekend if possible."

Ava wanted to stop herself, but she couldn't. She returned Keith's hug and added a soft kiss on the cheek.

"I would like that."

Chapter 34

Ava roamed around the kitchen, trying to think of the best way to approach the subject with her mom. Rita had been pestering her for months to get out and meet people. "Meet people," of course, meant meeting a man and start living again. She hadn't told her mother she went out to lunch and then to dinner with Keith last week.

"Hey, Mom. Do you know Keith Walker?"

Rita looked up from her iPad and answered. "Keith Walker, whose company won the construction contract at the hospital? I know *of* him. Why?"

Ava took her sandwich over to the table and sat across from her mom. She tread lightly, hoping her mother wouldn't read too much into her lunch and dinner date with Keith.

As Ava talked, Rita typed away on her iPad, which annoyed the heck out of her daughter.

"Mom, are you listening?" Ava huffed.

Ava's mom spun her iPad around with Keith's face beaming on the screen from his company's "About Us" web page.

"You're dating this hell of a fine-looking man."

Ava tried not to blush as she ate her sandwich. "One lunch and one dinner. That does not mean we're dating. Mom, I don't think I'm ready to start dating again. I don't know if I'm truly over DeAngelo."

Ava let out a sigh. "It would be too complicated. Keith's raising his nephew. I've never dated a man with a kid before."

Rita grinned. "Wait. Has he asked you out again?"

Ava should have known her mother would pick up on that piece of information. "Yes, for this weekend."

"Listen, honey, don't get yourself caught up in thinking too far ahead. It's a few dates. Go out, and have a little fun. I know DeAngelo hurt you, and if you're not ready, that's okay. I just don't want you to shut yourself off from the world and hide in your work."

Ava's nerves settled when she learned her next outing with Keith would be on the golf course. Golf was not at all romantic. Roses and a candlelight dinner would have freaked Ava out completely. A nice emphasis on a "friendly round of golf" she could handle.

Even better, Keith took her to a well-maintained, public course and not some stuffy, elite country club. Keith didn't seem like the snobby, country-club type, which Ava appreciated.

Ava adjusted her sun visor and took a big gulp of water

before she teed up. "I'm sure you can tell by my decade-old clubs that my game is rusty. I apologize now."

Swoosh. Ava hit a monster drive and hooked it into the rough. She looked back at Keith with a funny grin, laughing at herself.

"Told you."

"You haven't seen my game yet," said Keith with confidence.

Ava watched Keith hit a perfect drive off the tee, with the ball landing in the middle of the fairway. She thought Keith was being modest. Bringing a woman to anything sports-related to show off was a real guy-thing to do.

Ava managed to make it out of the rough, onto the green, and hole her putt. Keith, likewise, holed his putt. They both played the first few holes relatively well, but their games took a nosedive around the sixth hole.

Ava hit every bunker and lost three balls in the water, and Keith had zero short game. Poor guy couldn't make a putt to save his life.

"My game is heinous," Ava joked as she sipped her sparkling water with lime on the clubhouse patio.

Keith drank his unsweet iced tea. "At least you can putt. Funny how you can like something and be so horrible at it."

Ava noticed a group of young kids head to the course and remembered his son, Malcolm. "Do you take Malcolm golfing?"

"Occasionally. He's far more into basketball and baseball. I might get him in a league this summer if he promises to stick with it."

Ava didn't know what else to say. She wasn't used to talking to people about their kids. Danny didn't have kids yet. He and his wife had recently started talking about trying.

What was she going to talk to a man with a kid about? She knew nothing about kids. Heck, she didn't even know what grade a twelve-year-old should be in.

The longer she sat quiet, the more awkward and silly she felt. "Is school out already for the summer?"

That was a dumb question.

Keith nodded. "Yes, last week. Malcolm is with my parents in Knoxville for a week or so. He'll be back by the Fourth of July."

"I can get you more tickets for the event if you want to bring anyone else."

Ava remembered she had asked Keith the same question at dinner, but he didn't answer. She hoped he would take the hint that if he wanted to bring a woman—perhaps his girl-friend—it would be fine with her.

"No, it will just be Malcolm and me." Keith put money on the table to pay for their lunch.

"Would you like to have dinner tonight?" he asked.

Ava's decision went back and forth in her head like a tennis ball: yes, no, yes, no.

Dinner would seem too much like another date, and Ava wanted to keep things in the friend zone until she knew what to make of Keith.

"How about I throw a couple of steaks on the grill instead?" suggested Ava. No romance and no dressing up. This would be two new friends hanging out. Absolutely not a date.

The dinner was a no-brainer. Ava could grill up a steak better than most, and the sides she could do with her eyes closed. What she grappled with was what to wear. She needed to thread the needle carefully to look decent but by no means sexy.

Ava didn't want Keith getting any ideas their dinner was anything more than a friendly hangout. After much debate, Ava settled on a simple pair of black shorts with a blush-colored, sleeveless blouse and white sneakers. You can't get more "friend" than that.

Keith insisted on bringing something. Obviously, his mother raised him right. Ava had told him he could bring a dessert if he liked, but there was no need.

Keith showed up at Ava's with two individual-sized cakes. "One's chocolate, and the other lemon. I thought we could share."

Keep it in the friend zone was playing like a broken record in Ava's head as she walked Keith back to the patio. It was a simple, covered living space with a small but adequate kitchen off the side of her house.

Ava put the cakes in the mini-fridge and poured Keith and herself a tall glass of iced tea. She promptly added sugar to her drink and then walked over to the grill.

She glanced back at Keith. "How do you like your rib eye?"

Two nice, thick, juicy steaks seasoned with salt and pepper lay on a plate, ready for the grill. A mound of sliced mushrooms, mini potatoes, and asparagus had been prepped as well.

Keith surveyed Ava's setup. "Medium. I would ask if you need any help, but I sense I would be way out of my league."

In no time, Ava delivered a perfect backyard steak dinner. The steaks looked great with flawless grill marks, but Ava was a little nervous if she got the doneness correct.

"I hope the steak is how you like it," said Ava.

When Ava was seated and had begun to eat, Keith had already cut into his steak. She saw a perfectly-cooked steak, beautifully seared on the outside and spot-on pinkness inside, but wondered what Keith thought.

Ava waited for him to start the conversation. She had exhausted all hospital subjects, which was the only thing she could ever think to talk about. She hated not being able to hold a nonbusiness-related conversation.

Keith ate, took a sip of tea, and continued to eat. After several uncomfortable minutes of silence, he glanced up at

Ava. Only a tiny sliver of rib eye and two or three asparagus spears remained in front of him.

"I hope you don't mind," said Keith. "I'm a clean-plate kind of guy."

Ava laughed. "I don't mind at all. I appreciate a man with a healthy appetite, but you're eating rather fast."

Oh crap, Ava thought. She felt like she had stepped in it again. What she said sounded like flirting.

Keith laughed and slowed his pace. "Lunch at the golf course didn't go very far." He ate the last of his steak before continuing. "I made sure not to eat anything before coming over."

His comment ignited Ava's curiosity. "May I ask why you decided to starve yourself before coming over?" she teased.

Keith looked rather serious. "Are you sure you want to know?"

Ava gave a coy eye roll and playfully shrugged her shoulders. "Hey, if you're on some sort of weird diet, to each his own."

Keith had a gleam in his eyes. "I don't do diets. I was preparing myself."

Ava leaned in, giving him her full attention. "Preparing yourself for what exactly?"

"You see, I wanted to be hungry enough that even if you were a horrible cook, I could eat anything you put in front of me," said Keith, tilting his head and giving Ava a side glance.

"You said you were a good cook," he continued. "I had to take your word for it. So, good cook or not, I was prepared."

Ava covered her mouth with her hand so she wouldn't burst out laughing and spit iced tea everywhere. "Are you a clean-plate eater because you started with an empty stomach or because the food was actually good?"

"The food is excellent, and I know food. I would be happy to eat at your table every day of the week. You and I, we're going to get along nicely." Keith's engrossing stare and the sincerity of his words sent a tingle down Ava's spine.

After dinner, the two moved from the table to the patio loveseat. They talked about their shared experiences growing up in Texas. Keith showed interest in Ava's travels and business. He had only traveled once outside of the U.S. to Canada. Niagara Falls was his family's big international trip.

Ava kicked her sneakers off. She sat with her legs folded under her, praising the virtues of travel.

"International travel is amazing," she said. "I've learned so much and met the most wonderful people. It helped me think more broadly of the world."

"Do you think twelve is a good age to start traveling?" Keith asked.

"It's a perfect age. We took our first family trip to France when I was ten." Ava laughed as she got up to get dessert. "We better change the subject before I turn into your travel agent."

She put both cakes on one plate so she and Keith could

share. When she sat back down on the loveseat, she noticed Keith had moved. He was much closer than he needed to be to share the cakes.

"It's a deal. You can help me plan my first international trip for next summer," Keith replied as he stretched and rested his arm on the couch behind Ava's shoulders.

To Ava, it was a simple joke. When she looked at Keith, he had a determined, thoughtful look on his face. *Oh my goodness he is serious.*

"Where is a good place to go for a first international trip?"

Ava's mouth was open in surprise. "Well, let me think. I'm not sure. It all depends on what you like to do."

"A place with a lot of history and things to do outdoors. And good weather. I'm not into cold, dreary places." Keith replied as he moved even closer.

Ava couldn't think, sensing Keith was going to make a move to kiss her. Maybe if she kept talking and listing travel destinations, she could prevent it.

"Well, Mexico or anywhere in South America would work. The flights aren't that long. Spain, Italy, and Greece are also nice op—"

Before Ava could finish, she felt Keith's warm lips press against hers. Their mouths opened. Keith's firm hand slid across Ava's stomach and wrapped around her back. Before he had the chance to bring Ava into a full embrace, she jerked back and stood up.

Keith caught her hand before she could walk away. "Ava, what's wrong? I'm sorry if I made you uncomfortable."

Ava sat back down. Embarrassed, she looked down at the paved patio floor.

"No. I'm just not sure I'm ready for a relationship. Can we just be friends?"

Keith pinned his mouth shut to stifle a laugh. He kept silent while Ava chattered on.

"We just met. Don't you think this is moving too fast?"

Keith held her hand. "It was just one small, innocent kiss, Ava."

"That was no innocent little kiss, and you know it," said Ava with a cunning smirk.

Keith pulled Ava in closer. "We're already friends. I know we're meant to be much more."

Keith leaned in, and this time, Ava didn't resist. Their second kiss was Keith's one-way ticket out of the friend zone.

Chapter 35

The long-awaited Fourth of July celebration arrived. It was also the day Ava was to meet Malcolm for the first time. From what she already knew of Keith, she imagined Malcolm as a well-behaved and polite young man.

Ava forced Keith to promise to text her when he and Malcolm arrived. Keith resisted, knowing she would likely get pulled in a thousand directions as the event organizer. His assumption was correct, but Ava still wanted to make time and welcome Keith and Malcolm properly.

As she pictured, Malcolm struck Ava as a lovely young man who was raised to respect his elders. With a firm hand-shake and "It's a pleasure to meet you, Ms. Ava," Malcolm impressed her. But, like most twelve-year-old boys, Malcolm was far more interested in the carnival sights and sounds than hanging with Ava, or even Keith, for that matter.

After getting the okay from his uncle, Malcolm sprinted off to join a few of his school friends gathered around the dunking booth. The preteen boys were eager to dunk the clown and win a prize.

Ava stayed with Keith as long as she could before some emergency needed her attention.

"I promise to watch the fireworks with you and Malcolm."

Hours later, when the sun went down, the anticipation for the light show grew. Who didn't love a spectacular fireworks display?

Ava, Keith, and Malcolm were so close to the fireworks they could feel the blast pulse through their bodies. Ava felt as if she could reach up and catch as many twinkling lights as she desired. Keith and Ava exchanged glances as they heard Malcolm's roar of delight surpass the booms and thunders.

That sweet Texas night marked the beginning of a new chapter in Ava's life. As the summer progressed, Ava stayed busy with her work at the hospital and spent time with Keith and Malcolm. Her new summer activity was attending Malcolm's baseball games with Keith. Being an adult spectator at little league baseball was a completely new experience for Ava, but she enjoyed the mostly family-friendly atmosphere, minus the insanely competitive parents.

The sun was blazing in early August, and the temperature soared to a hot, hazy ninety-eight degrees. Ava could see Keith near the dugout, giving his nephew a pregame pep talk. A nervous Malcolm was about to play in his first semifinal game. If his team won, they would head to the championship game in Austin.

Ava handed Keith a bottle of water when he returned to his seat. "How's Malcolm?"

"He's nervous, but ready. I told him, win or lose, just do your best," Keith said as Ava looked toward the field with a delightful expression on her face. "What's so funny?, he asked."

Ava laughed. "I can't believe how exciting this is. I was never this nervous when Danny played sports. I always wanted him to win, but this is different. My heart is pounding. My hands are sweaty, and it's not the heat."

Keith laughed before turning his attention to the field. Malcolm's team was first up to bat.

"Now, what are you laughing at?" Ava asked.

"You being a bad sister and not rooting for your brother when you were kids."

Ava playfully shoved Keith on the shoulder. "Stop teasing me. I rooted for Danny, but I wasn't this nervous. I wonder why this is so different."

"Danny's your brother, and Malcolm is, well, not your brother. He's more like—"

"Let the games begin!" the announcer screamed through the speakers. All conversation ceased. The game had started.

At the end of the third inning, the score was tied. Malcolm's team, the Beaumont Tigers, had one run, and so did the South Texas Thrashers. Due to the heat, the umpire gave the boys a fifteen-minute break to rest before starting the fourth inning.

The game remained a nail-biter heading into the sixth and final inning. The Thrashers had a runner on second base, with the score still tied. Up next to bat was their shortstop. Ava clenched her hands together, closed her eyes, and hoped for the best. The Thrasher shortstop, Number 15 Temple, stood out throughout the game. He looked talented enough to be playing high school baseball.

"Strike one!" yelled the umpire at the first ball.

The crack of the bat on the second ball reverberated in the stands. The ball went flying toward the back fence. Ava's stomach sank.

No way. That kid just hit a home run. Before she could process the raw power of a thirteen-year-old boy and a loss for Malcolm, the ball hit the top of the fence and ricocheted back toward the field. The Beaumont Tigers still had a chance! The ball was picked up by the outfielder. It soared to third base and then home, but it was about three seconds too late.

"Safe!" yelled the umpire.

The game was over. The South Texas Thrashers advanced to the finals. The Beaumont Tigers' season was over.

Ava waited with Malcolm while Keith went to get the car. Disappointment held back Malcolm's tears.

"You played a wonderful game," said Ava.

"Thanks, Ms. Ava," said Malcolm. "But losing sucks."

Ava almost laughed at Malcolm's pinched brow and turned down mouth. "I agree. Losing does suck. But win or lose, your uncle is very proud of you, and so am I."

❧

Two Years Later

"All right, fellas, it's enchiladas tonight," announced Ava, sitting a hot, cheesy dish of chicken and beef enchiladas on the kitchen table. "We have some Mexican rice, corn salad, and guacamole. Who's ready to eat?"

"I am!" shouted Malcolm as he dumped a massive glob of guacamole onto his plate. "You cook the best food, Ms. Ava."

"My sentiments exactly," said Keith.

It always puts a smile on Ava's face to see anyone—but especially Keith and Malcolm—enjoying her food. Her heart was full. The work she was doing at the hospital satisfied her more than she thought. Initially, she had reservations about stepping away from the family business, but it was worth it. Happy and very much in love, Ava learned to balance both work and personal pursuits.

Halfway through his second helping of enchiladas, Malcolm proclaimed, "These enchiladas are even better than the ones at Señor Jalapeño, and I love that place. You should open a restaurant."

Malcolm took a big gulp of lemonade. "No, a food truck. That way, you can set up anywhere."

Ava embraced the idea with a giggle. She tipped her glass to Malcolm.

"I like the way you think. That can be my retirement plan: Ava's Enchiladas to Go."

"Ava's Supremo Enchiladas to Go," Keith chimed in.

Keith and Malcolm, both clean-platers, consumed two helpings inside of twenty minutes.

"I made chocolate and peanut butter brownies for dessert, and there is ice cream in the freezer," announced Ava.

"Is it okay if I take dessert to my room?" asked Malcolm. "I have some homework to finish and need to study for exams."

Keith gave the okay. But before Malcolm retreated to his room, he helped clean up and fixed himself a brownie sundae.

"Thanks again, Ms. Ava," said Malcolm with a grin. "Dinner was great, as always."

With Malcolm gone, Keith snaked his arms around Ava's waist while she wiped down the kitchen counter. His cheek touched hers as he leaned his chin over her shoulder.

"Why don't you stay the night?"

Ava wiggled her body around to meet Keith's dark, ebony gaze, suggesting more than just staying the night.

"What about Malcolm?" asked Ava, brows furrowing in concern. "It might be weird for him."

"Ava, baby, we've been together for almost two years now. You're over here just about every day. I love you, and I want to wake up next to you. Please stay."

The thought of waking up nestled in Keith's arms would be the perfect start to any morning. She had wanted to stay the night many times, but always made up some excuse not to.

"I love you, too, but me staying over will change everything. It's just been you and Malcolm, and now I'm in the picture. I don't want him to think I'm taking over."

Keith held Ava closer and kissed her. "Baby, you know Malcolm adores you. There's no way he's going to think that. You're a part of us now. You're family."

"I do love you and Malcolm, but it still makes me nervous."

Ava could tell Keith wouldn't drop the subject until he got a "yes" out of her. She decided to strike a deal.

"Christmas break is in a few weeks. If you promise to talk to Malcolm and see how he feels about me possibly staying over, I'll reconsider my position."

Ava backed up and extended her hand to shake on the deal. Keith grabbed her by the waist instead.

"I believe we can do better than a handshake," he whispered.

Chapter 36

"Malcolm really likes you," said Keith after he had had that promised talk with Malcolm. "He says you're the only one that doesn't baby him."

Ava almost wanted to cry. She had fallen in love with Keith and Malcolm, and she didn't want anything to mess that up.

It was New Year's Eve, and the only one painting the town red was Malcolm. Keith had agreed to let Malcolm attend the celebration downtown. Malcolm's best friend, Christopher, was going under his parents' supervision and had invited Malcolm.

Christopher's parents had rented a hotel suite with a perfect view of the festivities. They would keep the boys the entire night and get Malcolm back home in the afternoon on New Year's Day.

Like Keith, Ava was not a New Year's Eve person. She found the whole scene excruciating. Places were always too crowded, too loud, and the people too drunk. She'd much rather stay home and chill and wake up the first day of the new year in Keith's arms.

Ava cooked a nice dinner that night at Keith's. They cuddled together on the couch, watching movies and later, the countdown. Minutes away from ringing in the new year, Ava got the glasses, and Keith opened the champagne. The countdown began, "5… 4… 3… 2… 1 Happy New Year!"

Ava and Keith kissed and slow danced to the song streaming from the television. She rested in Keith's arms and listened to him talk about his hope for the new year. It was then that he said something she hadn't dreamed she would hear.

"Ava, will you marry me?"

Ava's knee bounced up and down as she glanced at the clock, waiting for Malcolm to come home.

"Ava, I didn't just talk to Malcolm about you staying over," explained Keith, trying to calm her nerves. "I also talked to him about asking you to marry me. He was ecstatic. He even went with me to pick out the ring."

Ava and Malcolm clicked from the beginning, but having her as a mother and not some lady his uncle was dating, was different. Their lives were about to change. Presumably, she would move into Keith's house and live with him and Malcolm.

Ava looked at Keith. "I know you're probably right, but this is a major change for Malcolm. I want to know for myself he's okay with it. It's almost noon. Malcolm should be home any minute now."

"When should we set the date?" Keith asked as he kissed and held Ava close.

She shook her head, resisting the idea. "No decision can be made until Mrs. Rita Marie Brooks has a chance to chime in. Waiting until this afternoon to tell her the news is already going to get me in trouble."

Ava jumped when she heard the key in the door. She turned away and then back to Keith.

"Okay, act normal," ordered Ava, posing like a mannequin. She stared forward, and her back was straight as a board. Malcolm didn't seem to notice when he ran into the living room with his eyes as big as a full moon.

Keith gave him a confirming nod, and Malcolm flung himself onto Ava for a huge hug. "You said yes, didn't you, Ava?"

Ava had tears in her eyes, shaking her head yes.

"Do you like the ring? I helped pick it out." Malcolm glanced up at Keith, then giggled. "I told Uncle Keith to get you the big diamond."

Ava wiped her eyes, laughed aloud, and gave Malcolm another hug. "Thanks for looking out for me. You did good."

Keith broke the two bosom buddies up. "Come on, you two, let's head over to Ava's parents' house. It's time we let everyone know this wonderful woman has agreed to be my wife."

When they arrived at the Brooks residence, Danny answered the door. "Happy New Year, you guys. Get in here; we're all ready to eat." He led the way to the kitchen.

"Hey everybody!" announced Danny, looking towards the living room. "Ava, Keith, and Malcolm are finally here. We can eat now."

After the customary Happy New Year wishes were exchanged, Ava asked for everyone's attention. She gave a loving glance to her fiancé. Keith did the honors.

"Ava and I are—"

Before Keith could finish, Ava screamed out, "We're getting married!" She waved her hand around, showing off her gigantic, emerald-cut, diamond engagement ring.

The next scream came from Ava's mom. "Oh, my lord, Clayton, our baby is getting married!" Then everyone joined in with shouts of congratulations, hugs, and a multitude of kisses.

The only other person Ava wanted to share the news with next was Caroline. She hoped her dear friend would be her maid of honor. Ava started to text, then stopped. *I'll wait until later,* she decided.

Ava, Keith, and Malcolm returned home in the late afternoon, exhausted. Malcolm crashed in his room. Keith relaxed in the family room to watch the college football championship game, and Ava took the opportunity to text Caroline. It was late in Germany, around 10:00 P.M. Ava hoped she would be alone and able to talk.

> Happy New Year. Have time for a quick chat?

Caroline replied five minutes later.

> Happy New Year. I can talk. Give me a call.

Ava called immediately.

"Happy New Year, Caroline. How are you?"

"I'm great. Happy New Year to you, too. How's Danny and your parents?"

Ava's nerves were building. "Everyone is fine. I have some big news to share." Ava paused and then blurted it out. "I'm getting married."

"Oh my God! Oh my God! That is so great. Congratulations! I'm so happy for you."

"I want you to be my maid of honor. Please say yes."

There was a loud scream, followed by, "Yes, yes, yes. I would be honored."

Chapter 37

In February, Ava decided she would be a fall bride so as to give the wedding planning partners, her mom and Danny's wife, Justine, enough time to plan. Ava had to slow her mom down from planning an over-the-top, expensive wedding.

Early on, Ava noticed that her mom intended to make her wedding day the event of the century. She had to wield a lot of love and patience to bring Rita back down to earth.

Ava slashed Rita's initial three-hundred-person guest list down to a mere one hundred with Keith's full support. Ava gave in to her mom's need for a party and allowed for an expanded reception guest list of an extra seventy-five people. Keith supported the compromise. As long as Ava was happy, he was happy.

After they settled on the guest list, the rest of the planning was smooth sailing until it came time to pick out the dress. Several appointments and three indecisive months later, Ava laid her eyes on the one.

By early summer, the trio solidified all the major wedding decisions. Ava made it a priority not to let wedding stress come between her and Keith. She handed the smaller details to her mom and Justine without a second thought. The summer was her's and Keith's to enjoy and ease into a blissful fall.

Enjoying their usual Friday date night out at a local restaurant, Keith revisited his new favorite topic.

"You know, the house is big enough for at least three more children," said Keith, giving Ava that look of "let's start tonight."

"We can start on the honeymoon. I promise," said Ava, rubbing her leg against his under the table.

For the first time in her life, Ava knew she was ready to have kids. Keith loved her, and she already considered Malcolm as her son. Marrying Keith and starting a family filled Ava with happiness.

The wonderful dinner and talk of their future lives together made for a perfect night. Ava danced in the passenger seat and sang along to "Everlasting Love" by Gloria Estefan on the radio.

She turned to Keith and belted out the next, slightly-modified verses, "Can't wait to be your bride."

Keith kissed Ava's hand, and his deep, raspy laugh filled the car as they sat at a red light.

Ava continued, "You'll never be denied—oh, did you feel that?"

Keith's laugh stopped, and his jubilant smile vanished. "Yeah, I think the guy behind us just bumped us."

He put the car in park, unhooked his seat belt, and opened the car door. "You stay here."

Ava screamed as a man from the car behind them pulled her door open.

"Get out of the car! Get out of the car!" demanded the stranger, his hand gripping the collar of Ava's shirt, ripping her from the vehicle and pinning her on the cement.

Keith reached for Ava, but his hand grazed her fingers. A second man violently jerked him from the car, as well.

Ava screamed and clawed, trying to free herself from the man's grip. Her face burned as the man delivered several blows. A stream of hot blood flowed from Ava's nose. Suddenly, she felt the pang of metal from the butt of a gun slam against her head above her right temple. A nauseating ringing in her ears left Ava unable to distinguish between all the chaotic sounds swarming around her.

Her vision blurred, and she collapsed to the ground. She tried to get to her knees, but two booted kicks to the stomach ended her effort. The man smashed her head into the road.

"Move again, and I'll kill you."

She laid motionless on the pavement. Keith's horrified yells reached her ears, but the car blocked her view of him.

Oh God, please help him.

Pop! Pop! Two loud gunshots rang out. An eerie calm held Ava captive.

Keith's Cadillac Escalade and the car that had bumped them sped away. When the exhaust fumes cleared, Ava craned her neck and saw Keith lying still in a pool of blood. The blazing heat of the asphalt burned Ava's palms as she crawled on her hands and knees to Keith. Her lips were badly swollen; she could hardly speak.

"Keith. Baby, please stay with me, please stay with me."

Keith's eyes were dim, but he was alive. Ava cried and pleaded more. "Keith, baby, I love you. Please stay with me. It's going to be okay."

People saw the scene and rushed to help. An ambulance arrived quickly. The paramedics tried to render aid to Ava, but she refused.

"No, my husband, please take care of my husband." She loved Keith completely. She didn't need a ceremony to love him as her husband.

Ava held tight to Keith's hand. She forced herself to keep up as the paramedics rushed him from the ambulance into the emergency room. The hospital staff knew Ava and Keith well. Word spread, and staff members notified her family immediately.

Ava looked on, feeling like she was in a hellish dream. The blood, shouting of orders, and bright, blinking lights of the equipment sent a terror through her.

Two bullets had pierced Keith's chest at close range. Bullet fragments had torn through his body, severing multiple arteries and causing massive internal bleeding. He went into cardiac arrest.

Standing at the foot of Keith's bed, Ava wept, hypnotized by the one thin, flat, red line. The doctor shouted commands.

"Clear!" *Beeeeeeeeeeeep.* "Clear!" *Beeeeeeeeeeeep.* "Again. Clear!" *Beeeeeeeeeeeep.*

A long pause.

"Time of death: 10:23 P.M."

Ava pushed passed the doctor. She flung herself across Keith's lifeless body.

"Please, Keith. Please, baby, don't leave me."

Frantic, Ava's mother ran to the emergency room's reception area.

"Ava Brooks. Where is my daughter, Ava Brooks?" she yelled.

The attending ER doctor, whom she knew well, approached, his face solemn and mouth cast down into a remorseful frown.

"Rita, Keith passed away. Ava needs medical attention, but she has refused. She won't leave his side."

Ava sat at Keith's bedside with his hand in hers. Rita's hand caressed Ava's shoulder, and she kissed the top of her daughter's head.

"Ava, it's me," said Rita. "I'm here, sweetheart. I'm here."

Without looking up, Ava responded to her mother's gentle voice. "He's gone, Mom," she cried. Blood and tears stained her face as she lifted her head. "Where's Malcolm? He can't see us like this."

Rita guided Ava to a private room. The nurses cleaned and stitched her wounds. Rita helped Ava remove her blood-soaked clothes, wash, and change into a clean pair of scrubs. Ava's dad arrived next, followed by Danny and Malcolm.

Seeing Ava's battered face, Malcolm burst into tears. "Uncle Keith. Where is Uncle Keith?"

The words lay trapped in her throat. So, she just held onto Malcolm and cried with him.

As the night flowed into the early morning, Ava heard voices. Her hospital room's door was ajar. With her right eye swollen shut, she saw through her left eye her dad and Danny talking to a man. She could tell by the dark tan uniform it was a Texas State Trooper.

Ava motioned to her mother. She whispered. It hurt to talk.

"What's going on?"

Rita eased Malcolm's head off her lap and onto the couch. He had fallen asleep. Rita went to Ava's bedside.

"Please, honey, rest."

Ava tried to speak again, but her mother stopped her.

"There was an off-duty officer nearby. He was able to call for help. They recovered the car and—"

"Our wedding," cried Ava. "What about our wedding? We have to let everybody know. Oh, Mom, I can't believe he's gone."

Chapter 38

"Can I please have a beer?" whined DeAngelo. He had spent the entire Saturday afternoon building new shelving for his mom's pantry and that was after dedicating the morning to mounting new kitchen cabinets.

Inspired to modernize their kitchens, Rosalynn and Momma Gretta used the men of the family as labor. DeAngelo, Rich, and Albert did the real hands-on work while Peter managed the tools and tried to read the instructions.

There was a little bit of a break after finishing the Kraus kitchen renovation three months ago. Now, the final touches for the Williams' kitchen were almost complete.

Rosalynn brought ice-cold beers to the table. Momma Gretta and Caroline followed with lunch.

After running out to the car to get a change of clothes, DeAngelo returned to Caroline's hysterical screams and cries ringing throughout the kitchen. Momma Gretta and Albert huddled around their daughter, trying to console her.

Rosalynn took DeAngelo by the arm. Her face was pale from shock.

"It's bad news from America."

Fear stabbed at DeAngelo's heart. His first thought was of Ava. He stood paralyzed. Five minutes. No, less than five minutes to grab his clothes from the car, and now this nightmare.

Distraught, Caroline broke down when she heard the tragic news. Peter grabbed her phone to find out what was happening. He was white as a sheet when he walked back into the kitchen with Caroline's phone in his hand.

Peter's voice was somber.

"That was Ava's brother, Danny. There was a carjacking. Ava and her fiancé, Keith—"

DeAngelo's voice shook with sheer panic.

"Ava, is she okay?" he yelled.

Peter's voice remained subdued. "Ava was severely beaten. Keith was shot twice."

Terror darkened DeAngelo's face. He had to know.

"Please, tell me she's still alive, please," begged DeAngelo.

Peter lowered his head, his voice trembling. "Yes, Ava is alive but in bad shape. Her fiancé died."

DeAngelo dropped his bag of clothes and eased his mom's hand from his arm. He walked over to Caroline and put his arms around his little sister, holding her for a short while. Then, without a word, he walked into the living room.

DeAngelo sat down, head in his hands. There was nothing he could do. He stared down at the floor. Those brief, horrifying seconds of thinking Ava might be dead were the most agonizing of his life. The thought that Ava was gone was inconceivable. Not her. Not Ava. Not so soon.

He had made peace with their breakup. He had to; she was never coming back. Yes, he knew she was engaged. Caroline had talked and prepared for Ava's wedding for months. She even had the privilege of being Ava's maid of honor. At the time, DeAngelo felt he was at the point of wishing Ava well.

She had moved on with her life, and he had done the same. Ava had found the man she deserved; the man he was unable, or unwilling, to be.

Peter's words echoed endlessly in his mind. *"Ava was severely beaten. She's in bad shape."*

How badly was she beaten? What is her real condition? Is she close to death?

DeAngelo cried in his hands. He wanted to see Ava with his own eyes and know she was alive. He wanted to run to her and comfort her. He wanted to hold her in his arms again, not as a lover but as a friend.

He remembered Ava's ultimatum years ago. *"We can move forward as friends or friends and lovers."* Now, they were neither. He hated himself all over again for pushing her away.

Rich eased into the living room and put his arm around DeAngelo. "Son."

DeAngelo sat up. His drawn, ashen face told the depth of his grief.

"Dad, she must be in so much pain, and there is nothing I can do. I still love her. She was the one," confessed DeAngelo, but everyone else already knew.

Chapter 39

Ava had prepared herself for this moment all morning. It was the first time she and Malcolm would be apart since Keith's death. From the day they had laid Keith to rest, Ava knew there was no way anyone was ever going to take Malcolm from her. It was an easy decision, and everyone knew it was what Keith would have wanted. Malcolm and his grandparents agreed that Ava should be his legal guardian.

"You can do this," Ava told herself. She promised to maintain her dignity and not embarrass Malcolm, no matter how difficult.

Ava spent that morning corralling Malcolm and his two friends, Christopher and Shawn.

She wondered if it was even possible to get three sixteen-year-old boys to concentrate for more than five minutes. The trio was far too hyped about the prospect of being on their own for two weeks.

Ava examined all the bags. "Boys, do you have everything packed?"

"Yes, Ms. Brooks," said Christopher.

Shawn gave a thumbs-up while texting with his other hand. "Yes, Mom," replied Malcolm.

Ava could clearly see shoes, clothes, socks, and other necessities scattered about the room and raised a brow. The urge to go through the boys' luggage and double-check for at least the basics nagged at her. But, she'd mortify the boys—and *herself*—depending on what she came across.

She knew they were good boys, especially Malcolm, but they were sixteen. Each one was young, carefree, and ready to take on the world.

"I hope you three packed everything you need. Do you have your money and all the contact information?"

Ava caught on that she was starting to embarrass Malcolm when he gave her a crazy look that begged, *please stop.* She smirked and gave Malcolm an eye roll in response.

"Fifteen minutes, boys, and then we need to head downstairs. That will give you all time for a nice breakfast before your bus arrives."

Fifteen minutes turned into forty as the boys joked and fooled around without a care in the world. Ava gave up and let them have their fun. Finally, they got downstairs. Ava couldn't help herself. Like any good mother, she double-checked the luggage tags before handing the bags over to the tour representative.

The sea of teenage boys and girls packed the hotel restaurant with their parents, all waiting for the same tour buses.

The breakfast buffet was the best option considering they were running late and the bus was now due in thirty minutes.

Ava hated running late for things, but she again reminded herself that this was the boys' trip. Besides, teenage boys can plow through two full plates of food in about five minutes.

Christopher and Shawn rushed up to the buffet first while Ava and Malcolm found a table. Ava took this rare moment alone with her son to remind him of his responsibilities.

"Malcolm, there will be a lot of nice, pretty girls on this tour, as well. I hope you're not planning on doing anything you shouldn't."

Malcolm covered the side of his face with his hand.

"Mom, please," replied Malcolm with a hushed voice of embarrassment. "You, Uncle Danny, and Grandpa Clayton already gave me *that talk,*" he said as his eyes doubled in size, *"several times."*

"I know, but—"

Malcolm talked fast, seeing his friends headed their way. "Mom, you know we're going to have chaperones watching us 24-7. I'm not going to be irresponsible. Promise."

That wasn't a no, but that was the best Ava knew she was going to get. She trusted Malcolm, but with teenage boys and girls mingling and traipsing around Spain, anything could happen.

Malcolm's a good boy. Ava knew he had the same deep, rock-solid respect for himself and others, just like Keith.

When Malcolm smiled, all Ava saw was Keith staring back at her. She almost burst into tears as Christopher and Shawn returned to the table with full plates.

Malcolm ran up, attacked the buffet, and brought back an enormous plate of meat, eggs, and potatoes. Her stomach jumped with nerves, Ava couldn't eat. She had a glass of orange juice and nibbled on a croissant.

She sat and watched the boys in amazement. It was like watching three industrial-sized vacuums inhale every crumb. Why she wasn't used to it by now, she didn't know. These boys were constant eaters, and she had the grocery bills to prove it.

The restaurant started to empty out as everyone flowed into the lobby. The tour buses had pulled up. Ava steeled her jitters and recommitted to her plan of a brief goodbye hug. She would hold Malcolm for a maximum of ten seconds. No, five seconds. And under heaven, no kiss on the cheek. No sixteen-year-old young man wants to get a kiss from his mom in public and in front of his friends.

The teenagers began loading the buses. Like the other parents, Ava shook with both excitement and nervousness. A two-week tour of Spain was the first of many adventures for Malcolm and his friends. The memories her son would make on this trip would last a lifetime.

Ava was glad she had agreed to escort Malcolm and his buddies to Madrid and then back to Texas. But now, as the boys were about to board the bus, it hit her. She felt a pit in her stomach. Two long weeks alone in Spain lay ahead of her.

"Mom, it's time!" yelled Malcolm with enthusiasm. "We need to get on the bus."

Ava embraced him. "I love you. Be safe and have fun." She counted down the five seconds, one heartbeat at a time, then set him free, but Malcolm held on.

She counted at least ten heartbeats, and he gave her the biggest kiss on the cheek. He shouted out not once, but twice, before disappearing onto the bus.

"I love you, Mom. See you in two weeks!"

Ava's heart swelled with joy. She waved like the proud mother she was until the bus was out of sight. As the other parents wandered off in all directions and the rumble of the bus engines faded, a tear wet her cheek.

"No, Ava, you are not going to cry." She headed back into the hotel, but instead of going up to an empty suite, she found her way to the small restaurant bar in the back corner. She needed to think about what to do next. Her lonely two weeks had begun.

Chapter 40

DeAngelo weaved his way through the crowded lobby of the hotel. He chose a table close to the bar. The sports director he was there to meet was late, but DeAngelo was too relaxed to be annoyed.

His phone buzzed with a text.

> Stuck in horrendous traffic.
> Can we reschedule?

DeAngelo was happy to do so. He wasn't in the mood for anything related to work. He felt the need to be free and roll with whatever the day would bring.

He looked over the drink menu and pondered whether he should get a glass of wine or a beer. He was about to settle on a beer when his ears pricked at a voice at the bar asking for sparkling water with lime.

DeAngelo froze.

It can't be. He was reluctant to look up, scared of what, or rather, *who,* he might see.

"Ava." His mouth hadn't spoken her name in years.

Ava turned, so stunned she lost her grip on the glass. It hit the counter and rolled along the granite bar top, splashing sparkling water everywhere. She turned to the bartender, mortified.

"Oh, goodness, I'm sorry," said Ava. "Please, I'm so sorry."

The bartender wiped up the mess and had another glass in her hand in seconds. Ava then turned to face the man she never thought she'd see again.

"DeAngelo."

"Ava."

A long pause rested between them.

"Would you join me?" asked DeAngelo.

"I can't believe it." Ava could hear the shakiness and hesitation in her voice. "What are you doing here? It's good to see you."

DeAngelo's heart pounded. His hands tingled. He could feel himself on the verge of spilling out every single thought that had gathered for six years in that small, closed-off place in his mind.

"God, Ava, I am so sorry."

A painful look marked Ava's gaze. This was not the time or the place.

"I can't do this," she said.

DeAngelo's heart failed him. He wished he had never looked up to see Ava standing at the bar. It would have been better never to have seen her than to know she still couldn't bring herself to even talk with him after so many years.

"I'm sorry, Ava," said DeAngelo, standing to leave.

She reached out, squeezed his hand, and stood. "Can we talk in private?"

DeAngelo hugged the elevator wall, giving Ava as much space as possible. He tried not to stare, but his eyes stayed fixed on her face. For too long, he had only seen that face in his mind's eye. The silent elevator ride to the tenth floor felt like an eternity for DeAngelo.

A fountain of tears broke free for Ava as soon as she stepped inside her suite. DeAngelo stood and wondered what he should do. Should he give her time, or should he hold her like he desperately wanted?

He moved forward to embrace Ava, but she stepped away. "Please have a seat. I'll be right back."

Ava then disappeared into the back room. DeAngelo fidgeted on the couch as he waited. He felt like a man who had been given a second chance to make things right.

Please, God, don't let me mess this up.

Ava returned with a clean face and puffy eyes. She grabbed the box of tissues from the table and sat in the chair across from DeAngelo. She didn't know where to start, so she began with the present.

"I'm here with my son, Malcolm. I just saw my teenage son and his friends off on their two-week tour of Spain. I'm a wreck."

DeAngelo hesitated. He searched his mind for the tiniest memory of Caroline mentioning Ava had a child. He tried to smile.

"So, you have a son." The uncertainty was thick in DeAngelo's voice, so Ava explained.

"Malcolm is Keith's nephew. Keith was raising him when we met. When Keith passed, I adopted Malcolm. This is the first time we've been apart since—"

DeAngelo wanted to reach for Ava's hand, but there was too much distance between them.

"I am so sorry for your loss. We were all at Mom's when Caroline received the news."

Ava's voice quivered as she apologized. "Thank you. It was a very difficult time." Ava's tears flowed once more, and she reached for more tissues. "I'm sorry, but I can't do this right now. I'm sorry—all of this. Malcolm leaving. Seeing you. It's all too much."

DeAngelo stood to leave. This was his second chance; he couldn't walk away without trying. He offered his hand for Ava to stand.

"Would you be willing to have dinner tonight?"

"Yes, I would like that." Ava agreed after a long pause.

DeAngelo gave Ava a friendly hug before leaving her

suite with a tiny spark of hope. He wasn't taking anything for granted.

He went downstairs to question the concierge about the best restaurants outside the hotel. He received three recommendations within walking distance. The concierge assured him that the food at each restaurant was superb, but their atmospheres were different. DeAngelo visited all three, again leaving nothing to chance.

He found the first restaurant to be far too trendy and touristy. Walking into the second restaurant, DeAngelo felt comfortable. A friendly young man greeted him.

"May I help you, sir?

After taking a moment to scan the room, DeAngelo answered, "Do you have any private rooms or booths for dinner?"

"We do, sir. Would you like to see one?" The young man walked DeAngelo farther into the restaurant to reveal a cozy area with a few tables and curved booths lining the wall.

"How crowded do you expect to be tonight?"

"Since this is June, not yet high season, and a weekday, I expect the front will likely be full, but not this space."

DeAngelo made a reservation for the back room at one booth in particular with a nice view of the plaza.

He decided to check out the third restaurant to make sure it wasn't a better option. It was white-table-linen formal and conveyed an overly romantic vibe, which was not what he wanted. DeAngelo now felt completely confident that the second restaurant was a perfect choice.

DeAngelo knew Ava loved flowers, but decided against taking any. For six years, he had worked to become a better man. Yet, he remembered regrettably he hadn't even given her flowers on their first date. *What an ass I was back then.*

Back in his hotel room, DeAngelo tried but couldn't relax. He stirred around, thinking of what he would say. Could he even hold it together through dinner? He nearly lost all his senses when he heard Ava's voice and realized it was her. There she was, in the same hotel in Madrid, out of all the places in the world. He thought maybe he would see Ava again at Caroline's wedding—if Caroline would ever get married.

Several times he thought about flying to Texas and just showing up at Ava's doorstep. Each time he ruled it out. Even for him, that was over the line.

Then the real thought hit DeAngelo square in the gut. What was Ava going to say to him at dinner? *Does she still hate me?*

He was sure Ava wouldn't yell or cause a scene. She wasn't that type of woman, but DeAngelo clearly remembered Ava could put anyone in their place with the mildest tone and demeanor. If Ava wasn't angry, DeAngelo thought she would be closed off and guarded. He refrained from reading too much into Ava's tears from earlier; it only led him to the negative side of things.

Before his thoughts ran away from him, DeAngelo got up and looked over his clothes. He had only packed to stay in Madrid for at most three days before driving to his sister Sophia's house. DeAngelo looked at his watch, relieved he had enough time to buy a new shirt, at least.

Luck was on his side. While scouting out the restaurants on foot, DeAngelo remembered passing several clothing stores. There was a store of every kind a stone's throw from the hotel. DeAngelo spent far more than he expected, but he reasoned he should be prepared to stay longer if Ava seemed comfortable.

Time slipped away as the morning faded into the afternoon. Their dinner reservations weren't until 8:30 P.M. He needed a distraction and quick before he thought himself into a dark place.

He shifted through a few emails and answered texts from his family. DeAngelo replied to the sports director to reschedule their meeting for the following day at 1:00 P.M.

Finally, his tempo and the passage of time synced. He steamed his new clothes, showered, and dressed. He stared at himself in the mirror and breathed in deeply, praying for the best.

Chapter 41

He kept staring. DeAngelo knew he had to say something, but what? For six years, he had dreamed about seeing Ava again. There she sat, across the table from him, looking as beautiful as ever.

"I know I'm staring, and I'm sorry, but I just can't believe it."

Ava lowered her head to hide her flushing face.

"I know," she said without looking at him. She paused for a second, not sure what to say herself. The shock of running into DeAngelo again after so many years had not worn off. Still anxious, she gazed into DeAngelo's charming, brown eyes. "I didn't know what to think when I turned and saw you."

The server brought their appetizers.

"I don't often hear someone order sparkling water with lime," said DeAngelo after the server had left. "When I realized it was you, I nearly fainted."

They both laughed, but Ava felt awkward. She was more than a little ashamed of her behavior that morning. Crying like a child. How silly she must have looked.

"I have to apologize for this morning," said Ava. "I tried but couldn't keep it together."

"No, please," said DeAngelo, shaking his head. "There is no need for you to apologize."

Ava took a deep breath to steady herself. "Malcolm and I haven't been apart since, you know, Keith," said Ava, swallowing hard to quell the well of emotions bubbling inside her. "I love that kid so much."

She touched her napkin to her eye and forced a little laugh. "At least I didn't cry like a baby in front of a bus full of high schoolers. All the memories of Malcolm growing up and us losing Keith were at the forefront of my mind. Then I see you." Ava shook her head. "Then I see you, DeAngelo Williams, and boy, did you bring back a boatload of memories."

DeAngelo fumbled with the fork next to his plate. He felt sad and guilty for intruding on such a private family moment.

"I'm sorry if I made things more painful for you."

Ava reached over and squeezed DeAngelo's hand softly. "The memories weren't too painful. It was more like wonderful nostalgia—thinking back and remembering all the good times that came and went too fast."

The server came to take the appetizer plates. Ava had hardly eaten a bite. Maybe she would stop talking long enough to eat the delicious entrée the server had placed in front of her.

"I can't believe how alone I feel with Malcolm gone. I thought I had prepared myself enough. I have to get myself together, or when he leaves for college, it'll be the end of me."

That gave Ava and DeAngelo a good laugh and eased the awkwardness. DeAngelo looked at Ava with a bit of amazement in his eyes.

"Motherhood suits you."

Ava's face brightened, and her smile widened at the compliment. "Can you believe it? Me, a mother? Sometimes I can hardly believe it myself, but yes, I agree; motherhood does suit me."

Her dinner was delicious, but Ava was more interested in hearing DeAngelo's story. "You know why I'm in Madrid, but why are you here?"

"So, you want the long or short version?" asked DeAngelo.

Ava gave a sassy glance. "Malcolm and his friends won't return for two weeks. I have plenty of time."

DeAngelo raised his wine glass, and Ava raised her water glass.

As the glasses clinked, DeAngelo toasted, "I shall start at the beginning. I've done a lot of growing up over the past six years."

His entire story unfolded over the two weeks. Each day and night, DeAngelo and Ava roamed around Madrid and the countryside like a pair of tourists. As they wandered along the cobblestone streets, he shared his life changes, and she shared hers.

DeAngelo had floundered around for a couple of months after Ava had left. He couldn't seem to find a direction that gave him purpose. His football career was over. He had destroyed the only relationship that meant something to him. He felt lost, but his family was there to keep him sane.

It didn't take long for him to man up and get his life together. He and Peter had both earned their degrees. The dynamic brother duo went to work building a highly-sought-after sports consulting firm. The part of the business DeAngelo loved the most was building athletic programs. That's what brought him to Madrid—the prospect of consulting on building a new modern sports program for a small college in the area.

It delighted Ava to see DeAngelo living his passion. She shared her work at the hospital and all the details of her life as a mother. She gave DeAngelo fair warning.

"I'm a proud mom. Please feel free to stop me if I go on too much about Malcolm."

She even shared her pain of losing Keith.

For Ava and DeAngelo, their two weeks passed by like a breeze. It didn't feel like old times—it was better. Through all their triumphs and tragedies, they both had grown into more mature and wiser versions of themselves. And there was no denying it. The connection and attraction that sparked between them at Henry Müller's cocktail party years ago still burned.

On the last Saturday night before Malcolm and his friends would return from their trip, DeAngelo and Ava reminisced over a quiet dinner. Then they strolled together around the plaza and returned to the hotel.

Ava invited DeAngelo into her suite. DeAngelo sat on the couch while Ava answered a few texts. When she joined him, he realized he was running out of time. There was a panic brewing inside him. The time they had spent together was wonderful. He couldn't let Ava walk out of his life again.

DeAngelo told Ava about a particular Sunday dinner at his parents. Emma Rose was excitedly reciting all she had learned at school that week to her auntie Caroline. Peter was rubbing Ingrid's stomach. She was pregnant again. This time, they were sure the baby was a boy. Momma Gretta and Albert talked about a cruise to Greece they were planning now that Albert had retired. And Rich was telling Rosalynn for the millionth time how much he loved her.

"I sat there, feeling so alone. The memories of you, of us, flooded my mind. I could see you cooking with my mom, conspiring with my dad for the Fourth of July party, and holding baby Emma Rose in your arms. I started to hate myself all over again for hurting you. I hate the man I was back then."

Ava held onto DeAngelo's arm. "Please, don't. I fell in love with that man. I never hated you. I tried, and I wanted to hate you, but I loved you too much. I hated what happened, but never you."

DeAngelo struggled to keep his tears in. "Thank you for that." He looked down and then back at Ava. "Ava, you were right. I did love the idea of the man I used to be more than the man I was becoming when I was with you. I was scared and intimidated. It was frightening to love and be loved so completely."

Ava kissed DeAngelo's lips softly. "Please don't."

DeAngelo took Ava into his arms. "My one regret in life was hurting you. But my second biggest regret would be to leave you tonight without telling you I still love you."

Ava cried into DeAngelo's broad chest. "I am terrified to love again. I've been close twice, only to have it taken away from me. I can't go through another loss. I just can't."

"Ava, please look at me," begged DeAngelo. "I didn't have sense enough to know it until you left me. I had to look at myself. I was arrogant, selfish, and far too immature to deserve you. You saw more in me than I saw in myself. I have spent these past six years growing into the man I should have been for you back then. Please, give me a chance to be the man you deserve."

Chapter 42

Peter cleared his throat and took the microphone. He had practiced at least fifty times. The stakes were high; he only had one chance to get this right.

DeAngelo clasped Ava's hand. "Are you ready for this?"

She kissed him with that sexy little smile on her face he adored so much. "I'm ready."

Peter's clear, smooth voice boomed as the doors of the tent swung open. "Ladies and gentlemen, it is my great pleasure to introduce Mr. and Mrs. DeAngelo Williams!"

His German accent sounded a little funny to the Americans and hard-core Texans, but Peter nailed it. DeAngelo and Ava entered with a roar of cheers and applause. Surrounded by their family and friends, they danced their first dance as husband and wife under a sparkling chandelier that cast thousands of pure-white reflections.

DeAngelo gazed at his wife. "Seven years later, and I finally get to say it. I love you, Mrs. Ava Williams."

Ava smiled as he twirled her on the dance floor. "I love you, too, Mr. Williams."

"Should we tell them tonight?" asked DeAngelo, excitement showing on his face.

Ava threw her arms around DeAngelo's neck. "Our moms and Caroline already know," she said, laughing. "It was a tight fit getting into this dress. It's going to be a struggle getting it off."

DeAngelo gave Ava a spin and then pulled her back in close. "You look amazing, and there won't be an issue getting you out of that dress tonight. Trust me."

Epilogue

Ava and DeAngelo made their home in Texas. Of course, they made annual visits to Germany. Momma Rosalynn and Momma Gretta wouldn't have it any other way. Their boys, Wesley and Thomas, were international travelers by their first birthday.

All grown up, Wesley, their oldest son, is learning the family business from his uncle Danny in Brazil. Thomas, their youngest, is at university in England with Peter's youngest son, Konrad. Thomas and Konrad are as thick as thieves like their dads. The boys are gone, but Ava and DeAngelo's lives are still full of laughter and joy. Malcolm and Isabel have given them a house full of grandbabies.

During that life-changing trip to Spain twenty-five years ago, Malcolm met Isabel. She was one of the beautiful, young, Spanish student ambassadors. They kept in touch and fell in love when Malcolm returned to Spain to study abroad during his senior year of college. They later married and blessed Ava with twelve-year-old Mateo, her reliable sous chef, for every Sunday dinner. Little ten-year-old Sanchez is their star athlete.

He takes after Malcolm and DeAngelo, known affectionally as "Papa D." And who can forget about two-year-old Nora? She's the little princess of the family.

The years have passed, but Ava and DeAngelo's love continues to grow. DeAngelo has been every bit the man she needed him to be. With him, Ava feels loved and complete. She lived it, and she knows it to be true. A broken heart will mend. Be encouraged and take the leap without reservation when you get the chance to love again.

www.ingramcontent.com/pod-product-compliance
Lightning Source LLC
Chambersburg PA
CBHW031443160726
47994CB00005B/1844